#1 *New York Times* Bestselling Author

SHERRYL WOODS

The Devaney Brothers

DANIEL

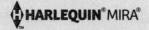

ISBN-13: 978-0-7783-1679-4

THE DEVANEY BROTHERS: DANIEL

First published in 2003 by Harlequin Enterprises Limited under the title DANIEL'S DESIRE

Copyright © 2003 by Sherryl Woods

This edition published June 2014

The publisher acknowledges the copyright holder of the individual works as follows:

Excerpt from THE SWEET MAGNOLIAS COOKBOOK
Copyright © 2012 by Sherryl Woods

Excerpt from SWAN POINT
Copyright © 2014 by Sherryl Woods

Recycling programs for this product may not exist in your area.

Printed in U.S.A.

Dear Friends,

Years ago, I heard a question on *Jeopardy!* about the most successful Disney movies of all time. It stated that they all had something to do with orphans. Well, who am I to argue with the Disney magic? Thus the Devaneys were born—five brothers, separated for years, thanks to a decision by desperate parents.

As each story unfolds and the brothers are reunited, more and more questions arise about why their parents allowed them to be separated. Readers have debated ever since about whether their reasons were valid or impossible to understand. As you come to know the brothers, I hope you'll share your thoughts with me, as well. Put yourselves in the parents' shoes and think about what you might have done under the same circumstances.

In the meantime, I'm delighted that the emotional stories of Ryan, Sean, Michael, Patrick and Daniel are coming back into print. I'll look forward to hearing from you.

All best,

Sherryl

The Devaney Brothers

DANIEL

1

It was just past midnight on the longest day of the year for Molly Creighton. Each time this particular anniversary rolled around, it stole another piece of her. Her heart ached, and her soul…well, there were times like this when she thought she no longer had one.

Over the years she'd come to accept the fact that life was unpredictable and sometimes cruel. She'd lost her parents at a very early age, but she'd survived thanks to the love of her grandfather. Jess had been a hard man, but he'd had a soft spot for her, and he'd raised her to believe in herself and to handle just about anything life tossed her way. There had been only one thing that had been too much for her, one loss that she hadn't been able to push aside so that she could get on with the business of living.

Oh, she went through the motions just fine. She ran Jess's, the waterfront bar in Widow's Cove, Maine, that had been her grandfather's. She had a huge circle of acquaintances and a tighter circle of friends, but she didn't have the one thing that really mattered. She didn't have her baby.

She blamed Daniel Devaney for that. Daniel had been the love of her life, though they were about as opposite in personality as any two people could be. Molly had always been—at least until a few years ago—a free spirit. She'd embraced life, because she knew all too well how short it could be. Daniel was an uptight stickler for the rules. He was logical and methodical. Maybe that was even what had drawn her to him. She'd enjoyed messing with his head, keeping him thoroughly off-kilter, almost as much as she'd thrilled to his slow, deliberate caresses.

They'd known each other practically forever, though his family lived in a small town a half hour away from Widow's Cove. They'd gone to high school together, where Daniel had been the star football player and she'd been the ultimate party girl, dating a dozen different guys before she'd finally gone out with Daniel. One date had put an end to her days of playing the field. One kiss had sealed their fate.

Even though Daniel had gone away to college and Molly hadn't, they'd been a couple, spending every free moment together. She thought she'd known his heart and his secrets, but she hadn't known the big one, the one that would tear them apart.

Finding herself pregnant four years ago, Molly had been ecstatic and had expected Daniel to be accepting, if not equally enthusiastic. Barely out of college and already established in a career he loved, he had been a do-the-right-thing kind of a guy, and he'd told her a thousand times how much he loved her. While they'd never discussed marriage, she'd believed that's where they were heading. If this pushed things along a little faster, what was the big deal?

But instead of reacting as she'd expected, Daniel had been appalled, not because he didn't love her, not even because they were too young, he'd claimed, but because fatherhood had been the very last thing he'd ever contemplated.

That was when he'd told her about the Devaney secret, the one that had ripped him and his twin brother, Patrick, apart, the one that had caused a rift so deep, Patrick hadn't spoken to their parents in years now.

As Daniel told the story, Connor and Kathleen Devaney had recklessly abandoned their three oldest sons in Boston and moved to Maine, bringing only Patrick and Daniel with them. For years they had raised the two boys as if the twins were their only children. Daniel had learned the truth only a few years earlier, when he was eighteen. He was still reeling from it.

With a father capable of abandoning three of his sons as an example, Daniel told her, how could he even consider becoming a parent himself? Any child would be better off without a Devaney in its life.

"I see too many kids whose lives are a mess because of lousy parents," he'd added to bolster his argument. "I won't do that to my own child."

Molly had tried to reassure him, tried to tell him

that he would make a wonderful father—wasn't he a child advocate for the state, after all?—but he'd flatly refused to take any role in their child's life beyond financial assistance. He'd insisted that she—and their baby—would thank him someday.

Rather than continue a fight she knew she couldn't win, Molly had let her pride kick in. Convinced she could raise the child on her own and stunned by Daniel's attitude, she had thrown his offer of money back in his face. Her baby would be a Creighton and proud of it.

And maybe it would have turned out that way, if Daniel hadn't broken her heart and her spirit. It was almost as if her body had understood what her heart had tried to deny, that a life without Daniel would be meaningless. The very night they'd tried to hash it all out, she had miscarried and lost her precious baby.

It was Daniel's brother Patrick who'd taken her to the hospital on that terrible spring night four years ago. It was Patrick who'd held her hand and tried awkwardly to comfort her. It was Patrick who dried her tears each year on the anniversary of that devastating loss. He'd been by earlier in the evening to check on her before going home to his wife. If she'd asked tonight, Patrick would have stayed.

As for Daniel, he and Molly hadn't exchanged a civil word since that awful night. She doubted they ever would. She blamed him almost as much as she blamed herself.

Unfortunately, that didn't mean she'd stopped loving him. Not a day went by that she didn't think about him and what they'd lost—not just a child, but an entire future. Seeing Patrick, who looked exactly like his twin, was a constant reminder. Not that she needed one. Daniel was so much a part of her, she could have conjured him up entirely on her own.

She sighed heavily and took one last cursory swipe at the bar with her polishing cloth.

Suddenly a faint noise in one of the booths caught her attention. Widow's Cove wasn't exactly a haven for criminals, but Molly instinctively picked up the nearest bottle as a weapon and slipped through the shadows in the direction of the noise.

She had the bottle over her head and was ready to strike, when a petite, dark-haired girl, no more than thirteen or fourteen, emerged from the booth, alarm in her eyes and her mouth running a mile a minute with a tumble of excuses for being in Jess's past closing.

Molly's heart was still slamming against the wall of her chest as she lowered the bottle and tried to make sense of what the girl was saying. The rush of words was all but incoherent.

"Whoa," Molly said quietly, reaching out, only to have the girl draw back skittishly as if she feared she was still in danger of being hit.

Molly set the bottle on the table, then held out her empty hands. "Look, it's okay. Nobody here is going to hurt you."

The girl stared back at her, silent now that the immediate threat was over.

"I'm Molly. What's your name?"

Nothing.

"I've never seen you around here before," Molly continued as if the girl had responded. "Where are you from?"

Still, the only response was that wide-eyed, solemn stare.

"Not talking now? Well, that's okay, too. It's a pleasant change after spending an entire evening with a bunch of rowdy men who can't shut up, yet have very little to say."

The girl's mouth twitched slightly, as if she were fighting a smile. Molly grinned, sensing that she'd found a kindred spirit.

"I see you know exactly what I mean," she continued. "Are you hungry? The grill's shut down, but I could fix you a sandwich. There's ham and cheese, tuna salad or my personal favorite, peanut butter and pickles."

"Yuck," the girl said, her face scrunched up in a look of pure disgust.

The reaction made her seem even younger than Molly had originally guessed.

Laughing, Molly said, "I thought that might get a response from you. So, no peanut butter and pickles. You are going to have to tell me what you do want, though."

The girl's shoulders finally relaxed. "Ham and cheese, please."

"With milk?"

"A soda, if that's okay."

So, she'd been taught some manners, and from

the look of her clothes, she'd been well provided for. They were wrinkled, but she was wearing the latest teen fashions, low-riding designer jeans and a cropped shirt that revealed an inch of pale skin at her waist. Her sneakers were a brand that cost an arm and a leg.

"I have money to pay for the food," the girl said as she followed Molly into the kitchen.

"This one's on the house," Molly told her as she made the thick sandwich and found a can of soda in the huge, well-stocked refrigerator.

The girl took the sandwich and drink, then regarded Molly uncertainly. "Aren't you going to have anything? You didn't eat all night."

Molly regarded her with surprise. "How do you know that?"

"I was kinda watching you," she admitted shyly.

"Really? Why?"

"I thought maybe if I could pick up on what goes on around here, you'd think about giving me a job."

"How old are you?"

"Eighteen," the girl said brazenly.

Molly frowned. "I don't think so. How about fourteen?"

"Close enough," she responded a little too eagerly.

"Which means you're only thirteen," Molly concluded, sighing heavily. Not that fourteen would have been much better, but thirteen definitely meant trouble.

"But I look eighteen," the girl insisted. "No one would have to know."

"I'd know," Molly said. "I try really hard not to break the law by hiring minors to work in the bar."

"Couldn't I at least bus tables or help you clean up after the bar closes? I could mop the floors and wash dishes. No one would even have to see me, and that wouldn't break any laws, would it?"

Technically, it wouldn't, but Molly knew better than to take on an obvious runaway, not without having some facts. And something told her this child was so anxious to make herself indispensable that she'd eagerly attempt all sorts of things that would break every rule in the book.

"Here's the deal. You tell me your name and your story. Then we'll talk about a job."

"Can't talk with my mouth full," the girl said, taking a bite of the sandwich to emphasize the point.

Molly shook her head, amused by the delaying tactic.

The girl gobbled down the rest of the sandwich, then looked longingly toward the fixings that were still on the counter. Molly made her a second sandwich, then held it just out of reach.

"Your mouth's not full now, and I'm waiting," she prodded.

The teen studied Molly's face and apparently concluded that her patience was at an end. "Okay, my name's Kendra," she said at last.

"No last name?"

She shook her head, a touch of defiance in her eyes. "Just Kendra."

"Where'd you run away from, Kendra?"

"Home."

Molly grinned. "Nice try. Now give me some specifics."

The girl sighed. "Portland."

"Do you have family in Portland that's likely to be going crazy looking for you?"

She shrugged. "I suppose." Though she attempted to achieve a look of complete boredom, there was an unmistakable trace of dismay in her eyes.

"Then call them," Molly said flatly. "If you want to stay here, that's not negotiable. They need to know you're safe."

Huge tears welled up in Kendra's eyes. "I can't," she said, then added with more belligerence, "I won't."

The ferocity of her response triggered all sorts of alarm bells. "Did someone at home hurt you?"

Kendra's eyes widened as Molly's meaning sank in. "Not the way you mean. No way," she said.

She sounded so genuinely horrified that Molly couldn't help feeling relieved. "Then what happened?" she asked, trying to think of other reasons a child this age might take off. Only one immediately came to mind. "You're not pregnant, are you?"

The girl regarded her indignantly. "I'm a kid. Are you crazy?"

Well, that was another relief, Molly thought. "Then what did make you leave home? Experience tells me that almost anything can be worked out, if everyone sits down and talks about it."

Rather than giving Molly a direct answer, Kendra

sent her a considering look. "Did you sit down and talk to whoever hurt you?"

Molly blinked at the question. "What are you talking about?"

"You were crying before, after you locked up. That's why I didn't speak to you sooner. People don't cry unless somebody's hurt them. Did you talk it out?"

Molly thought of Daniel's refusal to talk, his refusal to even take her point of view into account. And after the miscarriage, she'd been the one who'd fallen silent. He'd made one overture, one attempt at an apology—probably at Patrick's insistence— but she'd told him to stay the hell out of her life and slammed the door on him. So, no, she hadn't followed her own advice and talked it out. What was there to say?

"You didn't, did you?" Kendra prodded. "So why should I have to? Just because I'm a kid?"

"You have a point," Molly admitted, impressed by the girl's quick grasp of things. "But letting you stick around here and giving you a job could get me into a whole lot of trouble. You're a minor in the eyes of the law, even if you think you're old enough to be on your own."

Kendra gave her another one of those too-grown-up looks. "What's the alternative? You don't give me a job and I keep running," she said simply. "Do you honestly want that on your conscience? The next place I stop, the people might not be so nice."

Well, hell, Molly thought. She definitely did not

want that on her conscience. "One week, max," she said very firmly. "And you open up to me. I'll try to help you figure out the best thing to do."

"If that means calling my parents, it's not going to happen," Kendra said stubbornly.

Molly was equally determined to see that it did, but she merely said, "We'll see."

Now that her immediate fate was settled, Kendra gave her a hopeful look. "I don't suppose you have any of that apple pie left, do you? I could smell it when you brought it to those guys in the booth next to me. It smelled awesome."

"Yes, there's pie left." Her cook always baked enough for at least two days, because it was a customer favorite.

"And ice cream? I'm pretty sure there was ice cream on their pie."

Molly chuckled. "Yes, there's ice cream. When was the last time you ate?" she asked as she cut a slice of pie and set it in front of Kendra, then added a large scoop of vanilla ice cream.

"A trucker bought me a couple of doughnuts this morning," Kendra said as she dug into the dessert.

"Please tell me you were not hitching rides," Molly said.

Once again, Kendra regarded her indignantly. "What? Do I look stupid? I know better than to get in a car or a truck with a stranger, especially some guy."

"Well, thank heavens for that."

"This was a lady trucker, and she was in this place where my bus stopped. She must have felt sorry for me or something, 'cause she offered to buy the doughnuts. I could have bought them for myself, but I figured I should hang on to all the money I could, since I wasn't sure how long it would be before I could get a job." She gave Molly a thoughtful look. "So, how much are you paying me?"

"We'll work it out in the morning."

"Meals are part of the deal, right?"

Molly bit back a grin. "Yes."

"And I can sleep here, too?"

"Yes. Were you by any chance a negotiator in a previous life?"

Kendra shrugged. "Just looking out for myself. If I don't, who will?"

Indeed, Molly thought. Wasn't that a lesson she'd had to learn the hard way?

The saddest eyes Daniel Devaney had ever seen stared back at him from the latest missing-child poster to cross his desk. Kendra Grace Morrow had huge, dark, haunted eyes. Only thirteen, according to the information on the fax, she looked older and far too wise.

Believed to be somewhere in Maine, she had run away from her home in Portland two weeks earlier, no doubt leaving behind frantic parents and baffled police. Daniel's heart broke for all of them, just as it did every single time he looked over one of these posters. At least this time there seemed to be no question that the girl had taken off on her own. She hadn't been kidnapped. She'd left a note that hadn't said much and packed a bag. There had been a few sightings reported to the police, and in each the girl had been spotted alone.

Still, runaways never seemed to understand the dangers that awaited them, or else the situation they were leaving behind was so desperate, so awful, that anything seemed to be an improvement. He didn't know the facts of this particular case, but they all had one thing in common—a kid who needed help. And each time he saw one, he wondered if there had ever been posters like this for his three older brothers, the ones he hadn't remembered until he'd accidently found the old photos in the attic, the brothers his parents had abandoned years ago.

Sometimes when he thought of what had happened, of the choice that Connor and Kathleen Devaney had made to keep Daniel and his twin, Patrick, Daniel's heart ached. What had Ryan, Sean and Michael thought when they'd discovered that they'd been left behind? How long had they cried? How long had it been before they'd stopped watching and waiting for their mom and dad to come back for them? Had foster care been kind to them? Or had the system failed them, just as their own parents had?

He'd met them all recently, but they'd danced around the tough issues. One of these days they were going to have to face the past together and deal with the mess their parents had made of all their lives. It wasn't as if he and Patrick had emerged unscathed, not once they'd discovered the truth.

Patrick had taken it even harder than Daniel had.

He'd left home and hadn't spoken to their parents since. Nor had he been in touch with Daniel until recently, when he'd set up that first meeting with Ryan, Sean and Michael. He'd expected Daniel to have explanations by now for what had happened all those years ago, but Daniel was still as much in the dark as everyone else.

Oh, he'd tried his best to make sense of what had happened, but beyond revealing the existence of the three older boys, his parents had said precious little to try to justify what they had done. Even though Daniel had maintained contact with his parents, that didn't mean he'd worked through his own anger and guilt over having been one of the two chosen to be kept.

He supposed he owed his folks in one respect. Had it not been for the discovery of their betrayal, he might not have found the kind of work that he was doing now—saving kids in trouble, fighting for their rights, mending fences between them and their parents or finding them loving homes. The caseloads were heavy, the hours long, but it was important, meaningful work. And it could break a man's heart on a daily basis.

He coped by adhering strictly to the rules, by reducing messy emotions to black-and-white regulations. Sometimes it worked. Sometimes it didn't. Gazing into Kendra Morrow's haunted eyes, he instinctively knew that this was one of those times it wouldn't work. The girl was a heartbreaker. He hoped to heaven she was in someone else's jurisdiction, where she'd be found safe.

He sighed when his phone rang, relieved by the intrusion into his dark thoughts about a world in which kids ran away when they were little more than babies, too young to understand the risks.

"Devaney," he said when he'd picked up the phone.

"Daniel, it's Joe Sutton at police headquarters. Have you seen that poster for Kendra Morrow?"

"It's on my desk now."

"I was just having lunch over in Widow's Cove," the detective told him.

The mere mention of Widow's Cove was enough to make Daniel's palms sweat. And there was only one place in town worth going to for lunch… Molly's. "Oh?" he said as if his heart wasn't thumping unsteadily.

"I think Kendra Morrow's hanging out at Molly Creighton's place on the waterfront," Joe reported. "You know the one I mean? Best chowder on the coast?"

"Yeah, Jess's. Are you sure it was Kendra?"

"If it wasn't her, it was her double. I'd just seen the poster before I went over there."

"Then why didn't you pick her up?" Daniel asked, surprised by the lapse from a cop who was usually quick to nab runaways for their own protection. He and Joe had handled more than their share of these cases together, and he respected the older man's instincts.

"Because I looked through the file earlier, and

something's not quite right. I thought you might want to have a chat with the girl while I do some checking into why she ran away in the first place. You know as well as I do that sometimes these things aren't as cut-and-dried as they seem at first glance. If I'd thought she was at risk, I'd have brought her in, but she's not going anywhere. Molly will see to that. I didn't see any point in uprooting her until I have all the facts."

This time Daniel's sigh was even heavier. He and Molly got along like a couple of tomcats fighting for turf. Their relationship had been passionate and volatile for years, even before he'd let her down so damn badly. After what had happened the night she'd told him she was pregnant, the relationship had cooled to a degree that a glance between them could freeze meat. He regretted that, but he'd accepted it. He'd been a stubborn fool, and he didn't deserve her forgiveness.

Out of respect for her feelings, it had been a few years now since he'd set foot in that bar she'd inherited from her grandfather. He stayed away in part because Patrick tended to hang out at Jess's, but mostly because he couldn't bear the look of justifiable contempt in Molly's eyes.

"Can you take a run over there?" Joe pressed.

Daniel hesitated for just an instant, but when it came to work, he always did what he had to do, no matter how delicate the situation or how uncomfortable it made him.

"I'm on my way," he promised, folding the fax into quarters and stuffing it into the pocket of his jacket. "I'll check in with you later. You sure you don't want me to bring her over, if it is Kendra? If she figures out we're onto her, she could run again."

"Just alert Molly, in case she doesn't know anyone's looking for the girl. She'll keep her safe enough."

"She has a thirteen-year-old working in a bar," Daniel reminded him, an edge of sarcasm in his voice. It was just like Molly and her soft heart to take in a runaway kid and to hell with the consequences. Had she even once considered how desperate the parents might be or how many laws she might be breaking?

Joe chuckled at his comment on Molly's lack of judgment. "Loosen up. The kid's serving chowder, spilling more of it than she's serving, to tell the truth of it. I don't think there's anything wrong with that. Something tells me it's the best place she could be right now while we figure out what drove her to run away. The note she left didn't tell us a damned thing. I don't want to turn her back over to her parents and then find out there was some kind of abuse going on."

Daniel had his own opinion about this bending of the rules, but he bit his tongue. It was Joe's call, at least until the court got involved. Then Daniel would have quite a lot to say about a woman who put a teenage runaway to work, no questions asked, without reporting her presence to the authorities.

"The man you were talking to before, he was a cop," Kendra told Molly, her face pale and her eyes filled with panic. "I can spot a cop a mile away."

"It was Joe Sutton and, yes, he is a detective, but he's a good guy," Molly reassured her. "He drives over every few weeks for my chowder. If he'd been here to look for you, he would have said something. Besides, he's gone now, so obviously he didn't recognize you."

"Maybe he forgot his handcuffs and had to go back for them," Kendra said.

"Sweetie, he wouldn't handcuff you. You ran away. You're not a criminal. You have nothing to fear from Joe."

The words were barely out of her mouth when the door opened and Daniel Devaney came striding in as if he'd arrived to conquer the world. In her opinion, Kendra had a lot more to worry about with Daniel than she ever would with Joe Sutton. Daniel was a rigid, by-the-book kind of guy when it came to situations like this. How he and his twin brother, Patrick, had come from the same gene pool was a total enigma to her.

"Go in the back," Molly ordered the teenager, maneuvering in an attempt to keep Kendra out of Daniel's view. "And stay alert in case you need to get out of here in a hurry."

Kendra paled at the terse order. "What's going on? Is that cop back?"

"No. Just do whatever you have to do to stay out of sight. Tell Retta what I said. Tell her Daniel's here. She'll understand and she'll help you. I'll explain later," Molly promised, giving the girl's hand a reassuring squeeze. "Trust me. Everything's going to be okay."

Kendra followed the direction of her gaze and spotted Daniel. "He's a cop, too, isn't he?" she said at once.

"No, worse, in this instance. He's with a social services agency."

Understanding and alarm immediately flared in Kendra's eyes. "Then he's here for me?"

"More than likely." She couldn't imagine anything else that would have brought Daniel waltzing into her bar again, not after she'd made it clear that his presence here was unwelcome. "Just stay out of sight. I can handle Daniel Devaney."

When she was satisfied that Kendra was safely out of the bar, Molly strolled over to Daniel's table, order pad in hand, a neutral expression firmly plastered on her face. She ignored the once-familiar jolt to her senses. She would play this cool for Kendra's sake. If there hadn't been so much at stake, Daniel could have starved to death before she'd have given him a second glance.

"Fancy seeing you here," she said. "I thought you preferred classier joints these days."

Daniel frowned at her. "I never said that."

"You never had to. Your disdain has always been evident." And never more so than the night he'd declined to be a father to their child. Though he'd told her about his own father's failings, she'd always believed that at least some of his reluctance had stemmed from an aversion to her choice to run her grandfather's bar, rather than going off to some snooty college and pursuing some equally snooty career. Unlike his twin, Daniel was a snob in his fancy shirts with the monogrammed cuffs and his Italian leather loafers that were more suited to the streets of downtown Portland than the waterfront in Widow's Cove. He was definitely no longer a small-town boy.

He didn't even flinch as her barb struck him. "Save the judgments. I didn't come here to fight with you. Just bring me a cup of chowder, please."

Molly noted the order but didn't budge. He was acting too blasted casual and innocent. Something besides chowder had brought Daniel into the bar. Given Joe Sutton's recent departure, there was very little question in her mind that he was here because of Kendra.

"In town to see your folks?"

"No."

"If you're looking for Patrick, he won't be in till later," she said casually, in an attempt to get him to show his hand.

"I'm not looking for Patrick."

"Oh?" She sat down opposite him, sliding onto the booth's bench until her knees brushed his. The little spark of awareness that shot through her was an unwelcome surprise, but she tried not to show it. She couldn't control the sparks, but she could refuse to give him the satisfaction of seeing that his presence bothered her. Besides, there had been an answering spark of heat in his eyes. She could use that to her advantage, assuming she could manage to avoid choking on her own words. She had to try, though.

"Then it's my company you've come for? You have no idea how long I've been waiting to hear that one more time." She dropped her voice provocatively and made herself add, "What can I do for you, Daniel? Have you decided you missed me after all this time? Want to pick things up where we left off?"

He shook his head, clearly not taking her seriously. "As attractive as you make that offer sound, I'm here on business," he retorted dryly.

Molly stiffened, fighting the sting of hurt, even though the rejection was fully expected. "What business could you possibly have that involves me?"

His gaze swept over her, lingering just long enough to make her toes curl, dammit.

"That girl you've got hiding in the kitchen, for starters."

2

Daniel hadn't expected his conversation with Molly to go smoothly. Given their past history, he was probably lucky she hadn't hit him with a cast-iron skillet on sight. It was no more than he deserved after the way things had ended between them. Even so, he wasn't expecting her to flat-out lie to his face and judging from her expression, that was clearly exactly what she was contemplating.

"Well?" he prodded. "Cat got your tongue?"

He had to give her credit. She didn't even blink. In fact, she kept her eyes locked with his and managed a look of complete confusion. She never once glanced toward the kitchen.

"What girl?" she asked with all the innocence of someone whose heart was genuinely pure.

"You have a runaway working here," he said flatly, vaguely disappointed in her for the lie. It would have been more like the Molly of old to throw the truth in his face and dare him to make something of it.

Keeping his gaze on her face, he added, "Joe Sutton spotted her here earlier, and I saw her scurrying out through the kitchen when I came in. She's thirteen, Molly. Shall I count the number of laws you're violating by putting her to work in here?"

She visibly bristled, bright patches of color staining her cheeks. "*If* I had anyone that young working here, they wouldn't be serving alcohol. Nor am I running a sweatshop with child labor, Daniel, and you very well know it, so get off your high horse."

He reached in his pocket, pulled out the missing-child poster and slapped it on the table, carefully smoothing out the wrinkles. "Then you haven't seen this girl?" he demanded, his gaze locked on Molly's eyes, which always gave away her emotions. They were stormy now, but she didn't even blink at the challenge. In fact, she glanced at the poster without so much as a flicker of recognition.

Daniel bit back a sigh. She was good at lying. Damn good. She hadn't been when they were together. Something always gave her away. Was she this good now because of what he'd done to her? Something inside him twisted at the possibility that he was responsible for the hard shell she wore so easily now.

Her gaze never wavered as she said flatly, "Never seen her. What's she done?"

"She's a runaway, Molly," he explained patiently. "That's plain from the poster, or didn't you want to take a good long look at it? Were you afraid you might give yourself away if you had to read the fine print?"

"Go to hell, Daniel," she said, sliding from the booth. "I don't have to listen to this from you."

He snagged her hand, felt her stiffen and tried to ignore the slam of regret that hit him. "Then let me see her."

"You want to go poking around in my kitchen or even in my apartment upstairs, you do that," she said loudly enough to be heard in the next county. "I won't try to stop you, but I won't forgive you." Her gaze swept over him, cold as ice. "Oh, wait, that's right. I haven't forgiven you for a lot of things, have I? I can just add this to the list."

Daniel wanted nothing more in that instant than to pull her into his arms and kiss her until the ice melted and she molded herself to him the way she once had. He wanted the heat and excitement and passion back, if not the complications.

"Molly, this isn't personal," he said quietly.

"Funny, it feels damn personal to me. You're questioning my integrity."

"Only because I know what a soft touch you are when it comes to kids," he said. "You'd hide that girl if you thought it was the right thing to do, especially if you thought it would also tick me off. I'm telling you, it's not the right choice. She has a family. Think about them for a minute. Put yourself in their shoes. Their daughter's missing and they're scared. They're worried to death about all the things that could happen to an innocent kid out on the streets alone."

A faint flicker of emotion in her eyes told him he'd hit his mark, but then her expression returned to that neutral, cool one that told him he'd lost his one chance at getting through to her. Maybe Joe would have had better luck with her. Her guard wouldn't have been up with him. Her natural desire to defy Daniel wouldn't have been a factor.

"Like I said, you want to search the place, search," she said.

His gaze clashed with hers. "Do you think I won't?"

"No. I think you'll do exactly what you want to do," she said. "You always have."

He could have trusted her and let it go, could maybe have redeemed himself just a little in her eyes by walking out, but he turned and walked into the kitchen, because that was his job. Naturally, because of the commotion Molly had caused, the kitchen was empty except for the same cook who'd been working there for forty years. Though they'd once been friends, Retta could be as tight-lipped and taciturn as any female on earth with people she didn't like. She gave Daniel a look that spoke volumes about what she thought of him, but gave nothing away about any kid who might be hiding in the pantry.

"Have you seen a teenager in here?" he asked, even though he knew he was wasting his breath.

Retta made an exaggerated show of looking around. "Room looks empty to me."

"And earlier? Was she in here ten minutes ago?"

"I'm too busy cooking to keep track of people

coming and going. In case you haven't noticed, we're packed out there. Molly's doing a brisk business these days," she said proudly.

Daniel almost started to enjoy himself. Retta had an honest streak, and he could see that his questions were testing her innate desire to tell the truth. "Let's concentrate on the kitchen, Retta. Are you admitting that people have been coming and going in here today?"

"Did I say that?"

"Sounded like it to me. Where'd she go, Retta?"

She shrugged and stirred the chowder. "Like I said, I don't pay attention to the comings and goings around here." She frowned at him. "Come to think of it, I did take note of one person going."

"Oh?"

"That was you, and you broke my baby's heart." The look she gave him was fierce. "Don't go doing it again."

Daniel sighed. "I never meant to hurt her."

"But it happened just the same, didn't it?" Retta said. "Now get on out of here. I have work to do and I can't do it with the likes of you underfoot."

Daniel left, grateful to be away from Retta's accusatory looks and harsh words. He deserved all she'd said and more, but that didn't make it any easier to take.

Molly was behind the bar, pretending to wipe off the already shiny surface, when he emerged from the kitchen.

"Find anyone?" she inquired.

"Just Retta, looking as pleasant as ever," he admitted.

"She doesn't like you."

"She did once."

"So did I," Molly retorted. "Times change."

Daniel kept his gaze steady. "Do you want to hash out our old news here and now, with everyone looking on?"

Molly glanced around and evidently took note of the fascinated gazes turned their way. She shrugged. "Not particularly."

"Then give me your key."

She blinked at that. "What the hell do you want with my key?"

"I'm going upstairs to look for the girl. Not ten minutes ago, you said you had no problem with that."

"Well, I do now. You'll go upstairs over my dead body," she said, standing defiantly in his path.

His gaze never wavered. "Your choice."

The standoff lasted for what seemed like an eternity, but Molly clearly knew him well enough to realize that he wasn't going to leave until he'd completed his search. She reached in her pocket, then slapped the key in his palm.

"Have a ball," she said sarcastically. "When you get to the bedroom, be sure to spend a few minutes reliving old times. Of course, things aren't exactly the same. I've managed to rid the room of all traces of you."

He turned and stalked off before she could see that her jibe had hit home.

Upstairs, he opened the door to her private quarters, then sucked in a deep breath as a million and one memories assailed him. He'd spent some of the happiest nights of his life in this apartment.

It still bore the faint scent of Jess's pipe tobacco, the more recent scent of Molly's perfume. The carpet was worn bare in spots, and the overstuffed furniture had seen better days, but Molly had added touches that made the place feel cozy rather than shabby. There were fresh flowers in a vase on the table in the tiny kitchen, another vase beside the bed. There was a gallery of framed snapshots on her dresser, but the space where his had been was gathering dust. She'd tossed a bright red chenille spread across the back of the sofa and added a pile of pillows. A stack of well-worn paperbacks, mostly Louis L'Amour Westerns, still sat beside Jess's favorite chair.

Being here again, absorbing the atmosphere, made Daniel's heart ache. The pain was deeper because he was here not by invitation, but because he'd intruded. His lack of trust today was just one more thing to be added to the list of his sins he was certain Molly kept in some mental notebook. He doubted there was enough time left in either of their lives for him to make amends.

Worse, there was no sign of Kendra Morrow, so he'd alienated Molly yet again for no good reason. That didn't mean he believed for one second that Kendra wasn't around. He *had* caught a glimpse of her slipping into the kitchen when he'd first arrived—there wasn't a doubt in his mind about that.

If he'd brushed past Molly, he might have caught the girl, but he hadn't. One of these days he'd try to figure out why. Maybe he'd hoped that, despite everything that had happened between them, Molly would be straight with him. Maybe he'd just wanted an excuse to keep coming around.

But she hadn't been straight with him and it was plain that she intended to make this a whole lot more difficult for all of them than it needed to be.

"I'll find her eventually," he told Molly when he'd completed his fruitless search and joined her again in the bar. "Why not make it easier for everyone and cooperate? I'm not going to snatch her away from here. I just want to make sure she's okay. She can stay with you until Joe and I check things out at her home."

Molly evidently didn't buy the promise. She looked him straight in the eye and said, "I have no idea what you're talking about."

"Have it your way then," Daniel said with a sigh. "I'll be back."

"I'll look forward to it." She gave him a blatantly phony smile. "Does this mean you don't want that chowder?"

Daniel knew that was what she wanted. To be honest, leaving was what he wanted, too. Being around Molly under the best of conditions made him edgy, made him want her in a way that was so ridiculous it didn't even bear thinking about. But because he never took the easy way out, he met her gaze and said evenly, "Of course I want the chowder. Isn't it the best in Maine?"

Her gaze narrowed. "We like to think so. I'll get you a cup. Shall I fix it to go?"

"I'll have a bowl. And I think I'll stick around awhile and see who turns up."

Molly frowned at him, but made no further comment as she headed into the kitchen, no doubt to warn Kendra to stay put wherever she was hiding out.

When Molly finally returned, Daniel regarded her with amusement. "What took so long? Did you have to start from scratch? Maybe go out and dig some fresh clams?"

"Nope," she said cheerfully. "Had to find the arsenic."

Before he could comment on that, an expression of genuine relief spread across her face.

"There's your brother," she said as if Patrick's arrival were a good thing, rather than a complication. "I hope you two will play nice. It's bad for business when there's a brawl in here."

Daniel followed the direction of her gaze to where his twin brother stood perfectly still near the bar. Patrick looked as if he'd like nothing better than to flee, but he sucked in a deep breath, then crossed the room and slid into the booth. That, at least, was progress, Daniel thought. A year ago, Patrick would have acted on his first impulse and left. Their one attempt at making peace appeared to be holding, as long as it wasn't tested too often.

"I'll get you a beer," Molly said to Patrick, then gave his shoulder a squeeze.

They sat there in silence until she'd returned with

the drink, then hurried away again, clearly relieved to have someone else dealing with Daniel.

"You look good," Daniel said finally.

"Being in love does that for a man," Patrick said. "Maybe it's time you tried it." He waited a beat, cast a pointed look toward Molly, then added, "Again."

Daniel didn't miss the significance of the comment or the look. He wasn't going to get drawn into that particular discussion, not if he could help it. "Not likely," he replied. "Too many bad examples all around me."

Patrick gave him a wry look. "So, how are the folks?"

Daniel hadn't expected him to be so direct. He answered in kind. "They miss you."

"The same way they missed Ryan, Sean and Michael?"

"As a matter of fact, yes. I think not a day has gone by in more than twenty years that they haven't missed our brothers. I think we suffered for that. What do you think caused all that resentment we never understood?"

Patrick frowned. "I don't think about it. Maybe you should get together again with Ryan, Sean and Michael and ask them if they feel any sort of pity for our parents. Trust me, they don't."

"I don't know. They seemed like reasonable men to me."

"Reasonable, yes," Patrick agreed. "Not gullible."

"When are they coming back up here? Mom knows they were here for your wedding. I think it broke her heart that she didn't get to catch at least a glimpse of them. I think she would have risked coming to the wedding uninvited, if it hadn't been for Dad. She knew how it would upset him…and you. Maybe she should have, though. Maybe a confrontation then would have put an end to all this."

"I'm surprised you didn't encourage her to do it."

"I might have, if you and I hadn't just started to make peace. I didn't want to risk that. I thought it was a first step. Only trouble is, we seem to be avoiding taking the next one."

Patrick sighed. "You're right. As soon as I start thinking about the folks, I get this sick feeling in the pit of my stomach again."

"See them. Maybe it would go away. Seeing them for the first time is bound to be hard. It'll get easier after that. Tell Ryan, Sean and Michael that, too. Ask them when they're coming."

"I'm not going to push them," Patrick said.

"But you are in touch with them?"

"Why not?" he said defensively, as if Daniel had implied disapproval. "I like them. They feel like, oh, I don't know, family, maybe."

Daniel ignored the sarcasm. "I'm your family, too," he said quietly. "Maybe it's time you remembered that."

Patrick sighed again. "Okay, you're right. I am the one who's being a hard-ass, but you don't make it easy, Daniel, not when you insist on acting as if the folks did nothing wrong."

"Dammit, I know what they did was wrong. So do they, if you get down to it. People make mistakes."

"This was a helluva lot more than a mistake," Patrick countered heatedly. "They didn't just forget to bring in the morning paper or leave an umbrella behind at the office. They forgot three sons and left them to fend for themselves in another state."

Daniel frowned. "Don't you think I know that?"

Patrick held up his hands. "Okay, let's not go down this path again. Why are you here? I assume you didn't come just to hassle me."

"Business." When Patrick regarded him with blatant disbelief, Daniel explained about the runaway he believed was working for Molly. "Have you seen her?"

Patrick's expression remained perfectly neutral. "As far as I know, Molly waits on all the customers herself. Always has."

"And you wouldn't tell me if that had changed, would you?" Daniel said.

Patrick didn't have to respond. It was clear that Daniel wasn't going to get any more information from his brother than he had from Molly or Retta. It was as if they'd formed this tight little circle to keep him in the dark. He dropped the subject. An uneasy silence fell again, the kind that had driven him to stay away in the first place. It had been too painful after all the years when he and Patrick had shared everything.

He regarded Patrick wearily. "When is this going to stop?"

"What?"

"The tension between us. I didn't abandon anyone. The folks did, and we both know they regret it, that they've regretted it every day of their lives."

"I've told you this a million times, but I'll say it once more. You're not going to get me to feel sorry for them," Patrick said bitterly. "They made a choice, dammit. It could just as easily have been *us* they left behind. Would you be so blasted forgiving if that had been the case?"

"But it wasn't the case," Daniel reminded him. "They gave us a home and their love."

"At the expense of three other sons," Patrick argued. "Have they bothered explaining why yet? Or have you even asked?" At Daniel's silence, Patrick shook his head in apparent disgust. "Obviously not."

"Any explanations they have are owed to Ryan, Sean and Michael, assuming they even care at this late date."

"Oh, they care."

"Then why haven't they set up a meeting? I thought they'd want to see the folks when they came up for your wedding, but when I suggested it after the ceremony, they backed off."

"Maybe because it's not so easy working up the courage to confront the parents who abandoned you. Maybe because they're afraid of what they'll do when they see the sorry excuses for human beings who walked out on them."

Daniel understood his brother's pain, but he wouldn't listen to him bad-mouth two people who'd done their best for them, if not for their brothers. Kathleen and Connor Devaney were flawed. They weren't monsters.

"Watch it, Patrick. Those two people gave you life and their love for eighteen years. I won't listen to you talk about them as if they're the scum of the earth. They deserve more respect than that from you."

"Yeah, they gave us everything, all right," Patrick said, his tone scathing. "But at what cost?"

"It must be nice to be so perfect that you can pass judgment on other people's mistakes," Daniel retorted.

Patrick gave him a hard look. "While we're on the subject of mistakes, are you ever going to give Molly the apology she deserves?"

The sudden shift caught Daniel off guard. He knew Patrick was protective of Molly, but he hadn't expected his brother to call him on what had happened four years ago, not at this late date. "I tried. She doesn't want to hear it," Daniel said. "Besides, what good are words?"

"Not much," Patrick agreed. "But she deserves them anyway. She doesn't deserve you coming in here and hassling her over some runaway. There's too much history between the two of you. Next time, send someone else."

"There *is* no one else. It's my job. I'm trying to make sure the girl is safe and gets back to her parents. The fact that Molly has chosen to get herself involved is an unfortunate coincidence."

"Maybe the girl's parents are no better than ours,"

Patrick countered. "Have you considered for one second that she might be better off here with Molly?"

Daniel sighed heavily. "That's not my decision to make, not without all the facts. And if we're just going to go round and round in circles, I might as well get out of here. I'm probably wasting my breath, but I'll ask anyway. Let me know if you see this Kendra Morrow, okay? Try to persuade Molly to get her to talk to me. And warn me if you hear that our brothers are planning to show up on Mom and Pop's doorstep. I'm not sure Dad's heart could take it. Do they know he's had bypass surgery since they were here?"

"I told them," Patrick said tightly. "I doubt they're going to come to the front door and shout, 'Surprise!' Not that I'd blame them if they did. Turnabout's fair play and all that. It couldn't be any more of a shock than what Mom and Pop did to them, letting them come home from school to find an empty apartment."

Daniel winced at the reminder. He didn't like surprises any more than he thought his father's health could tolerate them. "Give me a number. Let me contact them. When they're ready, I'll set up a meeting. That way you won't have to be caught in the middle."

Patrick scowled at the suggestion. "I'd say this is their call…and mine, for that matter, Daniel. After all these years and everything that happened, I'd say they have the right to set the time and place. You don't get to control it, the way you like to control everything else in your life."

Patrick set down his half-filled mug of beer, stood

up, then leaned down to look Daniel directly in the eye. "While you're at it, leave Molly alone. She's a good woman and you've hurt her enough. If it were up to me, you'd pay through the nose for what you did to her, but she's more generous than I am."

"If I'd known about the miscarriage, I would have been there that night," Daniel said, knowing that even that wouldn't have been enough. "You didn't call me."

"Because you didn't exactly step up to the plate when she told you she was pregnant," Patrick reminded him, his accusatory gaze unrelenting. "You were the one responsible for putting her in the hospital in the first place. She didn't want you there. And she doesn't want you barging in here now. She sure as hell doesn't deserve to have you harassing her with your suspicions. Either come back with a genuine apology for what you did back then and today, or stay the hell away from her."

"I can't do that, not while she's hiding Kendra Morrow," Daniel replied. "I'm sorry, but I can't."

"That's right—the rules," Patrick said, his eyes filled with scorn. "If it's written down in black-and-white, you know what you have to do. When it comes to anything else—our folks, Molly, a baby—you don't have a clue."

As Patrick left, Daniel stared after him, sorrow building in his chest. Dammit all, he'd tried to see both sides of this mess with their parents, but sometimes reason lost out to fury. Sometimes he could hate his parents for doing this to all of them. He won-dered what his brother would say if he knew that.

He glanced across the bar to where Molly stood, watching him with a wary gaze. He'd do as Patrick asked and steer clear of her, as well…as soon as she admitted that she was hiding a runaway somewhere on the premises.

3

Molly wanted to smash something, preferably over Daniel's stubborn, hard head. Fortunately, he was gone…finally. And she was left with all sorts of contradictory emotions raging inside.

She went into the kitchen and slammed a few pots and pans around, creating a satisfying cacophony of sound. When she was through, she looked up into Retta's worried face.

"You done now?" the cook asked.

"For the moment," Molly said, her expression sheepish as she faced the woman who'd worked for Jess for decades and served as a surrogate mother to her.

"Daniel get under your skin?"

"As if I'd let that man have any effect on me," Molly said, then sighed at Retta's disbelieving expression. "Okay, yes. He got under my skin, I'll admit it. But only because he was being so pigheaded and arrogant. He came in here and accused me of hiding Kendra."

Retta grinned, clearly amused by her indignation. "Daniel wasn't exactly wrong about that, you know. You are hiding the girl."

"Yes, but he didn't know that, not for a fact," she said, not willing to be swayed by logic. "As if he has any reason to distrust me. He's the one who's not trustworthy."

"Honey, Joe Sutton saw Kendra right here, and unless Daniel's not as sharp as he once was, he saw her, too. He wasn't lying about that," Retta told her quietly. "He was already through the front door when you sent her flying through here and out the back door."

Molly frowned. "Are you saying I should have admitted that Kendra's here and turned her over to him? I don't know why she ran away, but I do know she's scared about something and doesn't want to go home."

"I'm just saying you can't blame him for thinking you had her stowed away somewhere."

Because it was futile to continue arguing the point, Molly asked, "Where is Kendra, by the way?"

"I sent her over to my place. Leslie Sue will keep her occupied till I give the word that it's safe for her to come back. Want me to call over there now?"

Molly nodded. "Make sure Leslie Sue comes back over here with her. If Kendra's scared because of Daniel's visit, she could take off. I need to talk to her. I have to get to the bottom of what drove her to run away from home in the first place. I told her she had a week, but it appears we've already run out of time. Daniel's coming back, no question of that, and I need to prepare her for that, too. I can't protect her if I don't know the truth."

"You think she'll tell you?"

"No," Molly admitted.

"You could call her folks, tell 'em she's safe," Retta suggested.

"I don't know how to find them."

"You do know," Retta corrected. "The name was plain as day on that poster Daniel was waving around." She picked up a slip of paper from the counter. "I made a note of it right here. Got the phone number, too."

Molly hated it when anyone called her on an evasion. No one did it more often than Retta. She scowled at the woman who took pride in serving as her conscience. "I can't betray Kendra like that."

"Well, honey, you'd better do something unless you want Daniel underfoot every time you turn around. The man's not going to leave this alone, no matter how uncomfortable it makes either one of you. When it comes to those kids he looks out for, he's like a pit bull. He doesn't let go."

"I know that."

"Well, then."

"Fine. Call Kendra and get her back over here," Molly said. The prospect of trying to pin the girl down was only minimally more appealing than trying to throw Daniel off track day after day after day.

In the meantime, she went back to tend to her long-neglected customers. When she finished making her rounds, she found Alice Devaney sitting at the bar. Molly frowned at her best friend.

"I imagine your husband sent you over here to find out if his brother had turned me into a basket case," she said.

"Patrick mentioned that Daniel had been here," Alice admitted. "I figured out all on my own that it would probably be an uncomfortable meeting. Are you okay?"

"I survived the first round, but there will be more unless I give him what he wants," Molly told her.

"Which is?"

"He wants me to turn over the runaway who's been staying here."

"I see. Are you sure you're doing the girl any favors by hiding her?"

"Don't you start on me, too. She's better off here than she would be on the streets," Molly said defensively.

"No doubt about it," Alice agreed. "But maybe she'd be even better off at home."

"Or not. How can I be sure?"

"Maybe this is one area where you can trust Daniel to know what's right," Alice suggested cautiously. "I know that goes against the grain with you, but he is the expert."

"At rules and regulations, not human beings."

Alice reached for her hand. "Molly, I'm sorry he hurt you so deeply, but it *is* his job to find and help runaways. From everything I've ever heard, he's very good at it."

"I'm not letting him take another child away from me," Molly retorted without thinking.

Alice gasped. "What are you saying? When did Daniel take a child from you?"

"Forget I said that," Molly said at once. Patrick and Retta were the only two people other than herself and Daniel and the doctor at the local hospital who knew about the miscarriage. It wasn't something she'd wanted spread around the small town of Widow's Cove. She'd insisted that Patrick keep the details from his wife. After all, it had happened long before he and Alice had even met.

"You can't unring that bell," Alice said forcefully. "I'm your best friend, or at least I like to think I've become your best friend since I came back to Widow's Cove and married Patrick. You can tell me what happened."

Molly shook her head. "I don't like talking about what an idiot I was."

"You could never be an idiot," Alice said fiercely. "Come on, Molly. Spill it. You'll feel better if you talk it out. I don't imagine Patrick's all that good at listening. His strong suit would be threatening to knock his brother's teeth down his throat for hurting you."

Molly grinned. "He did offer once or twice. I turned him down, something I sincerely regret at the moment."

"Maybe you shouldn't have. Maybe you'd both have felt better if Patrick had taken some action."

Molly stared at her in shock. "You're advocating I let the two of them brawl?"

"It might have helped them get back together if they'd worked off some of the anger that's been between them for the past few years," Alice said. She waved off the suggestion. "But they're not the point. You are. Tell me what happened between you and Daniel, Molly. I haven't pressed you on this before, but I think it's time you told me."

Molly sighed, thinking back to her first big mistake. "I thought Daniel loved me."

"That's not so awful," Alice said. "Are you so sure he didn't?"

Molly weighed her options and concluded that she could use the advice of a woman who'd had her own struggles with a Devaney man and that complicated family history before finally winning Patrick's heart.

"Okay, here it is in a nutshell," she said at last. "You know that Daniel and I were together for a while."

"I gathered that, yes. And I know it ended badly. You've made no secret of that."

Molly drew in a deep breath, then summed up what had happened in as few words as possible. "It ended because he went ballistic when I told him I was pregnant. The same night we argued, I had a miscarriage and lost the baby."

Tears promptly filled Alice's eyes. "Oh, sweetie, I am so sorry. You must have been devastated."

"I survived," Molly said grimly. "But I won't let him take Kendra away from me, not unless we know for a fact that it's the best thing for her. The kid is hurting. It's not that I intend to keep her for myself, for heaven's sake, but I do want to know why she left home before I send her back to the same situation she ran away from."

"Don't confuse giving up Kendra with losing your baby," Alice said gently. "The two things are not the same at all."

"Maybe not. I just know that Daniel's involved in both of them," Molly replied stubbornly.

"Okay, what can I do to help?"

Molly forced a smile. "Nothing that I can think of, unless you want to stand guard at the front door and keep him out of here."

"I doubt I'm much of a match for Daniel," Alice said. "Anything else?"

"No, and don't worry about it. I'll handle Daniel."

"You wouldn't have to handle him if you'd just do as he's asking and let him see Kendra. I'm sure the three of you could work this out."

Molly knew it was a reasonable suggestion, but if *she* was afraid of risking it, how could she convince Kendra to trust Daniel? "I'll try to persuade her to talk to him," Molly finally conceded, not even trying to hide her reluctance. "But I won't force her to do it."

"Not good enough," Alice said. "She's thirteen. That's too young to be making the kind of decisions that could affect the rest of her life. You're the adult. You need to be smart about this, for her sake and your own."

It was good advice and Molly knew it. In fact, when Alice had gone and Kendra emerged from the kitchen, Molly led her directly upstairs where they could have some privacy.

"Stay put," she ordered. "You and I need to talk as soon as I serve another round of drinks."

Kendra's eyes widened with alarm. "Am I in trouble? What did that guy say to you? I didn't do anything wrong. I'm not wanted for anything. I didn't knock over some convenience store. I never even shoplifted a candy bar. I swear it."

Molly's heart promptly melted at the girl's rush to defend herself. "I know that. But we do have to talk, okay?"

Kendra nodded.

"Watch TV or something till I come back. Whatever you do, don't come back downstairs tonight."

"Is that man coming back?"

"I doubt it," she said, then felt compelled to add, "but Daniel's unpredictable." She'd learned that the hard way.

Even though he was feeling cranky and completely out of sorts, Daniel detoured past his parents' house on his way home. He told himself he wasn't going to go inside, not when he was still worked up by his conversation with Patrick and his war of words with Molly, but as soon as he saw that every light in the house was blazing, he changed his mind and pulled into the driveway. Checking on his parents had become a nightly ritual, one he couldn't break so easily.

Worried by all the lights, he ran up to the front door and let himself in, calling out for his mother and father as he entered.

Inside, nothing more seemed out of the ordinary. The house was filled with the scent of dinner…pot roast, if he wasn't mistaken. The TV was blaring from the living room, a testament to the fact that his father's hearing was worsening, though he refused to admit it.

Since he wasn't up to competing with the evening news for his father's attention, he wandered into the kitchen and found his mother just removing the roast from the oven. She jumped when he spoke to her.

"Daniel Devaney, are you trying to scare ten years off my life?" she demanded, a hand pressed to her chest. A pink blush tinted her pale complexion and gave her more color than usual.

"Sorry, Mom," he said, grinning. "I thought you heard me come in. I yelled for you."

"Who could hear a thing over that racket from the TV?" She brushed a strand of still-black hair back from her face and studied him. "You look tired and worried. Can I fix you something to drink? Dinner will be ready in a few minutes. Will you be staying?"

He shook his head. "I've already eaten. I had a bowl of chowder over at Jess's."

Her blue eyes filled with curiosity. "Oh? What were you doing there?"

"Business," he said, but he could see that she didn't believe him any more than Patrick had. "It's true. Molly's got a runaway hiding out over there."

"Seeing Molly must have been awkward for you," she said, watching his face intently.

"And then some," he admitted. If she'd known the whole story, she would have realized just how awkward. He'd never told her the reason behind the long-ago breakup, most likely because he'd been too embarrassed and ashamed of his part in Molly's miscarriage, to say nothing of the fact that he'd inadvertently left Patrick to deal with the fallout.

"I don't suppose…" she began wistfully, avoiding his gaze.

He knew what she was asking. "Yes, Mom, I saw Patrick."

"How is he?" she asked. "Is he well? Is he happy? Was his wife there?"

It made his heart clench to hear the eagerness in her voice. If Patrick had heard it, he'd never have been able to stay away as long as he had. "Alice wasn't around, but he's well and happy, I think. He still doesn't say much to me."

"And that's our fault, your father's and mine," she said with apparent regret. "I'm sorry for that, Daniel. You two were always so close. If I could change things, I would."

"You could tell him—tell both of us—why you and Dad left our brothers in Boston and brought us here with you." It was the first time since the night he'd made the discovery that he'd put the question to her so bluntly.

"How would that help?" she said, tears in her eyes. "It was so long ago. You were little more than babies."

"We could try to understand, at least. Mom, you are going to have to come up with answers sooner or later. Ryan, Sean and Michael will come here eventually, and they'll insist on it. If you try to stonewall them, it will end any chance of a reconciliation for this family."

Her gaze turned toward the living room, and worry creased her brow. "Your father...he can't cope with that, Daniel."

"He'll have to," Daniel said, his own gaze unrelenting for once. "You owe them, and us, an explanation. Maybe once all the secrets are out in the open, this family can finally start to heal. Don't you want that?"

"Of course I do, it's just that your father feels so much guilt," she said. "He blames himself for everything that happened, even though we made the decision together. You can't possibly imagine how difficult it was, Daniel. No one can."

"Then tell us. Help us to make sense of it. I always thought you and Dad were such good, honorable people. Is it any wonder that this secret of yours took Patrick and me by surprise? What you did was so completely out of character."

She shook her head, as stubborn as all of the Devaneys. "It's up to your father. He's locked that part of our lives away, and I can't go against his wishes."

"But you can talk to him, persuade him that talking about this is for the best. What you did back then is still having repercussions today."

"You said Ryan, Sean and Michael seemed happy and well-adjusted when you met them," she said defiantly. "And Patrick's married now, too. How bad can the repercussions be? They've all moved on with their lives. Some of them even have children of their own now."

"They moved on in spite of what happened, Mom. It's not as if they made peace with it. And those children are your grandchildren. Don't you want to do whatever you can to be a part of their lives?"

"I'm sure your brothers would never allow that," she said, her expression bleak.

"But they might. Isn't it worth taking a chance? And what about me? I've lost four brothers and the woman I loved because of what happened all those years ago."

She gasped at that. "What does you breaking up with Molly have to do with anything your father and I did nearly thirty years ago?"

"It just does," he said. "Take my word for it. The decision you and Dad made has cost all of us. Maybe it's cost the two of you most of all."

"We've learned to live with our choice," she told him, still not backing down.

"And that means you have no regrets?" he asked bitterly.

"Of course we have regrets. We've had regrets every day of our lives since we left Boston, but we can't go back in time and undo what we did."

"You can't undo it, but you can make it bearable for the rest of us."

She reached out to touch him, hesitated, then drew back. "Talking about it might make things worse. Have you considered that?"

"How? How can the truth possibly be any worse than the explanations that each of us has been forced to consider? Were Ryan, Sean and Michael so unlovable? Or did you just draw straws and choose me and Patrick? Were we cuter than the others? Or less trouble? Maybe you meant to leave us behind, too, but we clung too tightly."

Tears were spilling down her cheeks as he spewed out all the questions that had tormented him, questions he knew that his brothers must have asked themselves a million and one times, as well. How could boys of nine, seven and five have been expected to cope with being abandoned? It would have been natural for them to have blamed themselves, to have grown up thinking they didn't deserve to be loved. It was a miracle they'd opened their hearts to anyone.

"Oh, Daniel, don't do this," she whispered. "Not to yourself. Not to us."

"Why not, Mom? You and Dad did it to us." He pushed away from the table. "I've got to get out of here."

"Daniel, don't leave. Not like this."

"I can't stay."

"At least say hello to your father before you go," she pleaded.

"I can't. If I do, I'll say something I'll regret."

He left through the kitchen door and went for a walk, too angry and upset to get behind the wheel of a car. Why couldn't they see that their secrets were destroying their family? What could have driven them to make such a devastating decision all those years ago?

As badly as he wanted answers, he knew that his brothers wanted them even more. They deserved them. He'd tried to warn his mother about that. One of these days, there was going to be a confrontation, and it was going to get ugly. And as much as he loved his parents, as much as he felt he owed them, he wasn't sure he was going to be able to bring himself to mediate, to be the cool voice of reason in such a volatile situation. At that moment, if he had to choose sides, he was going to be on his brothers'. His parents were dead set on not giving him even the tiniest excuse to be on theirs.

Molly was bone weary by the time she climbed the stairs to her apartment. She'd meant to get away sooner, but the bar had been busy and Retta had been on her feet too long as it was. Molly hadn't been able to ask her to fill in waiting on tables.

When she opened the door to the apartment, the TV was on, but Kendra was sound asleep on the sofa, her dark lashes like smudges of soot on her pale cheeks. If Molly wasn't mistaken, there were dried traces of tears there, as well.

"Oh, Kendra, what's going on with you?" she whispered as she pulled a blanket over the girl. "I can't hide you forever, not with Daniel breathing down my neck."

Not that Molly minded the prospect of going a few rounds with Daniel. In fact, if there was some way she could turn his life into a living hell, she was all for it. It would be downright exhilarating.

And maybe a little too much like the old days, she admitted honestly. That could be dangerous. She wasn't over Daniel, not by a long shot. If she hadn't already known that, the sparks flying between them this afternoon would have been a wake-up call. Anyone with any sense knew that hate was the flip side of love, that so much passion could turn on a dime into the opposite emotion. Hating Daniel was a habit, but so was loving him. It was easy enough to hate him deeply and thoroughly from a distance, but proximity had a way of confusing things. Hormones kicked in, and common sense flew straight out the window.

So, she needed to get him back out of her life for her own protection. And the only way to do that was to resolve the situation with Kendra. Easier said than done.

In just a couple of days the girl had stolen a piece of Molly's heart. She was smart and full of life. She was eager to help, desperate for praise. She was all the things Molly had been when she'd come to live with her grandfather. Jess had been there for her, steady as a rock. Now it was her turn to do the same for another scared child.

Resolved to stand by Kendra, no matter what, she went into her room and tried to see it as Daniel must have seen it earlier. Had he remembered the times they'd spent together in her bed? Had he noticed that his picture was no longer on her dresser?

She reached into a nightstand drawer and found the photo, taken on a rocky cliff overlooking the Atlantic. His hair, normally so neatly trimmed to keep the natural curl tamed, had been caught by the wind and mussed. A navy sweater made his blue eyes seem even darker. And his smile...she sighed just looking at it. It was a heartbreaker of a smile, complete with devastating dimples and a flash of pure mischief in his eyes. This was the Daniel she'd fallen in love with, the one with his guard down and nary a rule book in sight.

The Daniel who'd barged back into her life today was the hard professional without so much as a glint of humor in his eyes. When he was like that, it was easy enough to pretend that she'd never felt a thing for him. Of course, the pretense was just that, a lie to keep her safe.

Her hand instinctively went to her belly, covering the empty womb where her child—hers and Daniel's—should have been safe, should have grown until ready to face the world. She struggled against a flood of tears.

"I am not shedding one more tear over that man," she said staunchly. And she'd shed all she could over her lost child.

But despite her intentions, the tears fell anyway. She sank onto the edge of the bed, still clutching the picture, mentally cursing herself for not having thrown it away years ago.

A whisper of sound had her wiping her eyes before she faced Kendra, who was standing uncertainly in the bedroom doorway.

"Are you okay?" the teen asked worriedly.

"I'm just fine," Molly reassured her, then patted the edge of the bed. "Come sit here for a minute."

Kendra sat next to her, keeping a careful distance between them. "I tried to wait up for you. I guess I fell asleep."

"That's okay."

"We can talk now, if you want."

"Sweetie, I need to know why you ran away from home. That's the only way I can help you."

"I can't say," Kendra said, her expression apologetic. "I'm sorry. You're being real nice to me, but I can't. It will ruin everything."

What an odd thing to say. Puzzled, Molly studied her. "What will it ruin?"

"Can't I just stay here a little longer, please? I'm helping Retta. She said I was doing good. She taught me to make chowder today, and the customers liked it. I heard them say so."

"You are good, and if it were just about a job, you could stay," Molly told her. "But you have a home, Kendra. You have parents who are worried sick about you. I have to think about them, too."

"Is this just because you don't want to keep fighting with that man who came today?"

"No, it's because I feel guilty standing between you and your parents when I don't know what's going on." She tucked a finger under Kendra's chin and forced the girl to meet her gaze. "What did they do that was so awful?"

"It's not what they did," Kendra said at last. "It's what they're gonna do."

"I don't understand."

"They're going to send me away," she said, barely choking back a sob. "I'm just saving them the trouble."

And before Molly could ask a single question, Kendra was out of the room and out of the apartment, thundering down the stairs and out into the night.

Molly raced after her, then stopped when she got to the front door of Jess's. Kendra was outside, but she hadn't gone far. Molly pulled a chair over by the door and waited, leaving light from the bar spilling into the street. She wanted Kendra to know that when she was ready, this was one home she could come back to.

4

Daniel tried to spend as much time as possible burying himself in work. Even so, for the next few days he made it a point to stop at Jess's at various times, and at least once a day. He hoped to catch a glimpse of Kendra, but mostly he wanted to keep Molly rattled and aware that he was not letting her off the hook. He hadn't quite decided what time to show up today—probably around dinnertime, maybe not until just before closing when she'd be breathing a mistaken sigh of relief that he hadn't turned up.

In the meantime, he went out to do follow-ups on five cases, checking on at-risk kids to make sure that their situations at home were under control. The unseasonably hot temperatures could escalate tensions, and family members who'd been making positive progress could suddenly revert to old ways. He tried to show up unexpectedly often enough to make sure that didn't happen.

But as he went from home visit to home visit, he

couldn't shake the image of Molly from his head. Why the devil did she have to be so damned stubborn? Couldn't she see that she was just prolonging the inevitable? Sooner or later he would talk to Kendra. It would be best if their first meeting wasn't when he walked through the door with her parents. He liked to make sure such reunions went smoothly, but right now his back was to the wall, thanks to Molly.

He picked up a tuna on rye and a can of soda from the vendor in the basement of his office building in Portland, then climbed the stairs to his office. He found Joe Sutton waiting for him, his feet propped on Daniel's tidy desk, his chair tilted back precariously, his eyes closed. Though it was barely noon, he looked as rumpled as if he'd slept in his clothes.

"About time you got back," he said, startling awake when Daniel knocked his feet off the desk.

"Some of us spend our days out in the field checking on clients," Daniel said.

Joe stared hopefully at the sandwich Daniel was unwrapping. "Is that tuna on rye?"

Daniel sighed. Joe was notorious for always stealing whatever food was around. Apparently there was plenty to be found, because he was at least thirty pounds overweight. That didn't mean he couldn't move when he had to.

"Here," he said, handing the policeman half of his sandwich.

"No chips?" Joe asked, disappointment etched in the lines on his face.

"There's a vending machine at the end of the hall. You'll have to buy your own."

"It's out. I already checked."

"Then you're out of luck."

"So how's the Morrow girl doing?" Joe asked Daniel as he chewed.

"Haven't seen her," Daniel admitted.

Joe's eyes filled with surprise. "Why the hell not? It's not like you to brush off a case."

"I'm not brushing it off, believe me. I'm at an impasse. A *temporary* impasse," he corrected.

"How so?"

"Molly refuses to admit she's there."

"She's there. I saw her."

"I know that," Daniel said. "I spotted her, too. But it's as if the two of them have a sixth sense about when I'm going to walk through the door and, *poof,* Kendra vanishes out the back."

"Any idea why Molly's lying to you?"

"Because she thinks she's helping Kendra. She's not giving her up until she knows what's going on back at the girl's home. Have you made any progress on that front?"

"I've poked around the neighborhood and Kendra's school," Joe said. "From everything I've seen and heard, they're a model family. Mom's a chemist. Dad's a brilliant physicist. Everybody's squeaky clean, as near as I can tell. The kid's some sort of genius. She's skipped a few grades."

"Which is probably why she's been able to run circles around everyone who's been looking for her," Daniel concluded, then added, "with a little help from Molly, who's no slouch when it comes to making up her own rules."

Joe studied him quizzically. "What's that about?"

"What?"

"That edge in your voice when you mention Molly? I heard it the other day, too."

"Ancient history," Daniel said, trying to make light of it.

Even so, Joe reacted with dismay. "Why the hell didn't you say something about having a relationship with Molly when I asked you to go over there? I thought you were just reacting to the fact that the kid was serving chowder in a bar."

"What would have been the point?" Daniel asked with a shrug "You needed someone to go to Widow's Cove and check things out. That's my job. Besides, whatever there was between Molly and me ended a long time ago." Or at least it had, he acknowledged, silently, if you didn't count his reaction to seeing her again.

Joe shook his head. "There are other people in the department."

"But you came to me because Widow's Cove is my turf. Come on, Joe, we've got more important things to worry about than my history with Molly Creighton. Are you ready to pick up Kendra?"

"I've been thinking about it," Joe said. "That's what I ought to do. I ought to call her folks and say I've located their daughter and bring on the happy ending."

Daniel frowned, sensing the unspoken hesitation. "But you're not going to do that, are you?"

"No."

"Why not?"

"Gut instinct. Good kids—*smart* kids—don't take off from perfect parents just for the thrill of it. I want to know what's going on. It's got to be about more than them not letting her wear lipstick or go out on a date with some boy they disapprove of."

"The department could have your badge for not acting on this sooner."

"It's not my case. And I haven't actually seen Kendra Morrow close enough to ID her beyond a reasonable doubt," Joe said. "Have you?"

"No," Daniel admitted. "But we both know it's her."

"Do we really?" Joe pressed.

"Come on, Joe, we're breaking every rule in the book by not reuniting that kid with her family. You know that. Have you even spoken to the investigating officer and told him you think you've located her?"

"I've told him. He's willing to let me do some more digging." Joe leaned forward, his expression intense. "What's the goal here? Yours and mine? It's to keep the kid safe, right? She's not on the streets. She's with Molly. She's safe. We don't know that she would be if we sent her home. I want to know that, in my gut, before I shake things up over in Widow's Cove. I'm going to see the parents, see what my gut tells me about them. You keep trying to get close to the kid. Go around or through Molly, if you have to. Just see her."

Daniel chuckled. "You must not know Molly all that well if you think anybody goes 'around' or 'through' her. That doesn't happen unless she wants it to."

"Want to switch roles? You can go talk to the parents, and I'll work on Molly."

"No way," Daniel said quickly. Too quickly.

Joe gave him a knowing grin. "Didn't think so. Guess that history's not so ancient, after all."

"Go to hell."

"If I'm wrong about this and everything's peachy keen with the Morrows, I probably will," Joe said. "But every time I think I might be wrong, I take another look at that picture. That is one unhappy kid. Could be nothing more than hormones and teen angst, but I won't rest until I know for sure."

Daniel trusted Joe's instincts almost as much as he trusted his own. "Then let's get to work," he said, rising to his feet, his own half of the tuna sandwich still untouched. He could always eat at Jess's.

Joe grabbed the sandwich as they headed for the door. "No need to let this go to waste," he explained.

"You're gonna owe me lunch when this case is over," Daniel said.

"Chowder at Jess's?" Joe suggested slyly.

Daniel shook his head. "I'm thinking a good steak at the fanciest restaurant here in town."

"Boy, you do have it bad for Molly, don't you?"

"Don't be ridiculous."

"I'm never wrong about these things," Joe insisted.

"You're a forty-year-old bachelor, for heaven's sake."

Joe laughed. "How do you think I've stayed that way? Great instincts."

"Well, you're wrong about this," Daniel said defensively. "There's nothing between Molly and me. Not anymore."

"Never said there was. I said *you* had it bad. I'd have to spend a little time around the two of you together to say how she feels."

"Trust me, she's not interested in rekindling an old flame."

And much as he hated himself for giving a damn, the truth of that still stuck in Daniel's craw.

Daniel was about to drive Molly right over the edge. He'd been appearing at the bar more regularly than customers who'd been coming in for years. Midmorning, lunchtime, dinnertime…she never knew when she was going to look up and see him sauntering through the door with that grim, determined expression on his handsome face.

He'd been at it for a solid week now, and she was about to scream from the effort of being polite when what she actually wanted to do was throw a mug of beer in his smug face. At this very moment, he was sitting at the bar toying with the same soda he'd been pretending to drink for the past hour. He wouldn't even touch a real drink.

Molly braced herself and walked behind the bar. "Are you planning to move in? Given the amount of time you're spending in here, I should charge you rent, since the cost of that soda hardly compensates for the space you're occupying."

He leveled a look straight into her eyes. "You could get rid of me easily enough."

"Oh?"

"All you have to do is produce Kendra Morrow and let me talk to her."

"Give it a rest, Daniel," she said, grateful that she'd sent Kendra off for the day with Retta's daughter. Leslie Sue had taken a liking to the girl, and Kendra enjoyed spending time helping her out baby-sitting several neighborhood children, especially since it meant avoiding Daniel's impromptu visits to the bar.

"I can't give it a rest," he told her.

"Why not?" Molly asked plaintively. Lying to him was beginning to get to her. Honesty and trust were big issues to her, and Daniel knew it. She was violating her own sense of decency, and it didn't matter that Daniel didn't deserve any better from her.

"Because she's thirteen years old, Molly. She has a family."

"How much of a family could they be if she felt the need to run away from them?" She very nearly blurted what Kendra had told her, that her parents intended to send her away. Molly hadn't been able to get the girl to say any more than that, but it was just the kind of thing that might make Daniel leap to

Kendra's defense. After all, who knew more about the anguish of kids being sent away by their parents?

He met her gaze evenly. "Kids make some stupid decisions in the heat of the moment. This one could wind up with her getting hurt."

"That won't happen," Molly said, eyes blazing.

"Because she has *you* to protect her?" he asked quietly.

Too late, she saw the trap. So far she'd managed to avoid admitting that she'd ever seen Kendra, much less that she'd provided her with a safe haven. She'd kept their conversations about Kendra purely hypothetical, or at least she thought she had. All the lying was getting to be more and more complicated.

She tried to dance around any admission. "Because she's obviously a smart kid."

"How do you know that?" he pressed.

"She must be, if she's eluded you and Joe Sutton for all this time."

He gave her a wry look. "She's had help doing that, though, hasn't she?"

Molly refused to look away. "I certainly hope so. All children should have someone willing to offer a helping hand when they need it."

"You'll get no argument from me on that score. Usually that's what I am, a helping hand. I could be that for Kendra, if you'd stop standing in the way."

He said it as if there wasn't a doubt about Kendra being there, so apparently Molly wasn't half the liar she'd tried to be. Given the number of opportunities she'd had lately to practice, she was bound to be better before this mess was cleared up.

"I have a legal right and the experience to look out for her," Daniel added. "You have nothing. In fact, quite the opposite. You're interfering in a police matter."

Molly felt her temper kick in at his reasonable tone and at the suggestion that he could be relied on to be anyone's help in a crisis. "I know all about your kind of help," she snapped. "Believe me, wherever she is and whoever she's with, she's better off on her own."

Daniel actually winced at the cutting words. Molly hadn't thought he could ever be wounded by anything she said, but it was apparent that he was. Not that she was going to take back her words or apologize for speaking the truth.

"I'm sorry you believe that," he said quietly. "I won't hurt her, Molly, and I never meant to hurt you. I was trying to protect you."

"Is that what you call turning your back on your own baby and on the woman you claimed to love? Protection?" She could hear her voice climbing, so she turned aside before he could see the tears she was trying desperately to blink away.

She heard him move and thanked heaven that he had the sensitivity for once to go and leave her in peace. But before she could even finish the thought, she felt his hand on her shoulder, gentle, comforting.

"Molly, I'm sorry," he said, his voice thick with emotion.

When she finally risked looking at him, there was so much torment, so much emotion, in his eyes that it nearly stole her breath.

"I really am sorry," Daniel said, brushing awkwardly at the tear that slid down her cheek. He'd never been able to bear making her cry. "What I did was stupid and careless, but I honestly believed I was doing the right thing. I had no idea how it would turn out."

She sniffed. "It could hardly have had a happy ending now, could it?"

"No, but I never thought you'd lose the baby. I never wanted that." His hand cupped her chin. "Believe me. A part of me would have given anything for you to have my child, even if it meant watching him or her grow up from a distance. You would have been a wonderful mother."

Because she so desperately wanted to believe him, because a part of her wanted to block out the past and live in the moment, Molly brushed away his hand. "I can't talk about this anymore. Go away, Daniel. If you ever cared anything at all for me, stay away."

"I can't do that," he said, a hint of regret in his voice.

"Because of Kendra," she concluded, resigned.

He shook his head. "Not entirely. Because of you, too. I don't want things between us to end like this."

She almost smiled at that. "Like this? Daniel, they ended years ago. This? This is a piece of cake compared to the way they ended then."

"Maybe they should never have ended at all."

She stared at him as if he'd started spouting French or some other incomprehensible language. "You can't mean that."

He looked uncomfortable, as if he regretted saying it, but he wasn't taking it back. She waited and waited, but he let the words hang in the air.

Maybe they should never have ended at all.

What was he thinking? Was he crazy? He was the one who'd ended it. He was the one who'd been so insistent that she and their baby would be better off without him. And now, when it was too late to matter, he was saying he'd gotten it all wrong?

She gazed into his dark blue eyes and looked for the man she'd once loved, but she couldn't find him. Didn't want to find him. Not at this late date. It would make what had happened such a waste, even more tragic than it had been.

"Leave, please," she all but begged. "Just for tonight, go."

He lifted his hand, almost reached for her, then dropped it back to his side. "Good night, Molly."

"Goodbye, Daniel."

His lips curved slightly as he noted the hopeful distinction she'd made. "Not goodbye," he said.

After he'd gone, she sank onto a stool at the bar and rested her head on her arms. How was she supposed to get through day after day of having him around, deliberately goading her, trying to get under her skin, reminding her of what had once been between them?

There was only one sure way to get rid of him.

She would have to turn over Kendra. But that was not an option. Molly had made a promise and she intended to keep it, even if she lost her own sanity in the process.

She lifted her head as Kendra quietly slipped onto the stool next to her. Her dark eyes studied Molly intently.

Molly sighed. "I thought you were with Leslie Sue."

"I was, but it's late. I came back. Seems to me like I got here just in the nick of time."

"Why would you say that?"

"The guy was getting to you."

Molly frowned at her, refusing to admit what was obvious not only to her, but apparently even to a thirteen-year-old. "Daniel can't get to me," she insisted.

"Yeah, right," Kendra said, then fell silent.

The silence stretched out for what seemed like an eternity before Kendra said, "Tell me about this Daniel Devaney."

Molly knew what she was really asking, but she said only, "He's a child advocate for the state. That's all you need to know."

"He's not hanging around here just because of me," Kendra said with confidence. "He's got the hots for you. And it goes both ways, doesn't it?"

"Don't be ridiculous!"

"Not that I'm any expert," Kendra said, ignoring her denial, "but it sure looked that way to me. You get all flushed when he's around. And I saw that picture you were holding in your room the other night.

It was him, wasn't it? He's the guy who hurt you, the one you never talked things out with."

"That doesn't matter."

"Sure it does," Kendra insisted. "If you two had a thing once, it's no wonder he gets you all worked up."

"He gets me worked up because he makes me furious," Molly retorted. "He thinks he knows everything. Have you forgotten that he's looking for you? He wants to send you home."

Kendra paled, and Molly immediately felt guilty for reminding the girl of the threat that Daniel posed, when Kendra was thinking only of his effect on Molly.

"Sweetie, do you want to talk to him?" she asked Kendra. "Maybe you could explain why you ran away. Tell him that your parents intend to send you away. Daniel would help. He wouldn't make you go back, especially if your parents were about to abandon you. Believe me, he has some history that would make him very sympathetic to you."

Kendra's expression set stubbornly. "He doesn't look as if he'd be all that sympathetic. Besides, you just said he's here to send me home. I'm not going, not ever."

"He'd only insist on it if it's the right thing to do." She met Kendra's gaze. "Do you trust me?"

Kendra nodded.

"Okay, then. Here's the honest truth," she began, reassured by Alice's expressed belief that this was the truth in her view, too. "Daniel Devaney and I have our issues, but when it comes to helping kids with their problems, he's one of the best. No one's better at defending a kid if the parents are being neglectful or mean. He knows what that's like."

Kendra regarded her with shock. "His parents sent him away?"

"No, that's not exactly what happened, and it's something he should tell you about, not me. But he *will* understand—I can promise you that." She didn't like giving Daniel credit for anything, but she'd seen him spend too many sleepless nights worrying about his cases not to believe that. That's why his persistence now, as annoying as she found it, was both predictable and reassuring.

Kendra nodded slowly. "Okay, I'll think about it."

"You could tell me the rest of the story, and *I* could talk to him, if that would be easier."

Kendra shook her head. "You've been great. You've let me stay here and you haven't asked any questions. Not too many, anyway." Her eyes filled with tears. "I know you think I'm too young to be off on my own, but it's better this way, believe me." She swiped impatiently at the tears that spilled down her cheeks. "If I'm too much trouble, I can go. It's just that this is the first place I've felt really safe since I left home. You and Retta and Leslie Sue, you've been like family."

"Oh, sweetie, you could never be too much trouble. I just want to do what's right. Your parents have to be sick with worry. And you're missing school."

"I've got books in my backpack. I don't need some teacher to tell me what's in 'em. Besides, if

Mr. Devaney really knows I'm here, even though you haven't admitted it, don't you think my parents have been told I'm okay?" she asked.

"I doubt it," Molly replied. "Otherwise your folks would be demanding to see you."

Unless, of course, he and Joe Sutton knew more than they'd been letting on. Maybe that's why they hadn't made a major issue of Kendra's continued— if unacknowledged—presence. They could easily have served Molly with a subpoena for harboring a missing minor or used some other legal tactic if they wanted to play hardball. There had to be some reason why they hadn't. Whatever their reason was, Molly needed to know.

Much as she hated the idea of getting drawn into this any more deeply with Daniel, maybe it was time she made an alliance with one of the men to protect this fragile young girl.

Kendra was watching her intently. "What are you thinking?"

"That maybe it's time I got a little friendlier with the other camp."

"I don't like the sound of that," Kendra said worriedly. "What are you going to do?"

"You know the expression 'If you can't beat 'em, join 'em?'"

"Yeah, so?"

Molly gave Kendra a jaunty, reassuring smile and declared, "I'm going to make Daniel Devaney and Joe Sutton my new best friends."

5

Molly intended to start her new plan by going to see Joe Sutton. After all, Joe was about as close to a neutral party in this mess as she was going to find. But when she called his office at police headquarters, she was told he was out for the day on an investigation.

"If it's an emergency, I can track him down," the officer who'd answered his phone told her.

"No, thanks. I'll call back later if I need him," she said.

She hung up slowly and debated whether to wait for Joe or go to see Daniel instead. Because she didn't like the nagging little voice in her head shouting that she was a coward, she decided to go to Daniel's office. She wouldn't call, though. She'd leave it up to fate whether or not she actually saw him.

And in case fate was feeling particularly whimsical, maybe she ought to put on something fancier than what she wore to work every day. It always threw Daniel off-kilter when she dressed up, and she definitely wanted him off-kilter.

Her wardrobe didn't run to anything too dressy, but she did have a couple of power suits she could choose from when she had to meet with the town muckety-mucks for various permits. Used to seeing her in jeans and T-shirts, the officials were pretty much rendered speechless by the power suits. And the suits gave her a confidence she needed when she was away from her own turf.

She had the choices tossed across her bed when Kendra wandered in, rubbing her eyes sleepily.

"What're you doing?" she asked Molly, flopping down on the bed and only accidentally avoiding the suits.

"Picking out something to wear to see Daniel Devaney," Molly said, studying the suits with a critical eye. One was teal blue and fairly sedate. One was drop-dead red and had a neckline that plunged daringly. She usually wore it with a prim white blouse to negate the sexy effect.

Kendra, awake now, bounced off the bed and peered past her. "Red suit. No blouse," she said without hesitation. "It'll take him a week to get his tongue untangled."

Molly stared at her. "I'm not entirely sure that's the effect I ought to be going for. I want to project friendliness and reliability, not seduction."

Kendra grinned. "Seduction's always better." She said it with the assurance of someone much older.

"How on earth do you know that?" Molly asked.

"I'm female and I'm smart."

"So am I, but I didn't know that at thirteen."

"Maybe you weren't as smart as I am," the girl said, her expression suddenly turning oddly glum.

Something in her tone alerted Molly that the conversation had suddenly turned serious, though for the life of her she couldn't detect why being smart would be a problem.

"How smart are we talking?" Molly probed carefully.

Kendra shrugged.

"Kendra?"

"They say my IQ is off the charts, whatever that means. I don't see the big deal."

"It's something to be proud of," Molly told her, though it was evident Kendra didn't see it that way.

"Yeah, I guess."

Another piece of the puzzle clicked into place for Molly. Not only did Kendra's parents intend to send her away, but her friends at school were more than likely intimidated by her intelligence—assuming she actually had any friends other than kids who wanted to borrow her homework and have her help them cram for an upcoming exam.

"Does that have anything to do with why you ran away?" Molly asked.

"Never mind," Kendra said, her expression pleading with Molly to let the subject drop. "We're talking about you and that suit. Just wear the red one, okay? And I'll fix your hair. That straight style is way too sixties."

Willing to let the girl's reaction pass for now, Molly asked, "What do you know about the sixties?"

"Duh! We studied it in history. Hippies. Free love. Vietnam demonstrations. Woodstock."

For some reason Molly had a lot of trouble thinking of the decade before she was born as being history quite as ancient as Kendra seemed to be implying. Still, it seemed as if that was yet another discussion it would be pointless to pursue.

For the next hour Molly put herself in Kendra's hands. The girl seemed to be getting a huge kick out of playing beauty shop with a real-life woman to fix up. When she was finished with Molly's hair, she stood back and studied her with a critical gaze, then grinned.

"Oh, yeah, Daniel Devaney isn't going to know what hit him," she concluded, then turned the mirror so Molly could finally get a glimpse of herself.

"Oh, my God," she whispered, stunned. She actually looked as if she'd stepped out of the pages of *Vogue* or some other high fashion magazine.

The suit, which was dramatic enough with a blouse underneath, was a knockout with a hint of cleavage showing. The skirt was just short enough to make her legs look very long and slender. Kendra had adamantly tossed aside her flats and picked out her one pair of strappy summer heels.

"Too bad there's not time for a pedicure," Kendra said, eyeing her critically. "You could use some red polish on your toes."

"I think we've gone far enough," Molly said dryly, still overwhelmed by the swept-up hairdo with blond tendrils curling against her cheeks. She'd insisted that Kendra use a light hand with the makeup, but it was still more than she usually wore and her pale gray eyes stood out dramatically. Her lips looked soft, pouty and kissable.

"Now, remember, the lipstick is the kind that won't come off, so you can kiss him all you want," Kendra told her.

Molly scowled. "I am not going over to his office to make out with him. I'm going to poke around for information."

"Whatever," Kendra said. "But you might as well use what you've got." She grinned. "Let's go show Retta."

They went downstairs and walked into the kitchen where the cook was already working on lunch. She took one glance at Molly and dropped the spoon she was using to stir the chowder.

"Oh, my sweet girl, what have you done to yourself?" Retta asked, her eyes wide.

Molly faltered. "Too much?"

"Depends on what you're after," Retta said. "You want Daniel on his knees and weeping, I think you've got it just right."

"I want him talkative," Molly insisted.

Retta shook her head at that. "Doubt he'll get a word out. Poor man. I'd like to be there when you walk through the door. He deserves to get hit with all you've got. Past time for him to realize what he lost the day he hurt you."

Molly's enthusiasm for the makeover was slowly climbing. She wasn't entirely sure the approach was right, but she felt good. She felt like a woman for the first time in a couple of years now. And who better to use to get her confidence back than Daniel? Not that this meeting had anything to do with her. It was all about Kendra, she reminded herself piously.

Retta regarded her with concern. "You gonna be able to keep your head about you when that man starts drooling over you?"

"Believe me, Daniel can't get to me," Molly replied firmly.

"See to it that doesn't change," Retta said. "I'm not interested in picking up the pieces if that man hurts you again. This time I'll just whip his sorry butt. I imagine Patrick will help me."

"Yes, the two of you are quite formidable," Molly agreed wryly. "I'll remind Daniel of that if he gets any crazy ideas."

"Oh, he's gonna get 'em," Retta said. "There's not much question of that."

Molly sighed. "I guess I'd better go. I hope he's in his office after we've gone to all this trouble."

"Maybe you should call," Kendra said worriedly.

"Nope. I want the element of surprise on my side," Molly insisted.

"Honey, we're not talking surprise," Retta said. "We're talking shock. Once you've got him right where you want him and wheedled all that information out of him, you get right on back here and tell us every detail."

"That's right," Kendra added. "We want details."

Molly laughed at their enthusiasm. "I could always take pictures of his tongue hanging out."

Kendra looked around eagerly. "Where's the camera?"

"I was joking," Molly said.

"I'm not. I think I deserve a picture," Kendra insisted. "I could put a before and after shot in a portfolio and be a great movie makeup artist someday."

Now there was a career for a girl with a self-proclaimed IQ that was off the charts, Molly thought. "Well, you can forget the pictures. Let's try to remember why I'm going to see Daniel in the first place."

"To make the man crawl," Retta said.

"No," Molly retorted, scowling at her impatiently. "To make friends, so he'll keep us in the loop on Kendra's situation."

Retta frowned. "Honey, if that's all you want from the man, maybe you'd better put an apron over that outfit. No need to use flash and dazzle, when all you're after is some itty-bitty fish. I thought you were hoping to catch yourself a shark."

Molly hesitated. "Think I could catch a shark, if that's what I really wanted?" she asked, an annoyingly wistful note in her voice. She didn't want Daniel back. She really didn't. She just had to keep reminding herself of that.

"Is it?" Retta asked, her expression suddenly fiercely protective. "Despite all those protests a minute ago, are you thinking of giving that man another chance?"

"No," she said at once, her resolve reinforced by Retta's obvious dismay. "Of course not. I don't know what I was thinking."

Retta nodded approvingly. "That's better, then. You go along. Kendra and I will hold down the fort till you get back."

"Whatever you do, do not let Kendra serve alcohol," Molly said.

"You think I don't know any better than that?" Retta retorted. "I kept you away from the taps all those years, didn't I? Your grandfather always thought you looked real cute filling up an iced mug from one of those big old kegs."

Molly turned and went back to envelop the woman in a hug. "I love you, Retta." And because she caught the wistful expression on Kendra's face, she hugged her next. "Be good."

And then she went off to jump right into the tank with the biggest shark she knew.

Daniel looked up from the file he'd been going over for an afternoon court appearance to find Molly standing in the doorway of his office. For the first time he could ever remember, she looked uncertain. Maybe that was because she was dressed in an outfit that promptly sent his blood pressure soaring into the stratosphere. He swallowed hard and tried to pretend that he wasn't getting aroused just looking at that low-cut neckline and that endless exposure of her long, slim legs. For her to go to this much trouble, she was after something. Too bad it wasn't him.

"What brings you to enemy territory?" he asked, fighting to keep his tone casual when he wanted to leap out of his chair and sweep her into his arms and devour her. That glossy lipstick she was wearing all but shouted for a man to kiss her senseless.

She frowned. "Is that where I am, Daniel? Are you the enemy?" she asked bluntly.

"I'm not yours," he assured her.

"And Kendra? Are you *her* enemy?"

Her expression was so worried, her tone so serious, that he resisted the urge to smile. "We've been over this, Molly. I'd like to believe I could be the best friend she's ever had, if only she'd trust me."

Molly inched into his office and sat gingerly on one of the hard wooden chairs opposite him. She started to cross her legs, saw the hem of her red skirt climb and kept her feet firmly planted on the floor instead. Too bad, Daniel thought with real regret.

"Can she trust you? Can I?" she asked him.

"Only if I know what she's afraid of." He studied her face. She'd done something new with her makeup, too. Her eyes, which he'd always thought beautiful, seemed bigger, the fringe of lashes darker and more dramatic. But right now her eyes were troubled. "Do you know what's bothering her?" he asked. "Are you at least willing to admit to me that she's hiding out at your place?"

He could see the internal war she was waging over the direct question, but she finally made a decision. "Yes, she's with me, but you've known that all along."

"I have," he agreed. "But it's nice to have you trust me enough to tell me."

"I don't trust you, Daniel. Not entirely. But right now you're all we've got. We need you on our side."

He noted that she'd deliberately formed an alliance between herself and Kendra. He was going to have to keep that in mind, however he chose to handle things.

"Why did she run away, Molly? She must have told you by now."

To his surprise she shook her head. "She hasn't said much, not really. I just know she's terrified of going home. She flatly refuses to consider it. I tried to talk her into calling her folks to let them know she's safe, but she's refused to do that either."

He wasn't entirely convinced that was the full extent of Molly's knowledge, but he let it pass for now. "What's your instinct telling you? Has she been abused?"

"Not physically," she said at once. "She was adamant about that."

"You asked?"

"Of course, Daniel," she said with a trace of impatience. "I want to get to the bottom of this as badly as you do."

"And you're convinced she wasn't lying?"

"Not about that. I'm sure of it. She looked absolutely horrified that I'd even asked."

"There are all kinds of abuse," he pointed out.

"I'm aware of that. Hasn't Joe discovered anything?"

"He says that on the surface everything at home looks picture-perfect. She's from a nice middle-class family. She's the oldest. She's always had straight As, gotten involved in a lot of activities, seems popular enough."

"Then why hasn't he forced the issue?" Molly demanded. "You've both known she was with me for more than a week now. If things are so rosy at home, why haven't the two of you swooped in to take her?"

"Chalk it up to an abundance of caution." Daniel met her gaze. "Because it doesn't add up that a kid in that situation at that age would take off just for the thrill of it. There has to be a reason, at least one that seems valid enough to her. Joe's with the parents today. Depending on what he uncovers, we could be at the end of the line unless Kendra can give us some real reason for not taking her back. Can you talk her into meeting with me? I promise I won't pressure her. Maybe the three of us could have dinner, someplace away from the bar. Having you there might make her feel more comfortable. This is important, Molly. It can't be put off."

Molly nodded. "Okay, I get that. When?"

"Tonight, if possible. The sooner the better. Joe and I can't sit on this much longer. He's especially vulnerable because he's ignoring the fact that he could get a missing kid back home again. Cops have been fired for less."

"Then why has he been taking the risk?" Molly asked. "Why have you?"

Daniel met her gaze evenly. "Because, despite

what you think, we both trust your instincts. I know you would never have allowed Kendra to stay if you didn't believe in your heart that she was genuinely terrified of going back home. And Joe's got instincts of his own. He's checking them out. We're all putting ourselves on the line to protect her, Molly, you included. If this blows up and anyone finds out you've knowingly been keeping us in the dark, you-know-what could hit the fan."

Molly regarded him with surprise. "You've let it ride because of me?"

Daniel gave her a rueful smile. "Hey, don't let it go to your head. I've always thought you had your good points."

She dramatically clutched a hand to her chest. "Be still my heart."

His expression sobered. "Molly, convince Kendra to meet with me this evening. It's for the best."

"I'll do what I can," she promised.

"Then I'll pick you both up at six," he said with confidence. And if it happened that she couldn't talk Kendra into coming, having Molly all to himself wouldn't be so bad, either. It might be the last chance they had to make peace before both of their lives were turned inside out over the actions they had—and hadn't—taken to get Kendra Morrow back to her folks.

"Hey, Molly," he said as she headed for the door. She turned back. "Don't change. I like the suit."

She grinned. "It was supposed to make me irresistible."

"You didn't need the suit for that," he said with total sincerity. "I guess some things never change."

Molly's heart was thumping so hard as she closed the door to Daniel's office behind her that she was sure he must have heard it. So, she thought, the suit had done its job. And Daniel was solidly on Kendra's side, or at least making all the right noises. She hoped she could trust him. She had to—they had no choice. Time was running out, and he was the expert. He could make sure the system was on Kendra's side. He knew exactly which buttons to push with the proper authorities to keep Kendra safe.

Too shaky to go straight home, she decided to detour by the elementary school. Classes hadn't started again after spring break, but she knew she'd find Alice there, making preparations for her kindergarten students. She was the most conscientious, innovative teacher Molly had ever known.

At Molly's knock, Alice glanced up from the stack of brightly colored construction paper she was currently cutting into the shapes of spring flowers. When she caught her first glimpse of Molly, her mouth dropped open dramatically.

"Well, well, well, let me guess," she said. "You've just been to see Daniel."

Molly frowned. "How did you know?"

"That outfit shouldn't be wasted on anyone else. Did it do the trick?"

"It didn't render him tongue-tied," she said, vaguely disappointed.

"Devaneys are never tongue-tied," Alice said. "Unless it has something to do with their own family history. Then they can clam up with the best of them. What were you really after with Daniel?"

"I wanted him on Kendra's side."

"And?"

"I think he is, or at least that he wants to be."

"That's good, then. Why don't you seem more relieved?"

"Alice, you know the system when it comes to child protection better than I do. Can Kendra be forced to go back home?"

"She's a minor. Of course she can, unless there's a real danger for her there. Do you believe she's in danger?"

Molly considered the question. "Not the way you mean. I don't get any sense at all that she's afraid of her parents hurting her, not physically, but they have done something that has upset her."

"And you know what it is?" Alice guessed.

She nodded. "At least I have some idea of part of it."

"Did you share that information with Daniel?"

"I couldn't. She told it to me in confidence."

"Would it make a difference?"

"In court, I don't know," she said honestly. "But with Daniel it would. It would push all of his buttons. Should I have used it to make sure he fights harder?"

Alice sat back with a sigh. "That would have meant breaking Kendra's confidence, so no. How could you tell him under that circumstance? But you can encourage her to fill him in."

"I've tried, and I'm going to try to talk her into meeting with him tonight. He says time is running out. Pretty soon he and Joe aren't going to be able to hold back the fact that they know where she is."

"Then why are you here talking to me? Go home and persuade Kendra that she has to trust Daniel." She studied Molly intently. "Or did you really come here to talk about Kendra?"

"Isn't that what we've been discussing?"

"Sure, but I'm thinking that you might really be here to talk about the fact that you're beginning to have feelings for Daniel again and that you're scared."

Molly wanted to deny it, but she couldn't. "I never stopped having feelings for him," she said edgily. "I just buried them. How could I possibly allow myself to be in love with a man who would turn his back on his own child? What kind of woman would that make me?"

"Life is complicated," Alice pointed out. "And love is the most complicated thing of all. You found out the hard way that the man you love has flaws. That doesn't make him a bad person. That doesn't mean you shouldn't love him. It just means you have to weigh who he is against what you can live with."

Molly's eyes filled with tears. "I wanted our baby so much. And I wanted Daniel to be happy about it."

"Well, of course you did," Alice said, coming around the desk to hug her. "And down deep, I suspect Daniel did too. If there had been more time, he might have come around, but you lost the baby, and that robbed him of any chance to see things more clearly."

"Do you really think he might have?"

"Yes," Alice said with surprising confidence. "If he's anything at all like Patrick—and I have every reason to believe he is, since they're identical in every other way—then he would have come around. What the Devaneys did to all of their sons is down-right criminal. They left some of them thinking they weren't deserving of love, and they betrayed Daniel's and Patrick's trust by keeping a huge part of the past a secret from them. Imagine being eighteen before you found out you had three older siblings."

"Not exactly forgivable sins," Molly commented.

"No, but I'm convinced that if they'd all get together in one room and get everything out on the table once and for all, maybe things would be better."

"And everyone would live happily-ever-after?" Molly asked sarcastically.

"Hopefully, yes," Alice said defensively. "What's wrong with wanting that?"

"There's nothing wrong with wanting it, but maybe there are some situations in which that is a totally unrealistic expectation," Molly said.

"I refuse to accept that."

"Are you still pestering Patrick about a reconciliation with his folks?"

"Every chance I get," Alice admitted.

"And?"

"He's stopped telling me to mind my own damn business," Alice said cheerfully. "I consider that progress." She touched a hand to her stomach. "I intend to pull this off before our baby is born."

Molly's mouth gaped. "You're pregnant?"

Alice's cheeks turned bright pink. "I am." She studied Molly worriedly. "Are you okay with that?"

"Why on earth wouldn't I be?" Molly asked. "I adore Patrick, and you're going to be the best mother ever."

"But you—"

Molly knew where she was going and cut her off. "Losing my baby doesn't mean I can't be happy for you." She hesitated, then said honestly, "Okay, so I am a little jealous. I'll get over it."

"You and Daniel could reconcile and—"

"Don't even go there," Molly said sharply. The idea of another chance was too tempting to consider, not even for a moment. "Besides, the only child I can think about right now is Kendra. And I'd better get home and start pulling out every persuasive trick in the book to get her to agree to see Daniel tonight."

"Good luck with that," Alice said. "And, sweetie, don't be too quick to dismiss the possibility of getting back together with Daniel. I'm here to tell you that the Devaney twins might be a lot of trouble, but they are definitely worth it."

Molly grinned. "I believe that about Patrick. The jury's still out on Daniel."

"I don't know. One look in your eyes, and anyone with any perceptiveness at all can see that the verdict's already in."

Molly sighed. "Then isn't it a good thing that Daniel is not the most perceptive man in the universe?"

"You sure about that? He had the good sense to see through that hard shell of yours and fall for you once, didn't he?" Alice taunted.

"Maybe so," Molly admitted. "But I don't believe in lightning striking the same place twice."

"If you stick around a minute," Alice said, gesturing toward her bookshelf, "I'm pretty sure I can find the statistics to prove you wrong."

She probably could, too, which was why Molly had no intention of sticking around. Her opinion was keeping her safe for the moment. She definitely did not want to be confused by any contradictory facts.

6

"Have you lost your mind?" Patrick demanded the instant that Daniel answered his phone.

"Nice to hear your voice, bro," Daniel said wryly. He had a pretty good idea what the call was about, but he asked anyway. "What have I done now?"

"Are you taking Molly to dinner tonight or not?"

"That's the plan," Daniel said, not especially surprised by Patrick's reaction. He wouldn't have expected anything less than this evidence of his brother's protectiveness toward Molly. "How did you find out? Did she tell you?"

"No, she told Alice, who seems to find the prospect of you two getting back together very intriguing," he said, an undisguised note of disgust in his voice. "Of course, she wasn't here when you nearly destroyed Molly. If she had been, she'd be as bent out of shape over this development as I am."

"Patrick, I hate to tell you, but Molly's a big girl," Daniel said mildly. "She can have dinner with anyone she wants to."

"I know that, but does it have to be you? Dammit, Daniel, what were you thinking?"

"Not that it's any of your business, but I was thinking that I could get to the bottom of this mess with Kendra Morrow before the whole thing blows up in all our faces, Molly's included."

Patrick sighed heavily. "Then this is strictly a business dinner?" he asked, his skepticism plain.

Daniel thought of the impact Molly and her red suit had had on his libido. That pretty much ruled out an evening inspired by nothing more than business. If she wore that suit as requested, he'd have trouble keeping his mind on the reason for the dinner, no question about it.

"Pretty much," he said, choosing his words carefully.

Patrick promptly seized on his evasiveness. "What the hell does that mean? Is it or isn't it?"

"If you'd seen the suit she had on when she came to see me today, you wouldn't have to ask that."

"The red one?" Patrick asked, evidently familiar with the pure provocativeness of that particular suit. "She wore the red one?"

"That's the one."

"With a blouse, though, right? Please tell me she wore it with a blouse."

"No blouse."

"Oh, man," Patrick said with a groan. "She's apparently lost her mind, too."

"I will tell you this, if it's any consolation," Daniel said. "I really did arrange the dinner to talk about Kendra. And Kendra will be there to chaperone."

"Now there's a comfort," Patrick replied with an edge of sarcasm. "You've got a thirteen-year-old runaway who's supposed to keep two apparently mentally unstable adults on the straight and narrow."

"Which one of us don't you trust, Patrick? Me or Molly?"

"If Molly's wearing that red suit, I've got to say it's a toss-up. I don't think either one of you will use the sense God gave a duck. You never did when you were together the first time, or there wouldn't have been a pregnancy."

Daniel laughed. He could imagine Molly's indignation if she'd heard Patrick's low opinion of her common sense. Where he was concerned, however, he figured his brother had nailed it. He hadn't used a lot of brainpower when he and Molly had been together before. Then again, he'd never thought far enough ahead to imagine the impact a pregnancy might have. Once he'd been faced with the reality of it, all of his family's past history had kicked in with a vengeance to make him gun-shy. Not that he intended to go over that yet again with his brother. Patrick wouldn't buy Daniel's defense of his actions any more now than he had back then.

"Look, I've got a mountain of paperwork to plow through," Daniel told him. "If you're through being a worrywart, I ought to get back to it."

"Just one more thing," Patrick said.

"Oh?"

"Hurt her again, and this time I *will* knock you into the next county, no matter how she pleads with me not to do it."

"Warning duly noted," Daniel said. "And, Patrick, while I wish things had been different and Molly had turned to me that night, I'm glad she's had you for a friend. You've been a good one."

Once his brother had hung up, Daniel sighed. He would spend the rest of his life cursing the fact that Molly had needed to turn to someone else for comfort and support because of him.

The phone was barely back on the hook before it rang again. This time it was Joe Sutton, and Daniel could tell immediately that the news wasn't good.

"You saw the Morrows," he said flatly.

"I did. They're fine, upstanding people. I didn't get so much as a whisper of anything out of the ordinary. They have no idea why Kendra might have run away, and they're beside themselves that she did. There is no reason I can see not to get the girl back home pronto and give them some peace of mind."

Daniel winced at that. If Joe was convinced, he had no reason to question it, but Kendra's fear was real. Molly would have been able to see through it if it had been something the girl had made up or was dramatizing in some way.

"Give me till morning," he pleaded with Joe. "Can you do that?"

"What's going to change between now and tomorrow morning? Those people are going through hell worrying about their daughter. I felt guilty enough looking them in the eye and not admitting that I could take them straight to her. Any more delays and my goose is cooked. Yours, too."

"We're both already in this up to our eyeballs," Daniel pointed out. "Let's at least go the extra mile. I convinced Molly to set up a meeting with Kendra and me tonight. If I can get her to open up, tell me her side of things, we'll know for a fact that we're doing the right thing. With what you've just told me, I can ask the right questions, push a little harder for the right answers."

"I don't think Molly's going to let you lean on Kendra," Joe said dryly. "She's a runaway, not a criminal."

"And I'm going in there tonight as a friend, not an authority figure."

"Are you going to try to persuade her to go home voluntarily?" Joe asked. "The last thing I want to have to do is come in there with sirens blaring and haul her out."

"You're just worried Molly will ban you from the premises and you'll be cut off from your chowder fix," Daniel said.

"No, believe it or not, I'm worried about traumatizing the girl."

"Then we'll see to it that it doesn't go down that way, okay?"

"I'm heading over there at nine a.m.," Joe said finally. "I'll expect to find her ready, if not eager to go home."

"I'll be right there with you," Daniel promised.

"Thanks, Joe. I know you've gone out on a limb for this kid. I'll back you up in any way I have to."

Now he just had to convince Kendra and Molly that sending Kendra back home was for the best. He had no idea which of them was going to be the harder sell.

"You go," Kendra insisted when Molly told her about the dinner plans. "I can stay home and read. I've got lots of books. I'll be fine."

"You're missing the point," Molly said. "Daniel wants to get to know you."

"He wants to cross-examine me, you mean," Kendra said knowingly. "Thanks but no thanks."

"It won't be like that. I'll see to it," Molly promised.

Kendra regarded her skeptically. "The way I see it, the man wants two things out of this dinner…answers from me and a chance to spend a little quality time with you. He ought to be happy with a batting average of five hundred."

Some men might be, but not Daniel. "I promised him I would persuade you to come," Molly told her. "Sweetie, he could have turned you in by now, if that's what he wanted—he or Joe Sutton, either one. They haven't done it. That should tell you something. They both want what's best for you."

"I suppose," Kendra said with obvious skepticism.

"What will it take to convince you that I'm right about this?"

"Sworn statements that they're not sending me back to my parents," Kendra said without hesitation.

"I don't think you're going to get that, not until you've given them valid reasons why you don't want to go back there."

"Who gets to decide what's valid?"

"For now, they do. The court, if it comes to that."

"Now there's a reassuring thought," Kendra said. "Some judge who doesn't know me or my parents gets to decide what's best. Let's see, the judge would be a grown-up. My folks are grown-ups. I'm a kid. I wonder which way this will go?"

"I'm a grown-up and I'm on your side," Molly pointed out. "And Daniel and Joe have been on your side, even without all the facts, right? If you believe what you've done is the right thing, give us a chance to help you prove it."

Kendra seemed to weigh Molly's words for an eternity before finally nodding. "Okay, I'll come, but I'm splitting if I don't like the way things are going."

"Agreed," Molly said with relief. She had not wanted to spend an entire evening alone with Daniel. The prospect of that scared her at least as much as the prospect of all those questions terrified Kendra.

Downstairs, Molly filled Retta in on the plans and placed a call to her backup waitress and bartender. She wanted to be certain that nothing was left to chance now that Kendra had agreed to go along with meeting Daniel. Once satisfied that everything was in place, Molly called Daniel's once-familiar number and tried not to react at the sound of his voice.

"It's me," she said quietly.

"Hey, you," he said. "What's up? Are we all set for this evening?"

She could hear the smile in his voice and felt the familiar pang of yearning. "We're set. Kendra's skeptical about your motives and your intentions, but she's agreed to have dinner with us."

"Then I'll see you at six. How about pizza? All kids love pizza, right?"

"So do you, as I recall."

"This is about putting Kendra at ease," he insisted. "If I can get a pepperoni and mushroom pizza out of it for myself, so much the better."

"If we're going to Giorgio's, I'd better get upstairs and change," she said. "The red suit will be a bit much." She heard his sigh of disappointment with a sense of purely feminine satisfaction. "You did pick pizza," she reminded him.

"Obviously one more bit of evidence of just how big a fool I am," he said. He could name one person who'd be pleased, though—his brother. Patrick had really hated the idea of him spending time with Molly while she was wearing that suit.

"Daniel, this is going to be okay, right? You're not leading me down some garden path intending to betray Kendra the first chance you get, are you? Joe's not going to be lurking in the bushes to grab her, is he?"

There was no mistaking his slight hesitation.

"Daniel Devaney, you'd better tell me what's going on, because if I find out that this is some kind of ploy, I'll make you pay for it."

"It's not a ploy," he said at once. "But there has been a development. Joe saw the parents today. Everything checked out. He can't find a single reason not to take Kendra back home."

"She's scared," Molly retorted, barely managing to keep a lid on her temper. "Isn't that reason enough?"

"Not unless she can explain *why* she's scared," he said quietly. "That's what tonight is about, Molly. I swear to you that I'm going to give her a chance to tell me what's going on. If it gives me something to work with, I can hold Joe off. He's already given me till morning, which is more of a concession than we probably deserved. With the right ammunition, I can extend that."

"Or?" she asked, her heart in her throat. "What happens if Kendra doesn't give you something you think justifies her staying away?"

He hesitated, and she knew he was debating whether or not to trust her.

"Joe comes by in the morning to pick her up," he said finally.

Molly groaned. "Dammit, Daniel, why did you have to go and tell me that?"

"Because I don't want there to be any secrets between us. This is too important. I want you to know that I trust you not to do anything crazy, like running off with her."

For one insane minute that was exactly what had popped into Molly's head. She could pack up a few things and they could be gone in an hour. But she knew that Daniel would be on their trail in no time, as would Joe Sutton. They would be a whole lot better at tracking her down than she would be at evading them.

"Once you've heard her out, you have to tell Kendra the truth about what's going to happen next," she said finally. "She has to be prepared."

"Only if you'll promise to do everything in your power to assure that she's there in the morning if we agree that Joe picking her up is the way to go," he said. "The last thing any of us want is for Kendra to take off on her own again, right?"

"Right," she said emphatically. Molly would go with the teen before she would let that happen.

"I'll see you at six, then," he said.

"Daniel, why does life have to be so darned complicated?" she asked, unable to keep a wistful note out of her voice.

"I wish I knew the answer to that. Maybe over dinner we can all come up with some way to keep it simple."

"Sounds like a tall order."

"But we're smart people," he said. "And from what I hear, Kendra's a genius. Maybe she'll be the one to show us the way."

"She already has. She ran away. Apparently we're just not listening."

"I will listen," Daniel promised. "Trust me, Molly. When it comes to kids in trouble, I always listen."

She knew that was true. Maybe that's why it had been an even harder blow when he hadn't listened to her pleas on behalf of one innocent baby who couldn't speak for himself.

* * *

Knowing that Molly didn't trust him made Daniel ache inside. He wanted to blame her for it, but he couldn't. He had no one to blame but himself. He'd told her he loved her how many times? A thousand, maybe. But when she'd come to him on that fateful night, excitement and trepidation in her eyes as she'd told him about the baby, how had he demonstrated that love? By embracing her and the news? No. He'd rejected her and the baby, dismissing any possibility of becoming involved in parenting.

Oh, he'd had his reasons. Good ones, for that matter, but they weren't good enough. Any real man would have stepped up to the plate and accepted more than financial responsibility for his own child. In turning his back, he'd proved himself to be Connor Devaney's son. It was a regret he'd live with the rest of his life.

Sighing, he tried to get his attention back on his never-ending mountain of paperwork, but he couldn't concentrate. He couldn't fight the image of Molly in his head, fighting tears, her spine and shoulders rigid with pride as she'd turned and walked away. He'd stared after her, helpless, knowing what he should do, what he *wanted* to do, but lacking the courage to take the first step.

And then she'd been gone, not just out of sight but out of his life, a door slamming shut between them as securely as if it had been the impenetrable door of Fort Knox. Not until he'd heard the lock click into place had he realized how much he'd lost—the woman he loved, his child, his future.

The next day Patrick had told him about the miscarriage. It was one of the rare times since Patrick had left home when he'd initiated any conversation between them. He'd been all but trembling with outrage, his voice cold as he'd recited the bare facts about the trip to the hospital, then told Daniel in no uncertain terms to stay the hell away from Molly.

"You've done enough, more than enough," Patrick had told him. "I never thought I'd say this, not even after I moved out of the house and you stayed behind, but I'm ashamed to be your brother."

Even after all this time, Daniel could feel the words cutting through him, slicing his heart in two. He hadn't fought back, hadn't tried to explain. There were no acceptable excuses for what he'd done and they'd both known it.

Not that he'd listened to Patrick, not about staying away from Molly. He'd waited a day, then gone to see her, wanting her to know how sorry he was. He hadn't expected her forgiveness. He'd simply known that he owed her the apology. He hadn't been surprised when she'd thrown it back in his face.

Given all of that, it was little wonder that she couldn't wholeheartedly get behind advising Kendra to trust him. That she'd even arranged the meeting was something of a miracle.

He sighed when the phone rang, not in the mood to deal with a last-minute crisis.

"Hello, Devaney," he said curtly.

"Daniel, it's me." Kathleen Devaney's voice shook.

"Mom? What's wrong?" Something had to be. She never called him at work.

"Do you think you could come by the house?"

The uncertainty in her tone, the hint of a barely contained sob, scared him. He glanced at his watch. It was after five, less than an hour until he was supposed to pick up Kendra and Molly.

"Is it Dad? Is he having a problem with his heart?"

"No. It's your…there are some people here. Please, Daniel. I wouldn't ask if it weren't important."

A million questions tore through his mind at once. Had his brothers shown up out of the blue despite his pleas to Patrick? That had to be it. He weighed his options. None of them were attractive. He could blow off his mother's cry for help or he could call Molly and cancel, risking the fragile trust she and Kendra had in him. With a 9:00 a.m. deadline staring all of them in the face, postponement of tonight's meeting carried all sorts of risks. Even so, he'd always been a dutiful son, even when it hadn't been easy. He couldn't fail his mother now.

"I'll see what I can do about rearranging my schedule," he reassured his mother. "I should be there in ten minutes."

"Thank you."

He was already en route when he called Molly from his cell phone. "I need to postpone dinner," he told her.

"Just like that?" she asked incredulously. "I thought this was so important. I thought it had to be tonight."

"You're right," he admitted, never more aware of how impossible it was to struggle with divided loyalties. "It is important, but I just had a call from my mother. There's some sort of emergency at the house. I'm on my way there now. If it's something I can deal with in a few minutes, I'll get back to you and we can still make dinner."

He thought of his fear that he was going to find his brothers there. "My hunch, though, is that it's going to take longer. If it's not too late when I'm through there, I'll come by the bar and apologize to Kendra in person."

"And Joe Sutton? Can you put him off?"

"I'll work it out. I promise. Joe won't show up until I've had a chance to meet with you and Kendra."

"Fine," she said, her voice tight.

"Molly, I won't let you down," he told her urgently. "I won't. Mom said this is an emergency. I have to go."

She sighed. "Of course you do. I hope everything's okay when you get there."

He imagined the hell that might be breaking loose if this involved his brothers. "So do I," he said grimly. "So do I."

7

Molly slowly hung up the phone. She'd heard the genuine worry in Daniel's voice and knew he wouldn't be putting off this meeting with Kendra if there weren't a very real crisis at home. Still, she wasn't looking forward to trying to explain that to Kendra. The girl was suspicious enough. This would only reinforce her general distrust of adults, her belief that no one could be trusted to keep their word.

"Who was that?" Kendra asked, regarding Molly warily.

"Daniel," Molly admitted. "Now, I don't want you to get upset, but he's had an emergency. He's postponing dinner."

To her surprise, Kendra's expression immediately brightened. "Good! Then we can go out, just you and me," she said enthusiastically. "Who needs him?"

"At the moment, you do," Molly reminded her.

"You're not going to turn me over to that cop," Kendra said with confidence. "You know I'll just take off again if you try."

Molly tried to explain the position she was in, the position all the adults were in who were aware of Kendra's presence in Widow's Cove. "Sweetie, there are a lot of people who have to balance what's best for you against your parents' interests."

"Yeah, right. All they care about is protecting their own backsides in case my parents get mad at them."

"Is that what you think I'm doing?" Molly asked.

Kendra had the grace to look chagrined. "No, not really." Her chin jutted up defiantly. "But I'm not going back there. No one can make me."

"Actually, they can," Molly said, fighting for patience. "But they won't if you can give Daniel and Joe a valid reason why you shouldn't have to go."

"Why can't I just stay with you?" Kendra asked plaintively. "I could go to school here. My grades are real good, and I've been studying all along, so I could probably pass final exams in any classes, even if I haven't been here all year. Then everything would be great."

"There are probably a million reasons why that won't work," Molly said with regret. "For starters, I'm not a relative. Nor am I licensed to be a foster parent. I run a bar and live upstairs. I'm single and—"

"But you care what happens to me," Kendra replied, cutting her off. "Isn't that the most important thing?"

"I'm sure your parents care about you, too."

"If they did, they wouldn't be making me go away."

"Where, exactly, are they making you go?" Molly asked. Kendra made it sound as if they were sentencing her to hard labor. Molly couldn't believe it was anything other than what her parents thought was best for her, though where that could be, she couldn't imagine.

"Away," Kendra said flatly. "That's all that matters. They're sending me away and I don't want to go." She spun around and slid off the stool, then headed for the kitchen.

"You can forget about dinner. I don't want to go with you, either," she said, flinging the words back at Molly.

Molly stared after her and sighed. It was plain that Kendra wouldn't answer any more questions on that particular topic. Molly had to wonder if she would be any more forthcoming with Daniel.

In the meantime maybe Retta would have better luck probing for answers than she had had. Retta had always had a way of making Molly comfortable enough to talk about her innermost feelings, things she wouldn't have dared to share with her grandfather. Maybe Retta could work the same sort of magic with Kendra.

Molly had always heard that life with a teenage girl could be complicated. She was beginning to see the evidence of that firsthand. She could only pray that she wouldn't do or say anything to make Kendra's life—or her own—any more complicated.

* * *

Five minutes after ending his call to Molly, Daniel turned into his parents' driveway. There was a fancy, unfamiliar SUV parked in front, along with Patrick's easily recognizable pickup. As soon as he spotted the cars, Daniel's heart began to beat harder. There was no longer any question in his mind about what he was going to find when he walked through the front door. The only question mark was just how bad it was going to be.

He paused at the front door, drew in a deep breath, then stepped inside, expecting to be hit with a barrage of shouted recriminations. Instead, he was greeted with total silence. All those people and no one was making a sound? It didn't make sense. In fact, it was downright eerie.

He walked through the foyer to the living room, which they'd rarely used. It was kept spotless for company, not for use by rambunctious boys. Even after he and Patrick were older, the living room had remained off-limits, too stiffly formal to be inviting.

Now there were four men seated awkwardly on the sofa, their expressions dark and forbidding. His mother perched on the edge of an uncomfortable but prized antique chair, her hands twisting nervously in her lap. Naturally his father was nowhere in sight. He'd probably taken off at the first sign of tension.

Patrick glanced up when Daniel entered the room. "I imagine you were called in to save the day," he said.

Daniel ignored the barb and paused to give his

mother's shoulder a squeeze before crossing the room to greet his brothers.

One by one the others stood and shook his hand. First Ryan, the oldest. Then Sean, and last of all Michael. There was no mistaking the fact that they were Devaneys. They had his father's dark Irish looks, just as he and Patrick did. There was little of their mother in any of them, except for a slight softening around Ryan's mouth when he smiled, which he wasn't doing now, and in the paler blue of Michael's eyes.

Worried about his mother's pallor, Daniel turned back to her. "Mom, why don't you make one of your coffee cakes?" he suggested gently.

When Ryan and Sean exchanged a glance, Daniel studied them curiously. "What?"

"We've talked about those pecan coffee cakes," Ryan explained. "We both remembered how our mother always baked them on special occasions." He said it as if she weren't in the room, as if she'd died long ago.

Despite Ryan's distant tone, their mother hesitated in the doorway, the first faint trace of a smile on her lips. Her eyes shone with an unmistakable wistfulness. "You remember that?"

"I went out and bought one like it the first time Ryan came to see me," Sean said, looking vaguely uncomfortable at the hint of sentimentality. "It felt right, somehow."

Daniel glanced at his mother, but her eyes were filled with tears, and she seemed incapable of speaking. He filled the silence. "She still bakes them for

Easter and Christmas and birthday breakfasts, right, Patrick?" he said, hoping to draw his twin into the conversation.

Patrick merely shrugged as if it were no big deal that a mere coffee cake stirred memories for all of them. Daniel realized there would be no help from him. In fact, Patrick looked as if he'd rather be anyplace else at that moment.

"Are there other things you remember?" Daniel asked, looking from one brother to another, hoping to encourage more happy memories.

"Her spaghetti," Sean supplied, though he didn't look especially happy to be sharing that. "My wife's boss makes sauce that's almost as good, but there's something missing."

"A spoonful of sugar, I imagine," their mother said shyly. "It's a secret I learned from my mother."

Daniel turned to Michael, who'd remained silent. "Is there anything you remember?"

His expression still hard, Michael looked from Daniel to his mother and back again. "Being left behind," he said harshly.

Daniel hadn't expected the blow to come from Michael. When they'd first met, he'd had the impression that Michael remembered the least from the past, and that his foster family, the Havilceks, had made the intervening years good ones.

Tears welled up in his mother's eyes. "I'm sorry," she whispered, her anguished gaze on Michael. "You'll never know how sorry."

Daniel regarded his brother angrily. "Is that what you came for, Michael? All of you? Are you only interested in hurting her? In making her and Dad pay for what they did?"

"I think we have a right to be angry," Ryan said quietly.

"Damn straight they do," Patrick said heatedly. "Stay out of it, Daniel."

But he couldn't. He saw the torment on his mother's face, and he couldn't allow them to continue with a barrage of accusations that would accomplish nothing. He turned back to his mother with a forced smile. If the issues between them were ever to be resolved, they had to talk without bitterness, openly and honestly. He could see that wasn't likely right now, not when things had gotten off to such a rocky start.

"Mom, go on and bake the coffee cake," he told her. "Give me a few minutes with Ryan, Sean and Michael."

Patrick was on his feet at once. "Stop protecting her."

"Your brother's right," she told Daniel gently. "I don't deserve your protection."

"Well, you have it, anyway," Daniel said. "I won't let them come in here and hurt you."

"They're entitled to their say," she said.

"In a minute," he said flatly. "After we've talked. Please, Mom, leave us alone."

She started to leave, then turned back, her gaze on

Ryan. "It's been so long," she whispered, her voice shaky. "You won't leave, will you? Not right away."

"Not without saying goodbye," he promised.

She nodded, apparently satisfied that she could rely on the word of her eldest son, then left the room.

As soon as he was certain she was out of earshot, Daniel whirled on his brothers. "How dare you come into her home and badger her like this? I thought you were going to give me some advance notice, let me smooth the way." He focused on Patrick. "Didn't I talk to you a couple of hours ago? Why didn't you warn me?"

"Not that it matters, but I didn't know about the visit till they showed up at my house," Patrick retorted. "I already knew about your plans for the evening, so I didn't bother to call. I should have guessed that Mom would run to you the second we showed up."

"It's not as if she has anyone else she can turn to," Daniel said. "Dammit, Patrick, you should be more sensitive. We talked about this."

"Yeah, well, how dare you try to stop them from saying what's on their minds?" Patrick replied. "How the hell do you expect to smooth this over, Daniel? Platitudes and apologies aren't enough, not by a long shot."

Ryan stepped between them, one hand on Patrick's shoulder. "Cool it, you two. There's no need for you to be fighting because of us."

"There's every reason," Patrick insisted, clearly aligning himself with the brothers who'd been abandoned. "Daniel refuses to acknowledge that what our parents did was wrong. If it were up to him, he'd sweep all those years under the carpet. Well, I'll say it if he won't. What they did was unconscionable. It can't be ignored or prettied up." He scowled at Daniel. "You, of all people, have to know that. You deal with abandoned kids all the time. Our parents did that to Ryan, Sean and Michael, our brothers. How can you defend them?"

Patrick looked as if he wanted to take a swing at Daniel. Daniel would have done nothing to prevent it, but once again Ryan put his hand on Patrick's shoulder.

"It's okay," Ryan said.

Patrick shrugged off the contact. "It's not okay. Not what they did to you back then. Not what Daniel's trying to do now. I'm out of here. The rest of you can do whatever the hell you want."

The tension in the room was thick enough to cut as Patrick stormed out. Daniel tried to find the words to make things right, but there were none. None at all.

"I'm going to check on Mom," he said finally. He looked at Ryan. "Will you be here when I get back?"

"I promised that I wouldn't leave without saying goodbye," he said, glancing at the others for confirmation that they would go along with that. They nodded curtly, clearly reluctant to stay but unwilling to break Ryan's promise.

"Then give me a few minutes. Patrick's right about one thing. I think it's important for all of us to get past this."

Ryan regarded him with a shuttered expression. "I honestly don't know how that's possible. I'm not sure what I was expecting when we came here, but I don't think I'll find it. Seeing her again…" His voice trailed off. "It just brought all of it slamming back into me."

"Me, too," Sean said, his expression grim. "I guess I'd hoped that it would be different once we'd seen her, but it just makes the pain that much worse. We're not blaming you, Daniel. You had no part in any of this."

Daniel sighed heavily and glanced at Michael, who looked no happier than the others. Daniel could understand his brothers' reservations. He had a million of his own. "Please don't rule out giving them another chance," he said quietly, then went to see how their mother was holding up.

He found her in the kitchen, her coffee cake ingredients spread across the kitchen table, her hands idle, her eyes distant. It was evident that she was lost in memories, none of them happy.

She looked up when he came into the room. "Are they still here?" she asked anxiously.

"They're waiting to say goodbye."

She stared at Daniel helplessly. "I don't know what to say to them. How can I explain what their father and I did all those years ago?"

"Speaking of Dad, where is he?"

"He'd gone out earlier, thank the Lord. I don't think he could have handled this."

"Then he doesn't know they're here?"

She shook her head.

"When is he due back?"

"Not for a while yet."

"Mom, maybe you should go back in there and say goodbye for now. We can arrange another time to meet. You and Dad can talk over how you want to handle it, what you want to tell them."

She gave him a sad look. "They don't deserve anything less than the truth."

Daniel squeezed her hand. "Then that's what you'll tell them, but not today. I think you've been through enough, having them turn up here unexpectedly like this."

She touched his cheek. "You always want things to turn out for the best for everyone, but sometimes that's not possible, Daniel. There would never be an easy way or a right way to do this. And I'm not entitled to any compassion from those three men in there. They're my sons, just as you are, and I turned my back on them and walked away. It wasn't easy and it wasn't what I wanted, but I did it because your father insisted it was the only thing to do. I can hardly bear to look them in the eye and see the pain your father and I caused them."

She visibly drew herself together and stood up. "But I will face them. And I will answer their questions. I owe them that."

"Not today," Daniel insisted. "You've been through enough for today."

"They've been through more," she said with quiet resolve.

Daniel watched her walk slowly back into the living room, never prouder of her than he was at that moment.

But when they got there, only Ryan was waiting. He was on his feet, staring out the window. He turned slowly.

"The others are waiting outside, but I didn't want to go back on my promise. I'll say goodbye now."

Kathleen Devaney's step faltered, and she reached for Daniel's hand, her gaze on Ryan. "But you will come back, all of you?"

Ryan's gaze remained steady and unflinching. "I honestly don't know. I'm not sure I see the point."

She reached for him, then her hand fell back. "Please, you must. You've come this far. I know the answers must be very important to you. Come back tomorrow or next week. Whenever you're ready. I'll tell you whatever you want to know. You should see your father, too. He should see what fine young men you've turned out to be, despite what happened."

"I'll try," Ryan said, his tone even more noncommittal than his words. "Sean and Michael say they're through."

"Try to change their minds," she pleaded urgently. "It used to be they would listen to anything you said."

Ryan sighed. "That was a long time ago. For a lot of years, while we were apart, they blamed me for the separation almost as much as they blamed you and Dad."

She looked genuinely shocked by that. "How could they? You were a boy."

"It's not a rational reaction," Ryan said. "It's the reaction of two scared little boys who were abandoned by their parents, then separated from their big brother. They were sure there had to be something I could have done to keep us together at least."

Daniel tried not to feel the anguish his brothers had felt all those years ago, but it ate at his gut. He'd seen it too often in other frightened children who were facing an uncertain future. He'd seen it in Kendra Morrow's haunted eyes.

His mother was right. He spent his life trying to find happy endings for kids like that. He wanted one now, even though it was years and years too late. He wanted it for his brothers, even for his parents. They needed this as much as Ryan, Sean, Michael and Patrick did. As much as he did. They all needed to find peace, so they could move on.

"Ryan, they still look up to you. I saw it the first time we met on Patrick's boat. You can get them back here again," Daniel told him.

Ryan looked from Daniel to his mother, then back again. "I'll do the best I can," he promised. "If I can convince them to stay over, I'll call to set a time. If you don't hear anything, it's because they're determined to go back to Boston."

"Thank you for being willing to try," their mother said, her relief evident. "And, Ryan, I probably have no right to say this, and it might not even matter to you, but not a day has gone by that I haven't thought of all of you and prayed for you. You deserved better."

Ryan's gaze never wavered. "Yes, we did."

And then he was gone, and Daniel was left to deal with his mother's tears.

8

It was nearly midnight and the bar was empty as Molly wiped down the tables and put the chairs back into place, then gave the floor a more thorough scrubbing than usual. There was something comforting about the routine of it in the midst of the turmoil her life had become.

Kendra had gone to bed two hours earlier, still disgruntled over their earlier argument. Despite Molly's attempts to persuade the sulky adolescent, she'd continued to refuse to go out for pizza and had spent most of the evening in the kitchen with Retta, as uncommunicative with her as she had been with Molly.

Usually by now Molly would have gone upstairs herself, but she was feeling restless. She couldn't seem to stop wondering what had happened to Daniel. What sort of emergency had there been that had caused him to cancel an important first meeting with Kendra, especially with Joe's deadline looming over them? And why hadn't she at least heard from him by now? Surely the crisis couldn't have lasted this long…unless someone was seriously ill.

She made herself a glass of iced tea and sat at the bar, idly stirring in sugar, her thoughts a jumble. Maybe she should stop counting on Daniel to come up with a solution for Kendra and take matters into her own hands. There was still time before morning to bolt. They could be a few hours ahead of any search. Maybe that was all the edge they'd need.

"Don't even think about it."

The sound of Daniel's voice right behind her startled her so badly, she knocked her tea all over the just-mopped floor. She whirled around and scowled at him.

"Look at what you made me do," she snapped, going behind the bar to get a rag to mop up the mess and to put some distance between herself and Daniel.

He gave her a knowing, unapologetic look. "I wouldn't have startled you if you hadn't been trying to formulate a sneaky plan to take Kendra and make a break for it."

"I was not," she denied, though she could feel the heat of a blush climbing into her cheeks at the blatant lie.

"Oh, please. I might have been teasing, but your guilty conscience was written all over your face the second you heard my voice," Daniel said. "You've never been good at lying, Molly. Don't start trying it now."

"You startled me," she insisted, not giving up. "I

thought I'd locked the door against unwelcome intruders."

Daniel grinned. "Well, you hadn't, which meant you were still expecting me, whether you care to admit it or not." His expression suddenly faltered. He looked bone-deep weary. "May I stay?"

She regarded him with surprise. "You're actually asking my permission?"

He shrugged. "For a change. Consider it a peace offering."

She heard a rare note of uncertainty in his voice and saw the additional evidence of exhaustion and strain in his eyes. She put aside her damp cloth and gestured toward a stool. "Sit. What can I get you? You look as if you could use a drink."

"Decaf coffee if you have it."

Molly grinned at his idea of a pick-me-up. "It'll just take a minute," she said. "You'd probably sleep better if you had a beer."

He shook his head as he slid onto a stool at the bar. "I don't drink, not when I'm feeling like this. I don't want to risk it becoming a habit."

She cocked an eyebrow at him as she turned on the coffeemaker and scooped in the decaf coffee grounds. "Is that it? Or are you really afraid of losing control, especially around me?"

He frowned at her observation. "Why do you ask that?"

"Because you're the kind of guy who likes to weigh all the options, chart out a very precise course and then stick to it." She patted his hand. "That's okay. There are a lot of people like that in the world."

"But you're not one of them," he said.

"Lord, I hope not. I like surprises."

His gaze caught hers, held. "Oh, really?" he said, his voice filled with a challenge.

Before Molly realized his intention, he caught her chin in his hand, leaned across the bar and kissed her. It was a glancing kiss that barely touched her lips, but the shock of it sizzled straight through her. Memories tangled with the present, making her knees weak and her resistance weaker.

"That kind of surprise?" he asked, his voice husky, the dare in it still there to taunt her.

"For starters," she said, reaching for him and settling her mouth on his again.

She swept her tongue across the seam of his lips, heard the low moan deep in his throat, and then the kiss turned dark and dangerous and demanding. It was the kind of kiss she'd been craving since the moment they'd parted, all consuming and so hot it set her on fire. It had surprised her back then that Daniel Devaney could be the one to provide such a devastating kiss. Now it shocked her that he still could. She hadn't wanted that. She hadn't wanted the embers of her love for him to flare to life so readily.

Or had she? Wasn't this the anticipated ending of the dance they'd been doing for days now? Hadn't she been testing him? Testing herself?

Oh, what the hell, she thought. Enjoy the moment. She made herself stop thinking at all and gave herself completely to the wonder of having Daniel's mouth on hers again, of having his breath mingling with hers. For this moment the kiss alone was enough, even without its promise of so much more. She didn't have to have his hands roaming restlessly over her, didn't need to feel the deliberate caresses that could send her rocketing into another dimension altogether. The kiss brought heat and passion and more memories than she could count.

"Oh, my," she whispered, when it finally ended.

Daniel said nothing at all. He just sat there looking as if he'd been struck by a bolt of lightning. Molly grinned at him.

"Knocked you speechless at long last, didn't I?" she taunted happily, pouring his coffee and setting it in front of him as if nothing monumental had just occurred. "Told you, you had control issues."

He stared at her, his expression troubled. "Why did that happen?"

"Which part? Why did you kiss me? Or why did I kiss you back?"

"Any of it. Molly, this complicates an already complicated situation."

"Tell me about it," she agreed, though she was having a hard time mustering up the kind of regret he was obviously feeling.

"It cannot happen again," he said flatly.

"Okay."

He frowned at that. "That's all you've got to say? Just 'Okay'?"

She was beginning to lose patience with his attitude. "Did you want me to scream and holler and pout? It was a kiss, Daniel. I didn't declare my undying love. Neither did you. I can live without another one. I've been doing just fine without any contact at all with you. If it weren't for Kendra…" Her voice trailed off as she remembered the girl upstairs whose fate was in their hands. "Oh, my God, what about Kendra? Daniel, what are we going to do about her situation? That's why you're here. This other is just an untimely distraction."

He gave her a wry look. "I thought I was here about Kendra when I walked through the door. Now I'm not so sure. Maybe I could have settled the Kendra situation that very first night, if I'd been thinking straight. Instead, I let you play games for days, because it allowed me to keep coming back."

She scowled at the implication that he had unwittingly come for the kiss, that all of his visits had been about her. "Kendra is the only thing that matters. She has to be. Now, concentrate. Were you able to postpone Joe's visit in the morning?"

He shook his head. "He'll be here at nine. He refuses to postpone it even an hour."

Molly felt panic clawing at her. "We have to do something. He can't come in here and take her."

"He can," Daniel said quietly. "And there won't be a thing I can do to prevent it."

"But that's wrong. She's scared of going home. There's a reason for it. Doesn't that matter at all?"

"It might, if I knew the reason," he told her.

Molly considered telling him as much as Kendra had told her, but she didn't feel right betraying the girl's confidence, even for the best reason in the world.

"Let me go upstairs and wake her. Maybe she'll tell you now," she suggested.

But even as she spoke, she heard a rustle on the stairs, then caught a quick movement out of the corner of her eye. The front door of Jess's opened and slammed shut before she could even make sense of what she'd heard and seen.

"Kendra," she said, racing for the door, Daniel on her heels. "She must have heard us talking."

Outside, she saw no sign of the girl. Kendra had disappeared into the darkness of the waterfront. She was, no doubt, hiding in the shadows, remaining perfectly still until Molly and Daniel gave up.

"Kendra!" Molly called out. "Come back, sweetie. Talk to us. It will be okay. I promise."

"Dammit," Daniel muttered. "If we lose track of her now, who knows where she'll wind up? Where would she go, Molly?"

"To Retta's, maybe. She's been over there every day, helping Leslie Sue look after the kids she babysits."

"You call Retta. I'll keep looking out here," he said. "She's quick as a cat, but she can't have gotten far. She doesn't know her way around the waterfront like I do."

"Be careful, Daniel. She's already scared to death."

"Molly, I'm not an ogre," he retorted impatiently. "I know how to deal with a frightened runaway."

"Whatever," she said, going back inside to call Retta.

Unfortunately, the cook hadn't seen any sign of Kendra. It would only take a few minutes for Kendra to have reached her house, which meant she'd more than likely just run away again, panicked by what she'd heard Molly and Daniel discussing. The thought of her being out in the middle of the night, all alone, terrified Molly. Even in a town as safe as Widow's Cove, bad things could happen to an innocent young girl at that hour.

"Call me if she turns up," Molly told Retta.

"Of course I will, but that child won't go anywhere. Something tells me she's close by. She trusts you."

"She did until tonight," Molly said. "I think she heard me and Daniel talking about Joe taking her back to her parents in the morning."

"Oh, dear. There's no way around that?"

"Not that we've found yet," Molly admitted. "We were hoping she could give us one, but she obviously overheard just enough of what we were saying to panic."

"She'll come back," Retta said confidently.

"I hope you're right," Molly said, not sharing Retta's confidence.

But when she'd hung up and turned around, there was Kendra in the doorway, Daniel right behind her. She ran to Molly and threw herself at her.

"I didn't know where to go," she said, her voice catching on a sob. "It's so dark out there. What's wrong with this town? Why aren't there more street-lights?"

Molly hid a grin at the complaint. Leave it to Ken-dra to blame the lack of streetlights for her decision to come back to Jess's. "You did the right thing by not running away again," Molly said, holding her tightly.

"But I heard what *he* said," she said, scowling at Daniel. "I have to go home."

"Didn't you also hear him say that he might be able to change that if you can give him a good rea-son?" She urged Kendra toward a booth. "Sit down. I'm making you some hot chocolate and I'm getting more coffee for Daniel and more tea for me. We're going to talk this out."

"I'll come into the kitchen with you," Kendra said, staring at Daniel with evident distrust.

"Okay, fine," replied Molly, leading the way.

As she prepared Kendra's hot chocolate in the mi-crowave and poured the other drinks, she regarded the girl warily. "Sweetie, you have to trust some-body."

"I do," Kendra said. "I trust you. Not him."

"But he's the one who can provide a way out for you. Open up to him, please. Tell him what's been going on at home."

Kendra still didn't look convinced, but she took the hot chocolate Molly offered and followed her back into the bar, her feet dragging. Daniel was wait-ing for them in one of the booths, his legs stretched out, signs of exhaustion still plain on his face. Even so, he straightened when he saw them and smiled at Kendra. Under other circumstances, that smile could win over the wariest person, but Kendra's defenses were solidly in place. She stuck to Molly's side.

"Could you try not thinking of me as the bad guy?" he asked. "I want to help you."

"You want to send me home," Kendra said flatly, not giving an inch.

"That's usually where a girl your age belongs," he told her, "unless you can persuade me that there's some reason why you shouldn't be there. Can you?"

Kendra looked at Molly, clearly waiting for her encouraging nod. When she had it, she said, "I just don't see the point of going back there, when they're only going to send me away."

Just as Molly had anticipated, there was an immediate flash of sympathy in Daniel's eyes, a quick rise of temper. "Why do you think they're going to send you away?"

"Because they made all the plans," she said defiantly. "It's a done deal. I don't have any say in it." She glowered at him. "And I won't go back there, no matter what you say or what that cop says."

She bolted out of the booth and ran, but at least this time she headed for the stairs and ran up to Molly's apartment, not out into the streets.

Daniel turned to Molly. "What do you know about this?"

"Nothing more than what she just told you. I can't figure out where they'd be sending her that could possibly be so much worse than being on her own in a strange place."

"Neither can I. And it doesn't make a lick of sense. They didn't say a word to Joe about sending her away, or he would have mentioned it."

He pulled out his cell phone and punched in a number, clearly oblivious to the lateness of the hour. "Joe, it's Daniel. What do you know about the Morrows' plan to send Kendra away from home?"

Molly couldn't hear Joe's response, but she gathered from Daniel's frown that he wasn't satisfied by what Joe was saying.

"Ask them," he said tightly. "Then get back to me. In the meantime, the girl's not going anywhere. I'll go into court first thing in the morning, if that's what it takes to keep you from taking her. Or we can keep this unofficial till I hear from you. Your call." He nodded. "Okay, then. I'll wait to hear from you."

Molly felt her heart swell at the determination in his voice. When he'd hung up, she smiled at him. "I told her you'd never let her be sent away."

"Since you knew how that would get to me, why didn't you tell me yourself? It could have saved us all a lot of time."

"I'd promised I wouldn't betray her confidence," Molly said. "She needed to believe she could trust me."

"Did you tell her why knowing that would make a difference to me?"

"No. I just asked her to trust me, and you."

He ran a hand through his hair. "I've got to tell

you, none of this makes a damned bit of sense to me. The Morrows are good parents. Joe wouldn't make a mistake about something like that."

She leveled a look into his eyes. "Wouldn't you have said your parents were good people, too?"

He paled at that. "Below the belt, Molly."

"I didn't mean it that way. I was just trying to point out that even the best people aren't without flaws. You can't know what's behind a seemingly incomprehensible decision until they give you all the facts."

He sighed then. "You certainly got that right."

She studied his troubled expression, then asked, "What was the emergency at home tonight?"

"My brothers decided to pay a visit to my mother, en masse and unannounced."

"Oh, my. No wonder she was frantic," she said, feeling a surprising sympathy for all of them. She'd always liked Daniel's mother, had always felt at home in her kitchen and anticipated a time when they'd be sharing holidays and other family occasions. Even after she'd learned the truth about the past, she hadn't been able to reconcile that callous act with the warm and gentle woman she knew or even with the far more blustery Connor Devaney. She would have said he was a good man, who loved nothing more than his family.

"How did the visit go?" she asked Daniel.

"There wasn't any bloodshed," he said. "That's the best I can say for it. Patrick stormed out. I have no idea when he turned into such a hothead."

"He was always a hothead, just like your father. That's why you two were such a good team. You're calm, like your mother. That balanced him out. What about the others? Did they stay?"

He shook his head. "Sean and Michael left shortly afterward. Ryan stuck it out the longest, but even he looked tormented by being there and seeing her again. As for my mother, she was pretty amazing. She didn't fall apart, and she didn't blame any of them for the way they felt about her."

"And your father?"

"He was conveniently absent. If I didn't know better, I'd have to wonder if he hadn't had some instinct that they were coming. He's the one who's kept Mom silent all this time. I think she wants to get everything out in the open, but every time she dares to suggest it, he freaks. I know in my heart that everything that happened was his doing. Of course, she shares some of the responsibility because she went along with it, but he made the decision back then. I'd stake my life on that."

"If you're right, that means it's going to be that much harder for him to face his sons," Molly said. "It must have eaten away at both of them all these years. I'm amazed they stayed together."

Daniel regarded her with surprise. "They love each other," he said simply. "It's the one thing I've never questioned about my parents."

"But even the strongest love can be destroyed by something like this. It happens all the time after a child's death or some other tragedy," she said. Then she added, "Our love certainly wasn't strong enough to withstand what happened, and I would have sworn we were invincible."

Daniel flinched. "You can't compare the two situations."

"You turned your back on our child," she said. "How is that different?"

He was silent for so long she thought he might not answer, but then she realized he was genuinely thinking it over before responding.

"I did, but you have to understand that the baby wasn't real to me yet," he said eventually. "You'd known for, what, a day, maybe a little longer, when you told me. You'd probably suspected you were pregnant before that. You'd had time to accept the idea. I was caught completely off guard."

"Would your reaction have been one bit different if you'd had time to think about it?" she asked, unable to keep the bitterness out of her voice.

He kept his gaze steady. "I'd like to think so," he told her quietly.

"Easy to say now," she scoffed.

"No, it's not," he said. "Because it makes it so much worse that I put you through so much pain unnecessarily. If only I'd been a better man, if only I hadn't been the son of people who'd walked out on their own children, if only I'd been able to envision a little girl who looked like you, or a little boy playing ball like Patrick and me, maybe I would have done things differently that night and we'd have a family now." His gaze captured hers, held it. "Do you think it's been easy for me to live with knowing that I cost us that chance? Do you think it's easy admitting it to you now?"

Molly heard real pain in his voice, but she couldn't allow herself to feel any sympathy at all. It was one thing to kiss Daniel and let the old passions stir once again. It was quite another to forget the past and give him the chance to hurt her again.

"Molly?" he pressed. "Say something. Anything."

She looked into his eyes, saw the regret, but shook her head, anyway. "What's left to say?"

He opened his mouth and she could almost hear the unspoken words that were on the tip of his tongue.

"Don't say it," she pleaded. "Don't say you still love me."

For a moment she was afraid he might argue, might say it anyway, but he didn't. He merely nodded, a sad half smile coming and going.

"Not saying the words doesn't change anything," he told her.

Maybe not, but at least she could cling to the illusion that there was nothing between them now except anger. She needed to hold on to that anger with everything in her, because if she didn't, her heart would surely break. And that sizzling kiss they'd shared would take on a meaning she could not, under any circumstances, allow it to assume.

9

Two shocks in one day were almost more than Daniel, with his rigid code of self-discipline and planning, could cope with. The out-of-the-blue appearance of his brothers barely held a candle, though, to the stunning impact of kissing Molly.

All these years he'd thought she hated him for abandoning her when she needed him. Now he had to wonder if there wasn't at least the possibility of forgiveness. That kiss hadn't been about hatred. It had been a devastating reminder of the passion that they had once shared. That much, at least, hadn't died. Whether Molly was happy about it or not remained to be seen.

Not that he was in any way deluding himself that she was his for the taking. She might still have feelings for him—very strong feelings—but they were interwoven with distrust. It was going to take more than a few kisses, no matter how steamy, to win her back, to convince her that she could risk giving him her heart again.

If that was what he wanted, he concluded thoughtfully. This was no time for uncertainty. She'd made that plain when she'd prevented him from glibly saying that he loved her. She wanted proof this time, and words alone—especially words uttered in the heat of passion—weren't going to do it.

Of course, tonight could have been a fluke. It could have been one of those wildfires that erupted unexpectedly from mostly dying embers and burned itself out just as quickly. If he ever kissed her again, he probably wouldn't feel a thing.

Not that he intended to find out right away. He'd never been crazy about the out-of-control feelings Molly sparked in him. She was exactly right about his personality. He did like to keep a tight rein on the events in his life and on his emotions. He'd followed a different path when he'd fallen in love with her the first time, and look how that had ended. No, better to chalk this kiss up to a moment of insanity and not try to make anything out of it.

Satisfied that he'd analyzed the situation and reached the only sensible conclusion, he took a very cold shower and went to bed. He was certain he'd have forgotten all about the kiss by morning. He was just as certain that he would bounce out of bed ready to tackle the Kendra problem and solve that, too.

Instead, he awoke with an image of Molly—naked in his arms—taunting him. He was already restless, edgy and in need of coffee—the powerful, caffeinated kind—by the time he reached Jess's.

Retta met him at the front door. "What did you do

to my girl?" she demanded, arms folded across her ample chest as she blocked his way inside.

Daniel was not prepared to go toe-to-toe with Retta, not without his first cup of coffee. "What are you talking about? I didn't do anything to Molly." He figured the kissing didn't count, since she'd been a more than willing participant. Besides, he doubted Molly would have told Retta about the kissing.

"Then why isn't she here?" she demanded.

Daniel's heart thumped unsteadily. He grabbed Retta's shoulders and leveled a look directly into her worried eyes. "What happened? Where's Molly?"

"Do you think I'd be asking you, if I knew the answer to that?" she snapped impatiently. "What happened here last night after I talked to her?"

He tried to sort through the events of the evening. "Kendra came back. The three of us talked. Then Molly and I talked some more. I left. That's it," he said. "Nothing happened that should have sent her scurrying away. Are you sure she's gone?"

"Her bed hasn't been slept in."

"And Kendra's?"

"Her bed's a mess, but she's gone, too."

"Well, hell," Daniel said, raking his fingers through his hair. Why was it that whenever Molly was involved in his life, his hair invariably was a mess? Probably because there were too damned many infuriating moments just like this one. "Why would she take off? She knew I was coming back this morning to try to figure something out to help Kendra."

Retta studied him knowingly. "Maybe this wasn't about Kendra," she suggested.

"Then what…?" His voice trailed off. "You think it has something to do with Molly and me."

"Does it? I told you if you hurt her again, there'd be no stopping me from coming after you."

"I haven't hurt her," he swore.

"Then I'll ask you again, what happened between you two last night?"

"I kissed her, okay? Satisfied?"

Retta scowled at him. "Now why'd you go and do a dumb thing like that?"

"She was annoying me," he said, remembering the challenge in her eyes, the dare in her voice. "And before you climb on your high horse, you should know that she kissed me back. In fact, she initiated one whopper of a kiss herself. So, there's plenty of blame to go around her. She's messing with my head, too."

Retta sighed. "That's it, then. You cut through her defenses, she got scared and she ran. She's probably telling herself right this minute that she did it for Kendra's sake, but it's plain as day to me that she's running from her feelings for you."

Daniel sank down on a bar stool. "I need to think."

"A little late for that, isn't it?"

"Come on, Retta, give me a break. Bring me some coffee, please. I need to figure out where she would go. If Joe Sutton finds out she's taken off with Kendra, no matter why she did it, she's going to be in a whole pile of trouble."

"And whose fault is that?" she retorted, still not cutting him any slack at all.

He frowned at her. "Is casting blame going to

accomplish anything? Come on, Retta, help me out here."

She stalked behind the counter, picked up the coffeepot and poured him a cup. The one good thing about Retta being in charge of the coffee this morning was that it was bound to be strong. Retta didn't like the namby-pamby stuff that Molly passed off as coffee.

Daniel took his first sip and predictably it almost made his toes curl. "Good brew," he praised.

Retta grinned at him. "You always did like mine better than Molly's."

"If you were younger, I'd marry you," he said, as he had so often in the past, when they were on far better terms.

"Honey, you couldn't keep up with me now," she retorted. "You want some eggs and bacon? Something tells me it's going to be a long day around here."

"Sure. Make the eggs over easy," he said, already distracted by the dilemma of the missing twosome.

It would make sense that Molly would head for a big city, someplace where she and Kendra could get lost. But which city? Bangor? Portland? Or out of state? Maybe Boston or New York? Surely, though, she would be sensible enough not to take Kendra out of Maine. The charges could get a whole lot more dire if she'd crossed a state line with the girl, no matter how well-intentioned the journey. Wherever she was, he was going to kill her when he found them.

Retta plopped a plate in front of him. "Figure anything out yet?"

He stared at the scrambled mess she'd made of his eggs, then sighed and began to eat. "Nothing's coming to me," he said eventually. "You?"

"Do you think I'd tell you if I had a solution? I'd be more likely to call your brother."

"You'd tell me if you care about Molly," he said. "She could get herself into serious trouble this time, Retta. That child is only thirteen. The police know she was hiding out here."

"Do they know Kendra didn't want to go home?"

"We all know that," he said. "Kendra made her wishes very plain. I'm no lawyer, but I'm not so sure that'll be good enough to save Molly's hide when the lawsuits and legalities start flying."

Retta's eyes widened. "She could go to jail?"

Sensing that he'd finally gotten through to her, he pushed a little harder, hoping she would cough up whatever information she was holding back. "That depends on how the police want to play it," he said. "She could."

"But she's just trying to help that child."

"It won't matter." He caught her worried gaze, held it. "If you know something, anything, you need to tell me now."

Then he sat back and waited. And waited.

Retta scowled at him. "I don't trust you, you know that, don't you?"

He nodded. "That's a given."

"So if I tell you this and any harm comes to my girl…"

"I know. I know. You're going to take it out on me."

"And then some," she said fiercely. "Okay, then, I don't know what it means, but her car's out back. Wherever she's gone, whatever she's doing, she didn't drive."

That left the bus station, Daniel concluded, on his feet at once.

Or a boat. "Dammit," he said as understanding dawned. "Patrick. She's gotten Patrick to take them someplace."

"Well, I'll be," Retta said. "Of course she'd turn to him. Didn't I say that myself not fifteen minutes ago? She trusts him completely."

The unspoken implication that Molly didn't trust Daniel was unmistakable. Well, he'd brought that on himself, he thought, and they both knew it. What he did from this moment on was going to make the difference in whether Molly ever trusted him again.

"This is so cool," Kendra said as the wind whipped her hair.

She was leaning over the railing of the *Katie G.*, watching the wake as Patrick cut through the churning ocean. Molly watched her and concluded it was the first genuinely carefree moment Kendra had had since she'd turned up in Widow's Cove. At thirteen, her life should be filled with such moments, and not with worrying over staying safe while she was on her own.

"Molly!" Patrick's voice cut through the noise of the wind. There was no mistaking the command behind it.

Reluctantly Molly made her way to the front of the trawler where Patrick crouched, working the fishing nets, his expression grim.

"We need to talk," he said, continuing to bring in the haul as he spoke.

"Look, I really appreciate you letting us come with you this morning," Molly said in an attempt to appease him.

"Letting you?" he scoffed. "I didn't even realize you were on board until we were out to sea. I still haven't figured out how I missed that one."

"You got on board half-asleep," she teased. "You and Alice must have had a long night."

"Very funny," he said. "Maybe it had more to do with the fact that you broke into the cabin and stowed away down there until you were sure I wasn't likely to turn right back to the dock."

"Could be," she said cheerfully.

His gaze narrowed. "Why'd you do it, Molly? If you wanted to spend the day with me fishing, all you had to do was ask."

"Actually, I wanted to spend the day clearing my head. I have a lot on my mind."

"Such as?"

"Kendra, for starters," she said. "Look at her, Patrick. She looks like a kid should look."

He glanced toward Kendra and frowned. "Maybe a kid who hasn't run away from home should look like that. Kendra has cause to be worried. And something tells me I'm now in the thick of some scheme of yours to keep her away from her parents."

Molly winced. "It's only temporary. I just needed to buy a little time."

"In other words, the you-know-what was about to hit the fan with my brother," he said, rocking back on his haunches and leveling a look straight into her eyes. "Don't you think Daniel and I have enough issues without dragging me into the middle of this one?"

"I'm sorry," she apologized. "If I could have thought of anything else, I would have."

"Just how furious is my brother likely to be?"

"On a scale of one to ten? Maybe a forty," she admitted.

"Dammit, Molly!"

"I heard about last night at your folks' place," she said quietly. "I gather it was pretty bad."

He regarded her with surprise. "You heard about that?"

"Daniel told me."

His expression turned thoughtful. "I see. So he came running straight to you after he left there?"

She thought of the tormented look in Daniel's eyes when he'd walked into Jess's. "He hated what went on there. He hates being at odds with you, especially."

"Yeah, right."

"He does, Patrick. You know Daniel. He likes smooth sailing, and he loves you."

"He has a damn funny way of showing it," Patrick said bitterly.

"You don't have to agree with someone over everything to love them," she pointed out.

He gave her a steady look. "Does that go for you, too?"

She bristled at the suggestion that the situations were even remotely similar. "Daniel and I didn't just have some little disagreement," she said tersely, unwilling to relinquish the past so readily.

"Neither did he and I," Patrick reminded her. "These issues between us are a big deal."

Molly sighed. "I know that."

She stared out to sea, thinking of the way things had been between her and Daniel the night before. "He kissed me," she said eventually.

Patrick's head snapped up. "He what?"

"Locked lips with me," she explained, as if that weren't clear enough. "And I kissed him back."

There was no mistaking the fact that Patrick was fighting a smile. When he smiled, he had the same mischievous glint in his eyes that Daniel got. "Is that so? And?"

"And nothing," she muttered. "It was no big deal."

"It was a big enough deal to have you stowing away on my boat," he said knowingly. "That's the real reason you're out here, isn't it? That's why you need to clear your head this morning."

"I was worried about Kendra," she insisted.

"That, too, I'm sure, but it's really about you and my brother. You're scared, Molly. You're scared you're falling for him again." He frowned. "I knew this was going to happen. I told him myself that neither one of you has a lick of common sense when you get together."

She didn't like that he could see through her so easily, liked even less that he was calling her on it. "I should have gone to your wife. She wouldn't have been taunting me like this."

"I'm not taunting you," he denied. "I'm on your side, always. You know that."

She sighed more heavily. "Yes, I do." When she met his gaze again, she couldn't keep the wistful note out of her voice. "So, can we run away from home, Patrick?"

He blinked at that. "You want to run away from Widow's Cove with me?"

"And Kendra," she said, as if that would make a positive difference, rather than complicating things.

"I don't think so."

"Why not?" she asked, even though she could count at least a dozen solid, rational reasons against it all on her own.

"There's my wife, for one thing. There's my brother for another. And the long arm of the law. It's a bad idea all around, Molly."

"I figured you'd say that," she admitted.

"So you don't intend to tie me up and hijack my boat?" he asked, only partially in jest.

"If I thought I could get away with it, I'd consider it, believe me," she said. "But no. I'll go back quietly." She met his gaze. "Just not too soon, okay?"

"Good decision," Patrick said, looking past her. "Especially since the boat that's heading our way seems to be piloted by my brother, and he's looking none too pleased with either one of us."

Molly whirled around just as Daniel pulled alongside. The scowl on his face spoke volumes. Patrick was right. He was definitely not pleased. Even so, he looked incredibly handsome, with his cheeks colored by the wind and his hair mussed. She did love it when he was all rumpled. It reminded her that no one was as perfect as Daniel usually tried to be.

"Hello," Molly called cheerfully, standing her ground even though her heart was pounding.

Still scowling at her, Daniel took a rope and tossed it to Patrick. "Tie me up," he commanded.

Patrick complied without a word, then headed for the stern, where he spoke quietly to a wide-eyed Kendra, then led her below.

"You seem upset," Molly said to Daniel.

"Upset?" His voice climbed in a very un-Daniel-like way. "You don't have a clue. Retta's upset. I've moved on to livid. What the *hell* were you thinking?"

"I was thinking that a day on the water would be good for me and good for Kendra."

"That's it?" he asked incredulously. "This is some little feel-good outing?"

"That's it," she said.

"You intended all along to come back?"

"Of course."

His gaze narrowed. "Really?"

"Okay, there was a fleeting moment when I tried to persuade Patrick to sail us away to the ends of the earth, but he had all sorts of pesky objections."

"Such as?"

"His wife. You. The cops." She looked into Daniel's stormy eyes and added again, "You. That one bothered me, too."

He took a step closer until she could feel the heat radiating off him. "Then you did, at least for a moment, consider my feelings?"

She couldn't think, couldn't breathe, with him so close. He was deliberately crowding her, deliberately reminding her of the kiss the night before. All she could do was nod.

He reached out, traced the curve of her jaw and set off goose bumps. "How did you think I'd react when I discovered you were gone?"

She swallowed hard. "Furious," she muttered, then cleared her throat and faced him squarely. "I thought you'd be furious."

"But you left, anyway," he said flatly.

"I had to."

"Why? To protect Kendra?"

Now, she thought, now was the time to say it, to get it out and deal with it. "No," she said softly. "To protect myself."

She hadn't realized it, but he'd apparently been holding his breath, because he released it now, and for the first time since he'd climbed aboard the *Katie G.*, there was a smile on his lips. It was so like Patrick's, yet different. Charming. Compelling. Devastating.

"Ah," he said, cupping her chin. "Is this what you were afraid of, Molly?"

He lowered his head until his mouth was a tantalizing breath away from hers. He made her wait, and then wait some more, before finally closing that infinitesimal gap and touching his lips to hers. Gently, then more persuasively, coaxing her to accept the kiss, to open her mouth to the sweep of his tongue.

Oh, hell, she thought as she felt the kiss right down to the tips of her toes. She clung to him, trying not to sigh with the sheer pleasure of it.

She'd kept him from saying the words the night before, but there was love in that kiss and maybe just a hint of desperation. She knew how that felt, that neediness, combined with a fear that what she wanted most in the world was something she could never have.

When he finally pulled away, he muttered a soft curse. "I wish we were alone out here."

"Me, too," she admitted, then glanced toward the boat he'd borrowed, rented or stolen to come after them. "There is that."

Daniel chuckled when he realized she was actually considering the barely seaworthy vessel beside them as the appropriate place for a lover's tryst.

"I don't think so, darlin'."

"Where's your sense of adventure?" she asked.

"All used up just chasing after you in that thing," he said. "I'm sailing back on my brother's boat."

"Maybe Patrick could take that one back to shore," she said thoughtfully.

"And leave us with his precious trawler? Sweetheart, he doesn't trust either one of us that much."

Molly sighed. "I suppose you're right."

"Don't worry. I'll make it up to you once we're back on dry land," he promised.

"Something tells me once we get back to dry land, we're going to have other fish to fry," she said dryly.

Daniel laughed. "No question about that. Joe was all for calling out the Coast Guard. I talked him into waiting at the docks himself."

Molly took a step back. "He's there waiting for Kendra?"

"Not to take her," Daniel insisted. "To talk to her."

"Are you sure? One hundred percent sure?"

"I trust him," Daniel told her. "And I told him he could trust you and me to bring Kendra back. Don't even consider doing anything that would make a liar out of me."

If it was time to face her feelings about Daniel, it was also time to have a little faith in him. He knew he had a lot to prove to her. He wouldn't risk letting her down.

"Okay, then," she said, drawing herself up. "I'd better go below and talk to Kendra. I'll send Patrick up. You two could try mending some fences, as well."

"This is not the ship of miracles, darlin'. More like a ship of fools."

She frowned at him. "Only if you let it be. Talk to him, Daniel. He doesn't want to be so angry, not with you, not with your parents. Give him a reason not to be."

"I'm not sure I have one."

"You'll find it," she said. "That's what you do. You find solutions for people. I have complete faith in you."

His eyes widened at that. "You do?"

She nodded, probably almost as startled by the admission as he was. "When it comes to things like this, yes. Now it's your turn not to make a liar or a fool out of me."

10

Daniel watched warily as Patrick walked onto the deck and came toward him. There was little question that what was said between them in the next few minutes could make all the difference in their strained relationship. "You looking to throw me overboard?" he asked.

"Not unless I have to," Patrick replied.

"Molly thinks we should make peace."

"Yeah, she would."

"So do I."

"I'm not sure that's possible," Patrick said, sounding resigned. "Every time I think we're on that road, I see you take our parents' side again, the way you did last night."

Daniel chose his words carefully. He didn't want to make things any worse than they already were. He needed to find the middle ground, assuming there was one. Why was it he could negotiate a truce between rebellious kids and their families, but he couldn't solve anything when it came to his own? He had to try, though, and now was the time.

He met his brother's gaze. "Maybe there shouldn't be sides, Patrick. We're a family, after all. We've got our flaws, just like every other family."

Patrick's bark of laughter was derisive. "Is that how you see it? That there are a few little gnats in the ointment that keep us from having the perfect family?"

"I'm not going for perfect," Daniel corrected. "You're the one expecting that. I'll settle for seven adults who at least try to communicate, who can seek some level of understanding and forgiveness. We're not children anymore. We should be able to do this."

Patrick shook his head. "I don't know. For it to work, Mom and Dad would have to meet us halfway, and I don't see that happening. Do you?"

Daniel considered the question with the careful thought it deserved. "It won't be easy, but yes. I think they will. I think I can make them see that they're losing out on more than the sons who should have been in their lives. Ryan, Sean and Michael have taken that hard first step. I can tell them that it's up to them to take the next one. Maybe realizing that they're missing out on getting to know their grand-children will help, too."

"And you think they'll buy that?" Patrick scoffed.

"I do," he said, needing to believe in the goodness he and Patrick had seen in their parents all their lives.

"With a baby of my own on the way, no one would like to believe that more than me," Patrick responded.

"Alice's parents are dead. I'd like our child to have one set of grandparents in their lives, but I don't see it happening."

"Maybe we'll never have raucous, happy family reunions together," Daniel said. "But we might be able to pull off the occasional holiday without risking an all-out war."

"You're a romantic dreamer," Patrick said.

Daniel laughed. "No one's ever accused me of that before. I'm the hardheaded, practical one, remember?"

"Not about this," Patrick argued. "I know what you want, Daniel, and I know how badly you want it. I don't even blame you. I just think it's impossible."

"Nothing's impossible if you're willing to do whatever it takes to get it."

Patrick studied him intently. "Does that go for Molly, too? Do you want her back in your life badly enough to do whatever it takes?"

Daniel didn't want to go there, not with Patrick. "Maybe we should leave Molly out of this," he said. "You're a little too protective where she's concerned. And you've painted me as the bad guy."

"You *were* the bad guy," Patrick reminded him. "And someone had to look out for Molly."

The barb struck home, just as his twin had obviously intended. "Don't you think I know that? Don't you think I have some idea what a huge mistake I made?"

"Especially for a man who's making such a big deal about the importance of family," Patrick said.

"I know. I get it," Daniel said impatiently. "I know what I did was stupid and wrong and unconscionable. I think Molly's on the verge of forgiving me, though. Are you going to let her?"

Patrick gave him a hard, unrelenting stare, then shrugged. "It's not up to me. Molly's her own woman, in case you haven't noticed."

"Oh, I've noticed. Believe me, I've noticed." He studied his brother's face. "Will we have your blessing if we do get back together?"

"Do you honestly care?"

Daniel nodded. "Whether you believe it or not, I've always cared what you thought of me."

Patrick held his gaze, a challenge in his eyes, then finally released a sigh. "I love you," he said simply. "Even when I've been mad as hell at you, I've loved you. We're twins. How could I not?"

Daniel felt something ease deep inside him at his brother's words. "That goes for me, too," he told Patrick. "As long as we remember that, we can work out all the rest."

They stood there awkwardly for a minute, neither of them quite ready to take the first step. It was Patrick who finally moved, muttering, "Ah, hell," as he did so.

He pulled Daniel into a hard embrace, the first genuine show of forgiveness since they'd first begun speaking again months earlier. Daniel fought against the surprising sting of tears.

"Damn, I've missed you," Daniel said, his voice choked.

"Me, too," Patrick said. "You weren't just my brother. You were my best friend. I want that back again. I always thought when I had kids, their uncle Daniel would be there to help me celebrate and look after them."

"I will be," Daniel promised. When Patrick stepped back, his eyes, too, were damp, Daniel noticed. "I thought maybe after you'd met Ryan, Sean and Michael, I wouldn't matter anymore."

"Don't be ridiculous," Patrick said. "You always mattered. I wouldn't have been so furious with you if what you did didn't matter to me. You need to get to know our brothers. They're good guys."

"I got the impression they were fed up with me and the folks," Daniel said.

"I can fix that," Patrick said. "I'll call them. It's true that Ryan couldn't persuade them to stay, but I'll nudge them to try again." He grinned. "Maybe I'll call Maggie, Ryan's wife, and enlist her help. She's a steamroller when it comes to getting what she wants, and she wants to resolve things once and for all. When do you want them here?"

"The sooner, the better," Daniel said.

Patrick shook his head. "First, you have to convince Mom and Dad to agree to get everything out in the open this time. You let me know when you've accomplished that miracle, and I'll take the next step."

Easier said than done, Daniel thought, but he had to try, for all of their sakes. Patrick was giving him—and their folks—an opening. "I'll talk to them again as soon as I get this mess with Kendra straightened out," he promised. "Sooner if it looks as if that's not going to have a quick resolution."

"Speaking of Kendra," Patrick said worriedly, "how much trouble are Molly and I in for bringing her out here?"

Daniel gave him an innocent look. "To go fishing? What's the harm in that."

Patrick laughed. "None I can think of."

"Then that's our story and we're sticking to it," Daniel said, his gaze drifting to the steps down into the cabin.

"Go on," Patrick said, following the direction of his gaze. "I can get this boat back to Widow's Cove. Seems to me you, Molly and Kendra have a lot to talk about." He gave him a knowing look. "Unless you'd like me to give Kendra a fishing lesson and get her out from underfoot, so you two can…" He let his voice trail off on a teasing note.

"Thanks for the offer," Daniel said. "And no offense, but I want something a little fancier when I seduce Molly. She deserves champagne and flowers and candlelight, not a cramped bed on this tub."

"You'll get no argument from me on that score, bro. Glad to know you see it, too."

Daniel smiled sadly. "I always have. I just got a little mixed up for a while. Unfortunately, it happened at the worst possible time."

But he wasn't mixed up anymore. He knew what he wanted. He wanted Molly back in his life forever.

As the *Katie G.* approached the dock, Molly spotted Joe Sutton sitting on a piling, a deep frown etched in his forehead. He was not a happy man. She tightened her arm around Kendra's shoulders.

"Don't worry. He's on your side," Molly reassured the girl.

"Yeah, I can see that," Kendra scoffed.

"Joe's a good guy," Daniel added. "And you've got Molly and me."

Kendra stared at him with obvious surprise. "You're on my side? Or are you just trying to score points with Molly?"

He winked at her. "Can't I do both?"

Kendra shrugged, clearly not willing to be drawn into that discussion. "You can try," she said, but her shoulders relaxed a little.

"My, my, this is a happy little group," Joe said as Patrick tied up at the dock. "You running tours these days, Patrick?"

"Fishing charters," Patrick said, his gaze level, daring Joe to challenge him.

The detective shrugged. "Whatever." He turned to Daniel. "We need to talk…now."

"You two go ahead," Molly said. "I need to get back to Jess's."

Joe regarded her with amusement. "Nice try, Molly. I meant *all* of us. We'll all go to Jess's." He turned to Kendra, who was trying to slip behind Patrick where she might be less conspicuous. "You, too."

Kendra reached for Molly's hand and clung tightly. Her chin thrust up, she stared directly into Joe's eyes. "You don't scare me."

"I should," he said, but there was a twinkle in

his eyes that suggested he admired her brave show of defiance.

When Joe would have led the way to Jess's, Kendra dragged her heels. "I need to ask you something."

Joe turned back. "Anything."

"Are you going to send me home?" she asked bluntly.

"That's what we're going to discuss."

"Meaning you tell me what I have to do," Kendra said.

"No. Meaning we all talk about it and reach a decision together," Joe said.

"And I get a say?" she asked, clearly surprised and not entirely convinced.

He nodded. "An important say. Maybe not the deciding vote, but definitely a say."

Kendra seemed to weigh his words before finally nodding. "Okay, then, let's talk."

Molly exchanged a look with Daniel, who gave her a brief nod, suggesting that he thought things were going okay so far. She felt the first faint stirring of relief. Maybe everyone was going to be reasonable, after all.

When they walked into Jess's, Daniel and Joe headed for a booth as Retta flew out from behind the counter and hauled first Molly and then Kendra into an embrace. "You two scared the living daylights out of me," she scolded. "Don't ever do something like that again. Leave a note, even if you have to put it someplace *other* people won't find it." She cast a pointed look in Daniel's direction.

Kendra stared at Retta with shock. "You were worried about me?"

"Well, of course I was," Retta said.

Kendra immediately looked distraught. "I'm sorry," she whispered, her voice trembling.

"Oh, baby girl, it's okay," Retta said. "You're here now and you're safe. That's all that matters."

But Kendra didn't look reassured. Molly tucked a hand under her chin and studied her expression. "What's wrong?"

"I guess it just hit me," Kendra said. "If Retta was that upset because we went off fishing without telling her, my parents must be really crazed by now."

Molly nodded slowly. "I imagine they are. Does that mean you want to go home? Or at least call them?"

Kendra immediately shook her head. "No. Can't that cop call them and tell 'em I'm okay? Or Daniel? He could do it," she said, clearly warming to that idea.

"Ask him. That can be one of the things we discuss as soon as I get everybody something to drink," Molly said. She glanced at the booth where Daniel and Joe were clearly arguing, though trying hard not to raise their voices.

She put three cups of coffee and some hot chocolate on a tray, then carried it to the booth, Kendra trailing along behind.

"Okay, fellows, here you go," she said, setting the coffee in front of them. She glanced at Daniel. "It's still Retta's. Nice and strong, just the way you liked it."

Joe took a sip and nodded appreciatively. "Better than what I had in here the other day," he said, then regarded her apologetically. "No offense."

"None taken," Molly said, resolving to get Retta to give her lessons in making coffee to suit impossible men.

As she slid into the booth next to Kendra, the girl sat up a little straighter and regarded Joe without flinching.

"I want you to call my parents," she said.

Daniel choked on a sip of coffee, and Joe looked startled.

"That's it? You're ready to go home?" Joe asked.

Kendra shook her head. "No. And I don't want them to know where I am, either. I just don't want them worrying about me. Tell them I'm fine."

Daniel gave her an understanding look. "That's very thoughtful of you," he said. "But it's not that simple. If we let them know we've been in contact with you, then we're also obligated to take you home."

Her eyes widened. "But you said…" She frowned at Joe. "And you, too. You said I'd get to have a say in what happened."

Joe nodded. "Which is why I'm not calling anybody until we've heard your side of the story. Now's your chance to get everything out in the open, Kendra. Why did you run away from home? What did your parents do that was so awful?"

Molly gave her hand a squeeze, but Kendra just sat there, biting on her lower lip.

"Did they hit you?" Joe asked.

"No," she said at once.

"Punish you?"

"Not really."

"What then?" Joe prodded. "Is there a boy in the picture, someone they don't think you ought to see?"

Clearly, he was running through a litany of the usual reasons a teen might run away. Kendra maintained that none of them were the reason she'd left home.

"Kendra," Daniel prodded. "Stop stalling. Tell Joe what you told me."

"They're sending me away," she said, her voice catching. She looked imploringly at Molly. "Please, don't make me go back. I don't want them to send me away."

Molly glanced at Daniel, praying that he would signal her what the right response would be, but his gaze was on Joe.

"Where are they sending you, Kendra? I don't understand," Joe said, his tone gentle.

When she remained stubbornly silent, Joe turned to Molly. "Do you know?"

Molly shook her head. "She refuses to say another word."

Daniel regarded Joe with confusion. "I thought you were going to talk to her parents about this. What did they have to say?"

"I tried to talk to them, but they said going away couldn't possibly be the problem, that Kendra had agreed to all the plans."

Kendra said, her voice climbing, "They decided. They never asked me! They don't want me at home, so why should I go back there when I could stay with somebody who does want me?" She turned to Molly. "It's okay if I stay here forever, right? You want me."

"Honey, I'd let you stay here in a heartbeat, but it's not that simple," Molly said.

"Please, you've got to let me stay," Kendra pleaded. "I could help here, the way I have been, and I can go to school. I won't be any trouble."

Molly's heart was breaking at Kendra's increasing agitation. It was so plain that she didn't want to be sent back to her family, but at the same time she cared enough about them not to want them to worry about her. None of it was making a bit of sense, not that thirteen-year-olds were known for the depths of their logic. Too many hormones and not nearly enough life experience.

Molly turned to Daniel. "What do I do?"

"It's not up to you," he said quietly.

Kendra regarded him with alarm. "You're making me go back?"

"No," he said very firmly, startling Molly and Joe. "Here's what I think. Joe, you need to go and meet with the Morrows again. Get to the bottom of this. Tell them that without a straight answer, we're going into court to explore whether their custody needs to be challenged in Kendra's best interests."

"And what if they tell me they're going to have my badge for not turning her over the second I found her?" Joe asked. "Dammit, Daniel, this limb you and I are on is starting to crack."

"I'll call your boss," Daniel said. "I'll make it very clear why we've handled it this way, that there are some serious questions about what's going on between Kendra and her parents. I'm not saying they're bad parents, just that we both saw that there's an issue that requires some professional intervention."

"Yeah, that and a million bucks might not be enough to keep me on the force," Joe retorted.

Kendra's lower lip quivered. "I'm sorry I'm causing so much trouble."

Joe looked chagrined. "Kendra, it's not your fault. This is what I do. It's what Daniel does. I'd just like to know for sure that we're on the side of the angels."

"I think you are," Molly said quietly.

Kendra smiled. "Me, too."

Daniel grinned. "There you go, Joe. Two endorsements."

"Too bad they're not unbiased," Joe said as he slid from the booth. "I'll be in touch." He feigned a scowl for Kendra's benefit. "Don't get lost."

She shook her head and regarded him with a serious expression. "I'll be right here." She sketched a cross across her heart. "I promise."

He nodded. "Good enough for me."

As soon as he'd gone, Kendra turned to Molly. "Can I go in the kitchen with Retta?"

"Sure," she said at once, sliding out to let Kendra out of the booth.

To Molly's surprise, Kendra wrapped her arms

around her waist. "Thanks. You're the best." She beamed at Daniel. "You, too."

After she'd gone, Daniel gave Molly a brooding look. "That kid has a lot of people tied up in knots. I hope to hell we know what we're doing where she's concerned."

"We do," Molly said confidently.

His expression turned thoughtful. "What about us? Do we know what we're doing about us?"

Molly shrugged. "Probably not."

"And you're okay with that?"

She grinned. "For now, I'm fine with the one-day-at-a-time approach. Can you live with it?"

"If I have to."

"That's the only choice I see," she said, unwilling to commit to anything more, especially when Daniel was the one who was incapable of making the kind of commitment she might want at some time in the future.

"In that spirit, then, how about playing hooky with me this afternoon?" he asked.

Molly glanced worriedly toward the kitchen. "What about Kendra?"

"She'll be fine with Retta."

Molly knew he was right. In fact, it wasn't really Kendra she was anxious about. She couldn't help worrying about whether *she* would be fine with Daniel.

"I won't make you do anything you don't want to do," he said, a teasing glint in his eyes.

"That could leave a lot of room for flexibility," she

noted, thinking about just how badly she'd wanted to make love with him a few hours earlier.

His grin spread. "That's what I'm hoping."

"Okay, then. Let's say I were to agree to go out with you this afternoon. Where are we going?"

"Now that's the quandary, isn't it? Your place is pretty much out of the question, given the likelihood of unexpected traffic. Mine's a total mess."

"You're assuming that my agreement to play hooky requires privacy," she teased. "Did I give you that impression? Maybe I just want to go someplace for a burger and a game of pool."

He scoffed at that. "We could do that here. Retta makes a great burger, and the pool table's not in use. I think we need to improve on that plan."

"Steak, a glass of wine, maybe a chocolate mousse?"

"You're getting warmer," he said. "I hear they have excellent room service at the new inn on the outskirts of town."

Molly considered the suggestion. She'd heard about that inn, seen pictures of it in the local paper. No question about it, it was an idyllic romantic hideaway.

"Have I met the owners?" she asked.

"I doubt it. They lived in Portland till they bought the property."

"What about you? Do you know them?"

"Nope."

"That ought to eliminate the gossip factor, especially if you pay cash and register under a phony name." She grinned. "Sounds intriguing."

"You just like living dangerously. I knew the whole sneaking around bit would appeal to you."

She sobered at that. "It's not that I'm ashamed of what we're about to do, Daniel. It isn't."

He reached for her hand. "I know that. You just don't want to answer a lot of prying questions."

"Exactly, and there are bound to be a slew of them. From Retta. From your brother. Even from your folks. We're not ready for that yet. I don't even have all the answers for myself."

He lifted her hand and brushed a kiss across her knuckles. "Maybe we can start to figure out a few of them this afternoon."

"Maybe so." She grinned, getting into the spirit of things. It had been a lot of years since she'd had to slip out of the house to avoid her grandfather's questions about some boy. "Wait for me in the parking lot. I'll sneak out in about five minutes."

He laughed. "As if that's going to keep Retta from suspecting a thing."

"It's worth a try," she insisted. "Now go."

After he'd gone, she slipped into the kitchen and casually picked up a sliver of carrot intended for the vegetable soup Retta was making for dinner. Kendra was dicing potatoes with total concentration.

"Everything okay in here?" Molly inquired.

"Doing fine," Retta said, glancing up from the biscuits she was rolling out. "Daniel gone?"

"Uh-huh." She picked up another sliver of carrot. "Do you need me in here? I thought I might go out for a while."

"Kendra and I will be just fine," Retta assured her. "You go on and do whatever you need to do."

"I shouldn't be too long," Molly said. "A couple of hours, max."

"No problem."

"That's okay with you, Kendra?"

The girl blinked as if she hadn't even realized Molly was in the room. "What?"

"I'm going out."

"Okay, whatever."

Molly gave them a wave and headed for the door, convinced that no one was the wiser about her intentions. She was just congratulating herself on her subtlety, when Retta called out to her.

Molly glanced at her. "What?"

"I'm gonna want to hear *all* about that inn when you get back, you hear me?"

Molly regarded her evenly. "I have no idea what you're talking about."

Retta laughed. "We'll talk about you fibbing to me, too. Now go on and have yourself some fun. It's been a long time coming."

"It has been, hasn't it?" she said mostly to herself.

As for Retta and her ESP, Molly had known the woman her entire life. She should have realized she'd never be able to put anything over on her. Maybe it was for the best. Somehow it felt better going to meet Daniel and knowing that she had Retta's blessing. She knew full well that it wasn't something Retta was likely to give lightly, which meant she'd seen the same thing in Daniel that Molly had seen—a changed man, who was no longer afraid of love.

11

Daniel watched Molly emerge from Jess's, her cheeks flushed, her eyes sparkling with once-familiar excitement. How long had it been since he'd seen her in a carefree mood like this? Maybe she'd had happy times in the years since they'd split up, but he didn't think so. Nothing he'd heard suggested that she'd allowed herself to do something or to go out with someone for the sheer enjoyment of it. He had apparently robbed her of the free-spirited joy she'd always found in trying the unexpected. It was one more regret he'd have to live with.

He turned on the engine as she climbed into the passenger seat and faced him with pure, uninhibited mischief in her eyes.

"What?" he asked.

"I got caught," she said, grinning and sounding not the least bit repentant.

"Caught?"

"Retta's onto us. She figured out what we're up to."

Daniel stared at her, not sure he was comprehending what she was telling him, especially since she didn't seem particularly upset. To the contrary, she sounded like a kid on a lark. "Retta knows we're going to the inn to sleep together?"

"She does," Molly confirmed.

"How could she? She never heard a word we said. She was in the kitchen the whole time."

"What can I tell you? She's always had a sixth sense about these things."

"Then I'm surprised she didn't come charging into the parking lot with a meat cleaver," he said, barely able to contain a shudder as he glanced worriedly into the rearview mirror, not entirely sure that he wouldn't see Retta chasing after them, apron flapping, deadly cleaver in hand.

"Apparently she doesn't disapprove," Molly said.

He got it then. He understood why Molly looked so remarkably happy and at ease. "And that makes you feel a lot better about things, doesn't it? I mean things between us." He couldn't hide his own relief, either. Retta's approval meant everything to Molly, and a lot to him, as well.

She nodded. "I know it's ridiculous at my age to care about anyone's opinion, but I do. Retta was like a mother to me when I was growing up. She knows how badly you hurt me, so I know she doesn't take our relationship starting up again lightly. More than that, she's my one link to my grandfather. I guess it's a little like having his blessing, too."

"Then I can stop worrying about the meat cleaver?"

She grinned. "Unless you hurt me again."

"Then I will definitely try not to do that," he vowed. He glanced sideways at her. "Retta's approval aside, are you okay with this? We don't have to go to the inn. We could just go somewhere and talk. We haven't had a lot of time to catch up. Most of our conversations have been about Kendra."

She laughed. "I'm a modern woman, in case you haven't noticed. I can multitask. I can talk and have sex at the same time."

Daniel barely managed to bite back a smile. "Good to know. In fact, that's excellent."

Her expression suddenly sobered. "Daniel?"

"What?"

"Do you really think we can get it right this time?"

"We're going to try like hell," he told her. "Because this time losing you is not an option I can live with."

Apparently satisfied by his declaration, she settled back against the seat and closed her eyes. A minute later she was asleep.

Daniel sighed. Apparently, exhaustion from her all-night fishing adventure had caught up with her. A nap would do her good. It was a forty-five-minute drive to the inn. As he recalled, Molly could revive pretty quickly after even a brief catnap. Given his own state of near exhaustion, he would be doing well to keep up with her, but he intended to give it one hell of a shot. He'd been waiting way too long for this chance not to give it his all.

* * *

The inn looked as if it had been around for a century or more. The owners had done a fabulous job of creating a sprawling white clapboard country home that looked as though it had welcomed thousands of guests, even though its doors had been open only a few months.

Filled with guilty anticipation, Molly stood back while Daniel registered, then asked if it was possible to get room service at this hour. The young woman working behind the counter grinned.

"We're always willing to see that our guests' requests are met," she assured Daniel. "There's a menu in the room, or if there's something special you'd like, our chef will do his best to accommodate you."

"Two steaks, medium, a bottle of champagne and chocolate mousse," he said at once. "Is that possible?"

"Absolutely."

He turned to Molly, winked, then turned back to the counter. "Extra whipped cream?"

Molly nearly groaned aloud. She could feel the heat climbing into her cheeks, but the young woman didn't bat an eye.

"Not a problem," she said. "Will a half hour be okay?"

Daniel caught Molly's gaze again, held it, then said, "You'd better make it an hour."

The young woman remained completely unflustered. "Certainly, sir. Shall I have someone show you to your room?"

Daniel glanced at the key. "Third floor," he said. "Elevator's right there. I think we can find it."

"Then enjoy your stay. If there's anything else you need, call the front desk. My name's Colleen."

"Thank you, Colleen. I'm sure we will," Daniel said as he turned toward the elevator, suddenly being discreet enough to keep his hands to himself as Molly preceded him inside.

When the doors were closed, she poked him in the arm. "Tell the world, why don't you?"

"Tell the world what?" he asked innocently.

"That we're here for a secret assignation."

He laughed. "I thought we were here for sex and a nice lunch."

"I'm rethinking the sex part," she said, though even she could tell the claim was a little too half-hearted to be taken seriously.

"Bet I can change your mind," he said, already reaching for her.

"Daniel." The whispered protest died on her lips when he backed her against the wall of the elevator and brought his mouth down on hers in a kiss that could have convinced a saint to sin. She was vaguely aware of the elevator doors opening and closing, but the heat from Daniel's body managed to fog her brain. He was hard against her, ready for that sex she'd insisted she was going to deny him. And the truth of it was that she was every bit as ready as he was.

She'd missed this—the feel of his mouth on hers, the way her body molded to his, his woodsy, masculine scent, the sandpaper texture of his cheeks within hours of shaving. She'd been a tomboy as a kid, and she'd missed feeling surprisingly small and feminine next to his more powerful build.

It felt so damned good to lose herself on a sea of sensations, to be swept away to a place beyond thought.

This time, though, the sound of the elevator doors opening and closing was accompanied by a shocked gasp. Molly's eyes flew open to encounter the startled look of an elderly woman whose pursed lips suggested she was not amused by their behavior. Molly nudged Daniel and tried to extricate herself from his embrace.

"Sorry," she murmured, totally chagrined.

Daniel finally caught on. He recovered quickly. By the time he turned, he was wearing his most charming smile, the one that could win the heart of his sternest detractor.

As Molly watched, the woman's lips softened and a twinkle lit her eyes. Another conquest was clearly in the making.

"Honeymoon?" she inquired dreamily.

Daniel grinned. "Don't tell anyone, okay?"

"Not a word, but, young man, I do think you should take your bride into a room. Public displays of affection are so gauche, don't you think?"

Daniel looked suitably chastened. "You are absolutely right." He grabbed Molly's hand and hauled her from the elevator. "Have a lovely afternoon, ma'am."

"You do the same, young man," she said, the twinkle back in her eyes. She winked at Molly. "Much happiness, my dear."

"Thank you," Molly said, all but tripping over Daniel in her haste to get away before she burst into laughter.

She held her breath until the elevator doors closed and the woman was safely descending to the lobby before whirling on Daniel. "Is there any chance at all that the universe won't know about this little rendezvous of ours by nightfall? The story will be all over Widow's Cove, if not the entire state of Maine."

He grinned unrepentantly. "So what? Everybody loves a romance. Besides, no one here knows our real names."

"We may be anonymous in the gossip, but Retta knows we're here," she reminded him. "She can withdraw that blessing of hers just like that if she knew we were making a public spectacle of ourselves." She snapped her fingers.

"But she won't," Daniel said confidently.

"Why not?"

"Retta's the biggest sucker of all for romance." He leveled a look at her that made her tremble. "You can always back out."

Molly glanced at the key in his hand, then at the numbers on the doors. "Doesn't seem much point to that, since our room is right here and it's paid for."

When she would have taken the key and opened the door, Daniel held it just out of reach.

"Before we go inside, there's something you

should know," he said, his expression suddenly serious. "I love you, Molly. I know you said you didn't want me to say that, but you need to hear it. You need to believe it." He gestured toward the room. "That's what this is about. It's not just sex, not for me. I'm making a commitment to you, here and now, this afternoon. I'm not asking you to do the same, but I won't deny my own feelings."

Molly's heart pounded at the conviction in his voice. She wanted to believe him. She wanted to say the words back to him, but she'd done that once. She'd offered him everything, and it hadn't been enough.

She reached up and touched his cheek. "I believe you," she said. "It's about more than sex for me, too."

She stumbled over the idea of commitment, but Daniel seemed to understand that she wasn't ready to commit beyond this moment. She was a little surprised that he was so eager to talk about the future, but given the sad expression on his face, she couldn't deny that he seemed genuinely disappointed that they weren't on the same page.

He managed to put aside whatever dismay he was feeling, though. He grinned at her as he put the key into the lock, opened the door, then swept her up and carried her inside, kicking the door shut behind him.

"Here and now," he murmured. "That's all that matters."

Molly gazed into the troubled depths of his eyes. "It really is, you know. We can't control any of the rest, but we can make this moment count."

Daniel glanced past her at the clock on the bedside table, then grinned. "Especially since we only have about forty-five of those precious moments left before that lunch I ordered turns up."

Molly kicked off her shoes and reached for the buttons on his shirt. "Then I suggest we not waste another second."

Daniel didn't want to be rushed. He wanted to savor everything about this afternoon. He wanted to take his time stripping away Molly's clothes, lingering over each caress of her magnificent, familiar body. He wanted each minute to be memorable.

"Maybe I should call down and cancel lunch," he murmured as her fingers grazed his bare chest and made his pulse skip.

"Oh, no," she said. "I'm starved, first for you, then for food."

It was the way she'd always been, eager to make the most of whatever time they had. She could take her own sweet time tormenting him, or she could get caught up in a quick rush to pleasure that had them both gasping and breathless in a heartbeat. That was clearly her intention now, as she undid his belt and the button at his waist, then slid her hand down until his entire body jolted at the touch of her clever fingers.

Daniel spotted the quick rise of satisfaction in her eyes, the tiny frown of concentration on her brow, as she set about making him crazy. Maybe this moment wasn't about him. Maybe it was about Molly regaining her sense of control over their relationship. Maybe he simply needed to go along for the ride, let her take him wherever she wanted him to go. Being passive wasn't in his nature, but Molly seemed to have a plan and since at the moment his body seemed more than content with it, who was he to argue?

Her hands were everywhere and so was her mouth. He heard her catch her breath as she slid his pants down, releasing him in his full state of arousal. She touched the tip of him, sending a jolt through his entire body.

"I want you, Daniel," she said, looking up at last to meet his gaze. "Make love to me."

"With pleasure," he said, lifting her to the high bed with its thick comforter and soft, fresh-smelling sheets.

He stripped off his already disheveled clothes, joined her on the bed and then set to work undressing her, taking his time as he removed blouse, bra, jeans and, at long last, panties. It wasn't so much an exploration of her body—he already knew it as well as he knew his own—as it was a reawakening, for both of them. He wanted to remember—wanted *her* to remember—what it was like between them, how well they fit together, the pleasure that had always washed over them like a storm.

Already, though, she was restless, her hips seeking his touch. She was slick with perspiration, moist and ready for him to enter her. He'd waited so long for this, missed it in ways he hadn't even realized until now, but no more. He couldn't wait another second.

With one sure thrust, he was inside her, surrounded by her heat, feeling her contract around him with the first spasm. He waited as the waves subsided, then began to move, slowly, teasing her, then harder and deeper as her cries of pleasure mounted and his own body tensed, straining toward the promised release. When it came, it was shattering, the way it had always been with Molly…and only with Molly.

And with his climax came the equally shattering realization that the condoms he'd bought and kept in his wallet for this moment were still safely there. He waited for the panic to set in, waited for the awful fear that there might be another pregnancy that could come between them, but instead an amazing sense of peace stole over him. If there was a baby, so be it. Today was all about second chances. There could be no greater second chance than the opportunity to prove to Molly that he was ready for a family, that he wasn't afraid of testing his ability to be a husband and father. Not as long as it was with her.

Still joined with her, he gazed into her eyes. "Marry me," he said. "Be with me forever."

Alarm flared in her eyes, and he could almost feel her emotional withdrawal.

Her gaze shuttered, she said, "I thought you understood that I'm not ready for that, not ready for more than this."

"I do," he said.

"Then what was the proposal all about, Daniel?"

"I need you to remember that I asked, that I meant it."

She regarded him with confusion. "I don't understand."

"If…" He drew in a deep breath, then forced himself to continue. "If there's a baby, I want you to know now, this minute, that this time it will be different. I will be there for you."

Her expression faltered at that, then tears filled her eyes. "There won't be a baby, Daniel."

For a moment his heart stood still. Was there something Patrick hadn't told him about the miscarriage? Something she hadn't told him? He would never forgive himself if he'd destroyed her chances of having children forever. "Ever?" he asked, his heart in his throat.

As understanding dawned, she touched his cheek. "No, just now. I'm on the Pill."

His sigh of relief was deep. "Thank God."

She pulled away, her anger almost palpable. "So many pretty words, Daniel. Didn't you mean any of them?"

When she would have run, he held her tight, forced her to look into his eyes. "No misunderstandings this time, Molly. I didn't mean I was grateful that we hadn't made a baby. I was only grateful that I hadn't cost you the chance to have them. I couldn't have forgiven myself for that."

She searched his face, clearly wanting to believe him, but it was a long time before he felt her relax in his arms.

"I love you," he repeated. "And I do want to marry you, whenever you're ready, baby or no baby."

The tears spilled then, and she curled into him, clinging to him. The storm went on for so long, he was sure there could be no tears left, but when the sobs finally stopped, she looked more at peace than he'd seen her in years.

"We're okay?" he asked, trying to interpret what had just happened.

"We're okay," she said, then smiled at the knock on the door. "And definitely ready for lunch. I can think of all sorts of fascinating things to do with that whipped cream."

He frowned with mock ferocity. "Great thing to say when I have to go to the door," he said, grabbing a thick robe off the back of the bathroom door.

The waiter managed to keep a discreetly bland expression on his face as he set up the room-service cart in front of a large bay window. Daniel tipped him well, then gratefully closed the door behind him, barely hiding a smile at the sight of the large silver bowl filled with fresh whipped cream.

"What?" Molly said, studying him.

He picked up the bowl and carried it toward her. "Only the best," he teased, dipping up a spoonful and dropping it onto her breast.

Her eyes widened as he set the bowl aside and bent down to lick away every last trace of the cream. Her nipple was hard, her hips restless when he was done.

"More?" he asked.

"Oh, yes, please," she whispered, her voice husky.

"Our food will get cold," he reminded her.

"Nothing I like better than cold steak," she insisted.

"And warm champagne?" he asked.

She glanced toward the cart. "It's on ice."

"Ah, well, that's okay, then," he said, laughing.

She leaned back against the pillows and gestured toward the whipped cream. "Come on, Daniel. Get with the program."

This time he drizzled a trail of the sweet cream between her breasts and lower, then licked it away. "So good," he murmured.

"Me or the whipped cream?" she asked.

"You, of course. Always you."

Molly reached for the bowl. "My turn," she said, scooping up a large dollop, then studying him thoughtfully. "Where to start, though?"

Daniel fought a grin at her serious expression. "Doesn't really matter, you know. It's pretty much guaranteed to be a turn-on, whatever you do with that."

"Then maybe I'll start with a little right here," she said, dropping just a little on his mouth, then running her tongue over his lips. "You're right. It is good."

"Very good," he confirmed.

After that, she began to get creative, with a little dab here, a larger dab there, and that wicked mouth of hers making him completely crazy.

"Come here," he pleaded when she was sitting

back on her heels looking for some other part of his anatomy she could torment.

"I'm not through."

"Yes, you are," he said, snatching away the bowl and flipping her on her backside in a move that caught her completely off guard. "Time to pay up, darlin'."

She laughed. "Oh, really?"

"Yes, really," he said, lowering his mouth to hers and tasting her till she was writhing beneath him. "See, no need for whipped cream. You taste incredible just as you are."

"Good thing, because we were completely out of the stuff, and I, for one, am not about to call the front desk and ask for more."

"Scared people will think we used it for something other than a garnish on the chocolate mousse?" he teased.

"I don't think there was a doubt in Colleen's mind about its intended use," Molly said. "I think she was envying me because I was about to come upstairs and have wild, uninhibited sex with a very handsome man. I think our friend in the elevator felt the exact same way."

"She must have been eighty," Daniel said.

"Doesn't mean she can't be having a sex life of her own or a lot of very steamy memories," Molly said. "I think we'll still be having sex when we're eighty, don't you?"

Daniel gazed into her eyes at the admission that she saw a future for them. "That's what I want," he said seriously. "Sex or no sex, I want to be with you when we're eighty."

Molly sighed.

"Am I getting ahead of myself again?" he asked, even though she was the one who'd initiated the allusion.

"No, I want that, too, but I'm scared."

Daniel brushed a stray curl back from her cheek and gazed into her eyes. "Don't you think I'm scared, too? I'm terrified that I'll get it wrong again. I don't think we get but so many second chances in life. I want to make the most of this one. We have to make a vow to talk, Molly. If one of us is getting it all wrong, we have to get it out in the open. We can't run from it."

She regarded him with an unflinching gaze. "The way you did before."

"Yes," he said readily, more than willing to take responsibility for his own cowardice back then. "The way I did before."

She grazed his cheek with her knuckles. "Then maybe we really do have a chance of getting it right this time, Daniel." Her lips curved. "We could toast to that."

He grinned. "A very good idea," he said, getting the bottle of champagne. He popped the cork and poured them each a glass.

"To getting it right," he said, touching his glass to hers.

The crystal made a sweet sound, and the motion splashed just a little of the champagne. Molly studied the droplets on his chest intently, then grinned. "Whipped cream, champagne, what's the difference?" she asked as she put aside her glass.

Daniel groaned as she tasted him. She was going to be the death of him this afternoon, but oh, my, what a way to go.

When he was breathless and weak, she nudged him with her knee.

"What?" he asked.

"We need to get back."

"I don't think I can move."

"Of course you can," she said. She wafted the plate of now-cold steak under his nose. "Meat will give you your strength back."

"You can't just toss meat at a man you've all but destroyed and expect him to revive like some half-starved animal," he protested.

She grinned and set the plate aside. "You used to have more staying power, Devaney," she scoffed.

"No, you used to be demure."

She laughed at that. "Never. That must have been some other woman."

He pretended to think about it. "Oh, yeah," he said. "Must have been. I'll have to go through that endless list and try to figure out which one it was."

Molly smacked him with a pillow. "No more women. Not ever."

"None," he said, crossing his heart. He'd never wanted any other woman the way he wanted Molly.

Molly snagged his hand and met his gaze. "I'm serious. This time we're aiming for forever, right? We're going to do whatever it takes to make it work."

Right this second there wasn't a doubt in his mind. "Absolutely," he said with confidence.

He would die before he ever let Molly down again.

12

When Molly finally got back to Jess's, she kissed Daniel goodbye in the parking lot, then walked inside to face a quartet of worried faces all lined up on bar stools. Retta's scowl was mild compared to Patrick's. Alice's expression and Kendra's were more neutral.

"What did my brother do now?" Patrick demanded, obviously assuming the worst since Molly had returned alone.

Molly fought to suppress a grin. "You want details?"

His frown deepened. "Not *those* details," he said at once.

"Well, thank goodness for that," she said. "I'm not sure I'd be comfortable sharing them with you, especially with a teenager present."

"Where is he?" Patrick said. "Did you have a fight?"

"No," Molly replied evenly, then pointedly looked at the others. "Anybody need a drink?"

"I could use more coffee," Alice said in an obvious attempt to help Molly dispel the simmering tension. "Decaf, though. Can't have this baby jittery." She patted her stomach, which managed to divert Patrick's attention for a split second, long enough to give her a soft smile.

Molly refilled Alice's cup, then glanced at Kendra. "You want another soda?"

Clearly surprised at being offered soda this late in the evening, Kendra nodded eagerly. "Sure."

Molly turned to Retta. "Tea?"

"I'm fine with what I've got," Retta said tersely.

"What about you, Patrick? Another beer?"

"I'd prefer some answers. Where the hell is my brother?"

"On his way home," she said.

"If you two didn't fight again, why isn't he with you?" he asked. "Why are you covering for him?"

Molly met his worried gaze. "Do I look as if I've spent the afternoon fighting?"

Alice chuckled. "Actually, you look as if you've spent the afternoon..." She caught a glimpse of Kendra's wide-eyed expression and cut herself off. "You look happy."

"I am happy," she said, her gaze on Retta, who nodded slowly, then visibly relaxed.

Patrick wasn't as easily convinced. "Why didn't he come in here with you?"

"Because he had work to do," she explained reasonably.

"Stuff about me?" Kendra asked, her cheeks turning pale.

"He's going to call Joe, yes," Molly said, reaching over to give her hand a squeeze. "He said not to worry. We're going to work this out."

Kendra nodded slowly. "I guess he wouldn't want to make you mad by messing this up, would he?"

Molly chuckled. "Not a chance."

"Okay, then." A grin spread across her face. "Told you the guy had the hots for you."

Molly groaned. "Kendra!"

"What? It's not like it's a big secret or anything. The two of you snuck off in the middle of the afternoon and went to some fancy inn. Nobody here thinks you were gone for hours just to have lunch." She looked to the others for confirmation. "Right?"

Retta rolled her eyes. "Out of the mouths of babes. Come on, Kendra. Now that Molly's back safe and sound, you and I have work to do."

"It's late. Shouldn't I be going up to bed or something?" Kendra asked.

"You were wide-awake enough five minutes ago to be poking around in things that are none of your business," Retta responded. "I think you can stay up long enough to help me get the dishes put away so everything's ready for tomorrow."

"Slave driver," Kendra accused, but she grinned broadly as she followed Retta into the kitchen without further argument.

"So, it's official?" Alice asked, when Kendra and

Retta were gone. "You and Daniel are back together? Does that mean we could be sisters-in-law?"

"Whoa!" Patrick said. "Who said anything about Molly and Daniel getting married?"

Alice poked him in the ribs. "You married me, didn't you? Surely your twin is as smart as you are. He won't let the best thing to ever happen to him get away a second time."

Patrick swiveled around to look Molly in the eye. "Well? Is my wife right?"

"It's a little premature to predict how this is going to turn out," Molly told him honestly. "But it feels right. Will you be okay with it if we do stay together?"

Patrick seemed to waver, but he finally said, "Molly, you know how I feel about you. There's no one I'd rather see with my brother. I just wish I were as certain that he's the perfect man for you."

"I think he is," Molly admitted slowly. "Even though I felt betrayed, even though I was disappointed in him, I know I never stopped loving him."

"There you go," Alice said triumphantly. "Now stop trying to throw a damper on things, Patrick. I predict that one of these days we're all going to be family."

Patrick rolled his eyes. "Some family."

Alice frowned right back at him. "I'm happy enough with it, even if you are annoying me no end at the moment."

He grinned then, that devilish charmer of a smile that he shared with his brother. Alice was clearly as powerless to resist it as Molly was when Daniel turned the same smile on her.

"Want to go home?" Patrick asked his wife. "Maybe I can think of something to do that won't annoy you."

"I imagine you can," Alice agreed, then winked at Molly. "But you're going to have to work really, really hard at it."

"My pleasure," Patrick said, scooping her off the bar stool and throwing her over his shoulder.

"Put me down, you idiot," Alice said, laughing as she pounded on his back.

"Not till I can toss you on our nice, soft, feather mattress," he replied. "Besides, at the rate that baby's growing, I won't be able to do this much longer."

"How flattering," Alice said. "Maybe I should reconsider what we're about to do, since you think I already look like a whale and I'm not even four months along yet."

"Did I say that?" Patrick asked Molly. "Did you hear me say anything to suggest that I don't find my wife absolutely gorgeous and desirable?"

"Well…" Molly teased.

"Never mind," he replied irritably. "I guess I'll just have to work a little harder to prove how attractive I find her."

"In that case, your boat's closer," Alice pointed out.

Patrick laughed. "See why I love this woman, Molly? She's easily won over and she has no patience."

"And that's a good thing?" Molly asked doubtfully.

"In this instance, yes." With an arm clamped firmly across the back of his wife's thighs, he leaned across the bar and kissed Molly. "I want you to be happy—you know that, don't you?"

"I do."

Molly watched as Patrick carted the still-protesting Alice from the bar. She envied them the certainty of the love they'd found with each other. She believed in Daniel, believed that a future with him was possible, mostly because she wanted to so desperately. But deep in her heart, in a place she was trying hard not to go, she knew that real faith in the lasting power of their love was going to be harder to come by.

Daniel spent the better part of an hour on the phone with Joe Sutton, haggling over the next step to take in Kendra's situation. Joe's meeting with the Morrows hadn't gone well. They'd insisted once again that any problems between themselves and their daughter could be worked out once she got home.

"I told them I needed to know what those problems were, but they stonewalled me," Joe said, sounding thoroughly frustrated. "They still insist it's a family matter."

"Did you tell 'em it could become a court matter?" Daniel asked.

"I tried." He sighed. "I hate to tell you this, but it gets worse. They figured out that I'd only be so interested if I had a lead on her whereabouts. They're insisting that she be returned immediately or they'll sue me, the department and anyone else who's interfering in the safe return of their daughter."

Daniel uttered a profanity he rarely used.

"I agree, but it's going to get ugly if we stand in their way," Joe told him. "I filled my boss in, and he's bouncing off walls. He wants the girl back home yesterday."

"Hold 'em all off for twenty-four hours," Daniel pleaded. "Maybe I can convince Kendra to tell us everything so we'll have some ammunition to take to a judge. We need to know where the parents intend to send her. If it's some fancy boarding school where she'll get an incredible education, he might not be so sympathetic."

"And what if there is no ammunition?" Joe asked. "What if this is just a mixed-up kid? We wind up with egg on our faces and the department winds up in court."

"Always a possibility," Daniel agreed. "But you've met Kendra—do you think she's a kid who just wants to stir up trouble?"

"No," Joe said. "But we're running out of time. What if she won't open up?"

"Then maybe I can talk her into going home to confront her parents directly, with me there as mediator." He had a hunch Molly wasn't going to be happy with any reunion in which she didn't get to participate to reassure herself that Kendra was in good hands. He couldn't blame her, either.

He also knew that in some twisted way she was equating Kendra's fate to that of their lost baby. If he failed Molly again, there was no telling how she would react.

"Hold on," Joe said eventually. "Let me run that by the chief."

Daniel waited impatiently for him to come back on the line. "Well?" he asked when he heard the line reconnect.

"Devaney, this is Chief Williams. Why the hell are you dragging your heels about this?"

"Gut instinct," Daniel said at once. "I know that's not a lot, but there is a real problem there, Chief. I'd stake my job on it."

"You *are* staking your job on it," he retorted. "And Sutton's and mine, more than likely. That better be one helluva gut you've got."

"I believe it is, sir."

"Then take your twenty-four hours and not one second longer. This time tomorrow night, I want that girl tucked safe in her bed at home or I want one helluva reason why she's not there."

"Yes, sir," Daniel said. "Thank you."

"I'll put Joe back on so you can work out the details," the chief said.

Daniel sighed as he waited.

"Now what?" Joe asked.

"Leave it to me. You've done enough."

"Oh, no, you don't. Until this is resolved, we're joined at the hip."

Daniel thought of the way he'd spent his afternoon and felt an instant of relief that Joe hadn't decided to shadow his every move a few hours earlier. Still, Molly wasn't going to be much happier about this turn of events.

"I'll call you first thing in the morning when I'm ready to head over to Jess's," Daniel assured him.

"You're not going straight over there now?"

"And do what? Wake Kendra out of a sound sleep?"

"She might say more when she's half-asleep," Joe noted.

"Not with Molly yelling at both of us about being a couple of bullies for dragging them out of bed in the middle of the night," Daniel said with certainty.

"You have a point," Joe said, relenting. "But if I don't hear from you by daybreak, I'm coming looking for you."

"Never doubted it for a minute," Daniel told him, then hung up.

The receiver was barely back in place before the phone rang again. He was in no mood to deal with anyone, but a guilty conscience had him reaching for the phone, anyway.

He barked out a greeting that was met by silence.

"Dammit, is anyone there?" he demanded.

"Having a bad day?" a cool male voice inquired.

"I've had better," Daniel said, trying to figure out why the voice seemed so familiar.

"This is Ryan."

"Ah," he said, realizing then that there were faint traces of his father's Irish brogue in Ryan's voice even though he'd grown up in Boston. He doubted Ryan would appreciate being reminded that he carried any trait of the man he'd come to hate. "Sorry for jumping down your throat."

"Want to talk about whatever's bugging you?"

Oddly enough, he did. He could use the advice of a big brother right now, but it was confidential information and he wasn't free to share it.

"I wish I could," he said.

"Job-related?" Ryan guessed.

"Yes."

"That runaway who's been staying with Molly?"

"You know about that?" he asked, surprised.

"Patrick filled me in."

"Oh?"

"Only the basics, Daniel. He didn't share the details of your personal or professional business, though I gather there are some old, unresolved issues between you and Molly."

"We're working on that," Daniel said.

"Good. I liked her the first time I met her. For a bit, there, I wasn't sure if she was the one Patrick had his eye on or if it was Alice."

Daniel didn't know what to say to that. It felt strange to realize that Ryan knew so much about Patrick's life, that they'd begun to create a bond where none existed between Daniel and his big brother. It wasn't beyond the realm of possibility that Ryan knew more about Patrick these days than Daniel did, given the long-standing tensions between himself and his twin.

Feeling more than a little disgruntled about that, he said stiffly, "I'm sure you didn't call to talk about my life."

"Actually, I'd like to know more about your life," Ryan said. "So would Sean and Michael. It's the folks we're a little gun-shy about seeing again."

"Yeah, it's not like the last time went so well," Daniel said, unable to keep the sarcastic edge out of his voice. If his brother took offense at that, so be it.

"More like a disaster," Ryan agreed. "But Patrick believes there's hope. He thinks you can bring Mom and Dad around and make them talk to us."

"I told him I'd try," Daniel said. "To be honest, though, I haven't had time to do much about it. Are you planning to come back up here soon?"

"Well, you see, here's the thing," Ryan said. "If it were up to me, I could wait till hell freezes over, but I have this very precocious child in the house who wants to meet her grandparents. Once she found out that I know where they are, she's been relentless. Sean's son is curious, too. Being a bachelor, you may not be aware that there is nothing that can motivate a man quicker than a kid on a mission."

Daniel wondered if thrusting a couple of kids into the midst of all that tension would be wise. Then again, the grandchildren could provide exactly what the situation needed—a bridge. They had no axes to grind with Connor and Kathleen Devaney.

"Daniel, you still there?"

"I'm here."

"What do you think? Should we come up?"

"When did you have in mind?"

"This has dragged on entirely too long already. We need to get this over and done with," Ryan said flatly. "How's tomorrow for you?"

Daniel muttered that same rarely used profanity for the second time in less than an hour.

"Not good?" Ryan asked at once.

"It's just that I have a situation that needs to be resolved by this time tomorrow. It can't be put off." But neither could this, he told himself. "Look, I'll work something out. I'll make some hotel reservations for all of you. I'll do everything I can to get this other situation straightened out early in the day and set things up for a meeting between you and the folks for tomorrow night. If not, we'll do it first thing on Sunday. Will that work? Can you be a little flexible?"

"We'll make it work," Ryan said.

"You mentioned Sean and the kids," Daniel said. "Will Michael come, as well?" He recalled how bitter the youngest of the three had been.

"We'll all be there," Ryan said. "Even if I have to butt heads with a few people to make it happen. Our wives, too."

At Ryan's words, Daniel's heart began to beat a little harder. It was the reunion he'd dreamed of from the moment he'd found out about his brothers. For so many years now, even after he'd had his own all-too-brief reunion with them, he'd thought the odds were too long for all of the Devaneys ever getting together peacefully in the same room. To his astonishment, it was actually close to happening now. He intended to make sure that nothing went awry.

"When you get here, meet me at Molly's. You know the place, right? On the waterfront?"

"I know it," Ryan said.

"I'll be there all day, and I'll be able to tell you what I've set up. We'll probably get together with everyone there, too. I think it might be better if we do this on neutral turf."

"Makes sense to me. Barging in at the house last time was damned awkward," Ryan said. "And, Daniel, I really am looking forward to getting to know you, no matter how things turn out with the folks."

Daniel couldn't hide his surprise. He'd expected the same sort of blame from Ryan that Patrick had always assigned to Daniel in his loyalty to their folks. "Really?"

"You sound as if you didn't expect me to feel that way," Ryan said.

"It's just that the past few years Patrick has seen me as the roadblock, the chief defender of our folks. He's been so furious with me that we've barely spoken," Daniel explained. "I can't begin to tell you how much I regret that. I never wanted to be in that position. I just couldn't turn my back on them. Whatever they did to you, whatever the reason for it, they were good parents to me and Patrick."

Ryan sighed heavily. "I don't want to take that away from you. I really don't. No two people are ever going to see this mess exactly the same. Sean and I don't. Neither do Michael and I. We all had different experiences, some due to our ages, some due to what happened after the folks abandoned us."

"Patrick and I had the same one," Daniel said. "But he has no problem blaming our parents for everything without knowing the whole story. All he sees is the fact that they lied to us for so many years and let us think we were their only children. In my heart I know they wouldn't have done that if they'd seen any other way to handle it. I think they were scared of us losing all respect for them, which is exactly what happened with Patrick."

"You know something, Daniel, I have a good friend here who's a priest. He says it's a funny thing about faith. He says some people are born with it. They trust in God, trust in their fellow man, and nothing bad ever happens to shake that faith. Then there are the skeptics. They want proof. I think the ones who are born with unshakable faith are the lucky ones. Seems to me like you're one of those. The rest of us need our proof, our explanations. Doesn't make any of us wrong."

Daniel felt an amazing sense of peace steal over him as he listened to his brother. "How did you get to be so wise?"

Ryan laughed. "I'd like to say it came naturally, but a lot of it has to do with letting go of my anger and listening to people who are a lot wiser than I am."

"That priest," Daniel said.

"And my wife. Maggie sees the world and the people in it in a way that gives me hope every day of my life. You'll like her. You're two of a kind."

"I'll look forward to meeting her," Daniel said.

"See you tomorrow," Ryan said. "Hope you get that other situation resolved."

Daniel thought of the struggle he was going to face convincing Molly or Kendra to go along with what had to be done. "I hope so, too. Otherwise, you're likely to find me bloody and bruised when you get here."

He figured even if he managed to pull off a miracle with Molly and Kendra, that still left the battle with his folks to get them to meet with his brothers. He cast a gaze heavenward. "Hope You're not fresh out of miracles."

"What was that?" Ryan asked.

"Nothing," Daniel said, feeling foolish at having been caught saying the words out loud. "Just a little prayer."

"I've been doing a lot of that lately myself," his brother admitted.

"Has it helped?"

"I'll let you know after tomorrow," Ryan said.

Daniel sighed. Amen to that.

13

Daniel was in an astonishingly chipper mood, Molly decided when he walked into the bar early Saturday morning, swept her into his arms and kissed her soundly right there in plain sight of God and everyone. Apparently he was no longer the least bit concerned about Retta and her meat cleaver.

When he released her at long last, Molly stood back and studied his expression. Despite the outward appearance of exuberance, she thought she detected a few shadows in his eyes. She knew him well enough to recognize that that could only spell trouble.

"Come with me," she said at once.

"Where?"

"Upstairs."

He grinned at that. "Anxious to get me alone again? I guess that kiss was even better than I thought."

"The kiss was just peachy," she said, shaking her head at the size of his ego. "It's whatever else is going on in that head of yours that has me worried. Come on, buster. Upstairs."

He dragged his heels like a kid trying to avoid a lecture. "I haven't even had my coffee."

"Coffee can wait."

"Where's Kendra?"

"In the kitchen with Retta. She's learning to make omelettes. Now stop stalling and let's get moving."

Daniel cast a suspicious look toward the kitchen. "Swear to me that Kendra is in there."

Molly lost patience. "Oh, for heaven's sakes, see for yourself."

To her disgust, he actually went to the kitchen door and peeked in. When he turned back, there was no mistaking the relief in his expression.

"Okay, that does it," she said. "If you don't head for the stairs right this second, you and I are going to have the mother of all fights right here in the middle of Jess's. Word will get back to your brother, and this time I won't stop him if he wants to beat you up."

He held up his hands in a gesture of surrender, though there was a suspicious twitch at the corners of his mouth. "Okay, okay," he said, heading for the door that led to her apartment above the bar.

When they got upstairs, Molly faced him, hands on her hips. "Mind telling me what was going on just now?"

Daniel regarded her with apparent confusion. "I looked in on Kendra. Is that what you're upset about?"

"Part of it," she conceded. "You're acting weird. Very un-Daniel-like."

"You're going to have to explain that one."

"When you first walked through the door and planted that kiss on me, I thought everything in your universe had to be just fine. But it was just an act, wasn't it? You're hiding something."

He frowned, and for a moment she actually believed he might tell her that she was crazy, that she'd gotten it all wrong, but then he sighed heavily, blowing that theory to bits.

"Tell me," she demanded.

"You'd better sit down."

"I don't want to sit down," she said, pacing around the small living room as she awaited whatever bad news he was trying so hard not to tell her. "Tell me."

"Okay, here it is, and I know you're not going to be happy about it."

"Will you just get to the point?"

"I have until this evening to prove that Kendra shouldn't go home or I need to reunite her with her parents," he said, looking miserable. "I'm sorry, Molly, but there's no more wiggle room on this. Her parents figured out that Joe knows where she is and are threatening lawsuits against everyone involved. That could include you, by the way, since you've known from the beginning that she was a runaway with family looking for her. I'm no lawyer, but I figure there's a case against all of us for obstructing justice—at the very least."

She stared at him, not entirely comprehending what he was saying. "So, what? You're going to take her home and that's that?"

"Yes. I have no alternative."

"You would turn that girl over to her parents, even though we both know something is dreadfully wrong, just to protect your own hide?"

"No, dammit, to protect yours."

She faltered at that. "No, I won't let you do it, Daniel. Certainly not for the wrong reason, not to protect me."

"You won't have a choice. Neither of us do."

"Oh, really?" she scoffed. "We'll see about that."

"Come on, Molly, be reasonable. Sooner or later, you had to know this moment would come."

"Don't use that patronizing tone with me," she snapped. "I will not let you force Kendra to do something when she's so obviously scared."

"And if I take her, anyway?" he asked quietly. "What then, Molly? Is it going to come between us?"

"Yes," she said at once.

He leveled an unflinching look straight into her eyes. "Because you'll see it as another betrayal?"

"Yes," she said, though her voice was barely above a whisper. She knew it was unreasonable, knew that it wasn't the same as before, but it felt the same. It hurt that he wasn't on her side, wasn't willing to protect yet another child who mattered to her.

"Sweetheart, this is my job. I take it very seriously. I will do everything in my power to protect Kendra if she needs it, but there is no evidence that she does. To the contrary, all the evidence suggests that she's from a good home. Her parents love her. They're frantic. Put yourself in their shoes for a minute."

She didn't want to think about the Morrows. Kendra was all that mattered. "Then why doesn't Kendra want to go back there?" Molly demanded, unable to keep the urgency out of her voice. "Come on, Daniel. Think about it. They're going to send her away. How much can they really love her if they're going to do that, knowing that she doesn't want to go?"

"Then help me find out where they're sending her," he pleaded. "Go downstairs with me now and lay it on the line for her. She opens up with us, here and now, or she goes home. Even at the risk of alienating you forever, those are the choices, Molly."

She heard the unmistakable finality in his voice and shuddered. He wasn't going to relent on this. Professionally, he'd been backed into a corner. And, much as she hated to admit it, she could see the position he was in. Kendra had given him nothing to work with, no truly solid reason he could take to the police or the courts that would justify not returning her to her parents.

"What do you need from her?" she asked at last.

"The truth," he said simply.

"What if you don't see the truth the same way she does?"

"We'll work it out," he promised. "The three of us."

Molly knew it was the best deal she could hope for. "Give me a few minutes alone with her, okay?"

There was no mistaking the hint of doubt in his eyes. She could even understand it. That didn't mean it didn't hurt. "You expect me to trust you, Daniel, to believe that you have Kendra's best interests at heart. You have to trust me when I tell you that I'm not going to grab her and make a run for it."

He nodded. "I do trust you. You've got fifteen minutes, Molly. No longer."

It was less than she'd hoped for, but probably more than she deserved under the circumstances. If Joe was about to turn up at any second, she doubted he would approve of any concession Daniel was making.

She nodded curtly. "I'll do what I can."

She left Daniel standing in her living room and went back downstairs, trying to think of some way to get through to Kendra and get the answers they needed.

Molly found the girl in the kitchen, close to Retta's side, watching the cook's every move as she made omelettes for the handful of customers already in the dining room.

Kendra glanced up. "This is fun. I think I'm gonna be a famous chef and run a restaurant when I grow up."

Molly grinned. It was a far leap from Jess's to fancy gourmet dining. "Good for you."

"Where've you been? I thought I saw Daniel here a minute ago," Retta said.

"He's here," Molly said. "Kendra, come with me for a few minutes."

Alarm immediately darkened her eyes. "Why?"

Retta put her arm protectively around the girl's shoulders. "What's going on?" she asked Molly.

"I need to talk to Kendra," Molly said.

"Now?" Retta asked, her expression filled with worry.

"Right now," Molly said.

Retta studied her face, then nodded. "Baby, it's okay. You go on and talk to Molly, okay? Remember she's on your side and do whatever she asks, you hear me?"

Kendra nodded meekly, then followed Molly into the bar, her gaze darting around nervously. "Where is he?"

"Who?"

"Daniel."

"Still upstairs, more than likely." Or outside trying to waylay Joe Sutton, but Kendra didn't need to know that.

When they were settled in a reasonably private booth in the back, Molly reached for Kendra's hand. "You know that I only want what's best for you, Kendra, don't you?"

Kendra nodded.

Molly debated her next words, then opted for the truth. Kendra was smart enough to see through any sugarcoating, anyway. She had to know this stalemate couldn't go on forever.

"Daniel and Joe can't put off taking you home," she said at last. "Your parents have guessed that Joe knows where you are and they're threatening to take legal action against him, Daniel and possibly against me, if we don't bring you home."

The color drained from Kendra's cheeks. "Can they do that?"

"I'm afraid so."

"But that's not fair. You're only trying to help me."

"The way they see it, we're keeping you from them. I don't care for myself, but I am worried about Daniel and Joe. Their jobs could be affected by this, and that's not fair, either."

Kendra stared down at the table. "I suppose."

"Sweetie, you know it's not."

"I could call them, from someplace where they couldn't trace the call," Kendra said, her expression brightening. "I could explain that I'm okay and that they shouldn't get mad at you guys."

"I think it's too late for that," Molly said. "Now, if there's a reason why you don't want to go wherever they're sending you, you have to tell us. Daniel will fight for you, but you have to speak up now. There's no more time." She tucked a finger under Kendra's chin and forced the girl to meet her gaze. "Is there a reason? Something besides the plan to send you away?"

Tears swam in her eyes, but Kendra remained silent.

"Did they ever hurt you?" Molly asked one more time.

"No," she said softly. "Never."

"Was there an argument of some kind?"

"No."

"Did they punish you for something?"

Kendra shook her head.

Molly regarded her helplessly. "Kendra, you're a good girl. You didn't just run away for no reason, did you?"

She shook her head but remained silent.

Molly sighed. "Then we have no choice. Daniel has to take you home."

Kendra's shoulders heaved with sobs. Tears spilled down her cheeks. "I don't want to go back," she whispered brokenly.

Molly felt her heart twist in her chest. She would have given anything to grab the girl and run with her, but she couldn't do it. She'd made a promise to Daniel and she had to honor it.

"It's time, Kendra. Your parents love you. Joe says there's not a doubt in his mind about that. Do you think he's wrong?"

"No, not really," she said without hesitation.

Molly felt relieved that Kendra at least believed that her parents cared about her. "Then going home won't be so bad, will it? Whatever happened, you can work it out."

Kendra regarded her hopefully. "Will you come with me?"

"If Daniel agrees, of course I will," Molly said at once. She was no more ready to say goodbye than Kendra was. She wanted to get a good look at the people who were going to send Kendra away again. Maybe they'd provide the answers that Kendra had been unwilling to offer.

Kendra sighed heavily. "Okay, then. I'll go."

Molly glanced up and saw that Daniel was approaching, alone, thank heavens. "Kendra says she'll go home," she told him. "She'd like me to come along."

There was no mistaking the relief in Daniel's eyes. "Fine with me," he said at once. He gave Kendra's shoulder a squeeze. "I know you feel bad right now, but it's going to be okay."

The look Kendra gave him was filled with despair. "I don't think so."

"Sure it will be," Molly said. "Daniel won't let you down." She was counting on that.

"Will you be able to come see me?" Kendra asked.

"We'll try to work it out with your parents," Molly promised. "Right, Daniel?"

"Absolutely."

Kendra finally managed a teary smile. "I guess we should go, then. Can I say goodbye to Retta?"

Daniel nodded. "Of course. I need to speak to her, too. I'm expecting some people here in a bit. I want them to know where I am."

Molly heard a mix of anticipation and dread in his voice and knew at once exactly who he was expecting. "Are you sure you can do this now? Joe could take us."

He glanced at Kendra, then shook his head. "Absolutely not. They knew I had some things to work out today. They'll be here when I get back."

His words spoke volumes about his commitment to Kendra…and to Molly. In that instant, knowing how long he'd waited for the reunion and that he was willing to wait a little longer to keep his promise to Kendra, Molly's last remaining doubts fled. This was a different man from the one who'd run out on her years ago. And their love was stronger than ever.

* * *

"I'm scared," Kendra admitted as Daniel pulled to a stop in front of a large Victorian house with a sprawling porch and a profusion of flowers spilling from window boxes on the railing. "They're gonna be so mad at me."

"I've called," Daniel reassured her. "They're grateful that you decided to come home, that you're okay. They can't wait to see you."

"I missed weeks and weeks of school," she whispered. "I'll probably have to take all my classes over again."

Daniel thought it a little odd that she didn't sound especially distraught over that. "It'll be hard, but you can do it," he reassured her. "Maybe you can even take in some subjects and get credit. We'll talk to the principal."

"No!" Kendra said so heatedly that both Daniel and Molly were caught off guard.

"Sweetie, why don't you want to take the make-up exams?" Molly asked. "You studied while you were with me. I saw you with your books. I know you could pass the exams."

"But that's just it," Kendra said, bursting into tears. "I don't want to pass."

Daniel exchanged a bewildered look with Molly. "Why not?" he asked. "I could understand if you were afraid of failing, but why are you scared that you might pass them?"

Kendra remained silent for what seemed like

an eternity. When she finally spoke, her voice was barely above a whisper. "I want to stay behind."

"You want to fail?" Daniel asked incredulously.

Kendra nodded. "I want to be with my friends, with kids closer to my own age. All the kids in my class are so much older than me. They treat me like a baby. I feel like some sort of freak."

Daniel sighed as understanding finally registered. How had he and Joe managed to miss the fact that this overachieving kid had been pushed too hard? They'd seen only how proud her parents were of her accomplishments. She had great grades, so great that they'd never stopped to consider that she was only thirteen and already a junior. One more year and her parents would be sending a terrified fourteen-year-old off to college to cope with situations that were far too advanced for her social skills. She was smart enough to recognize that she wasn't ready for that. It also explained her one repeated claim that her parents were going to send her away. They were... to college.

"That's why you ran away, isn't it?" he asked quietly, wanting to be sure he'd finally gotten it right. "So you would fail all of your classes and have to stay back?"

Kendra nodded.

"And that's what all the talk of being sent away was about, right? They're talking about college already, aren't they?"

Again she nodded. "They've already taken me to look at some schools and told me I'd be cheating myself of a better opportunity if I stayed home and went to a local college. They really want me to go to some fancy Ivy League school. I don't even want to go to college now."

"Oh, Kendra," Molly said, pulling her close. "I wish you'd explained this at the beginning."

"I couldn't. My parents are going to hate me. They're so proud that I'm smart. I didn't want to let them down, but it's awful. Everybody teases me, and it would be a million times worse at college. All the girls can think about is going to dances and dating and stuff, but nobody ever asks me, because I'm too young to date. I don't have any friends in my class because I don't have anything to talk about with them. They think I'm a baby, and I am." Her voice caught. "Compared to them, I'm just a baby who happens to be smart."

Molly hugged her fiercely. "You are exactly the way you're supposed to be," she said. "And you don't need to grow up too fast. Your mom and dad will understand. We'll make them understand, won't we, Daniel?"

Relieved that it was a problem that could be resolved so easily, when so many of the fears he'd had for Kendra had been so much more devastating, Daniel nodded. "We'll work it out. I promise."

Kendra swiped at the tears running down her cheeks and looked at him with eyes filled with hope. "Do you think you can, really?"

He saw the same hope shining in Molly's eyes and knew that he would do everything in his power, everything necessary to see that this had a happy ending.

"Let's go inside," he said. "There are two people who are anxious to see you, Kendra."

Kendra clutched Molly's hand tightly as they started toward the house, but when the front door flew open and her parents appeared, she dragged in a deep breath, released Molly's hand and ran to them.

Her mother gathered her close while her father wept openly.

"Thank you," her mother said at last. "Thank you for bringing my girl back home." She focused on Molly. "Thank you for keeping her safe."

"It was my pleasure," Molly said. "She's a wonderful girl. I'm sure you're very proud of her."

"We are," Kendra's father said.

"Could we talk for a few minutes?" Daniel asked. "I think it would be helpful if you understood why Kendra ran away." He looked at Kendra. "Right?"

She nodded. "Please, Mommy. Will you and Daddy listen? Please?"

The Morrows exchanged a look. Then David Morrow stepped aside and gestured for all of them to come inside.

"Would anyone care for tea or coffee?" Kendra's mother asked.

"No, thanks. We won't be staying that long," Molly said. "We don't want to intrude on Kendra's homecoming."

"That's right," Daniel said. "But you do need to understand what happened." He glanced pointedly at Kendra. "Will you tell them what you told us in the car just now?"

In a halting voice Kendra explained to them how she felt about being the youngest girl in her class, how scared she was about going away to college, how desperately she wanted to be with friends her own age. Then she sat up a little straighter. "But I don't want to disappoint you," she said bravely. "If you want me to graduate early and go to college, I will."

Mrs. Morrow looked stunned. "Baby, why didn't you say anything? I had no idea you were so unhappy. You've always done so well in school and you've always seemed so well-adjusted."

"Because she didn't want to let you down," Daniel explained. "Running away was all she could think of to do to make you take notice. She thought if she missed a lot of school and failed her classes, she'd get to stay behind and do her junior year over again. I'm sure if you spoke to her principal, there might be some way to reach a compromise, so she continues to get an education that challenges her but still allows her to be with kids her own age. Maybe she could take advanced placement courses, or even college classes one or two days a week."

"I'm sure we could work that out. Everyone at the school has been wonderful. They're all so proud of Kendra. I guess none of us ever saw that our pride was getting in the way of her happiness," her mother said. She squeezed Kendra's hand. "No more. We'll talk about it and work out the solution together."

"My vote will really count?" Kendra asked.

"It will be the most important vote of all," her father assured her.

Kendra threw her arms around her father and buried her head in his shoulder. "Thank you, Daddy."

Once again Daniel noticed that there were tears in David Morrow's eyes. He glanced at Molly. "You ready to go?"

She cast a wistful look at Kendra, but finally nodded. "I'm ready."

They left amid a flurry of thanks and promises to stay in touch. They were almost to the car when Kendra came running down the driveway and threw her arms around Molly's waist.

"I love you," she said.

"I love you, too, Kendra. You're the best. You can come work for me anytime."

"Maybe I could come this summer," Kendra said hopefully.

"If your parents agree," Molly told her. "You know, Retta's starting to count on you."

"I'll call," Kendra promised. "Every day. And tell Retta I'm gonna practice making omelettes."

Molly blinked back tears. "That will make her very happy."

Then Kendra turned to Daniel. "I guess you were right," she said. "You said everything would be okay and it is."

"You know how to reach me if that ever changes," he said. "But I think your folks are going to be listening to you now."

"Uh-huh," she agreed. Then she reached for his

hand and pulled him aside. She beckoned for him to lean down, then whispered in his ear, "When you ask Molly to marry you, can I come to the wedding?"

Daniel chuckled. "You're too young to be matchmaking, kid."

"And you're too old to be wasting time," she told him right back.

He glanced at Molly and knew that she was everything he'd ever wanted. "Since you're so smart, I guess I should listen to you."

"Then you're gonna propose?"

"I imagine so."

"When?"

"Soon."

"You'd better," she said. "I think a wedding would make the perfect ending."

It would, Daniel thought. But first he had a family reunion to pull off. If that went well, he just might put his heart on the line and go for a wedding.

14

Molly was still wiping away tears when Daniel started the car and drove away from the Morrows' house. He reached into his pocket, drew out a handkerchief and handed it to her. She stared at the neatly ironed square and found herself fighting a grin.

"Only you, Daniel," she said.

He gave her a puzzled look. "Only me what?"

"Only you would be wearing jeans and a flannel shirt and carrying a pristine handkerchief."

"I imagine Patrick has one in his pocket at all times, too," he said. "That's what our mother taught us."

"Patrick's gotten over it. Trust me on that," she said. "I was lucky to get a wadded up clump of tissues from him when I was bawling my eyes out over you."

"What can I say? I'm more of a gentleman than my brother. Is that a crime?"

"No, it's sweet," she said. "And I appreciate it."

He glanced over at her, his eyes filled with worry. "Are we okay?"

"You mean because of Kendra?"

He nodded.

"You handled it well, Daniel. You're good at your job."

"If I were good, I'd have found some way to get her to open up when I first talked to her. We could have avoided all these weeks of stress for everyone involved, especially her parents."

"Unless you want to resort to drugs or torture, I don't think you can make teenagers tell you anything they're not inclined to share," Molly said. "She trusted me, and she wouldn't open up to me, either. She knew exactly what she was doing. She was obviously trying to buy herself enough time to miss the end of the school year so she could fail her classes."

He sighed. "I suppose."

"You know it's true."

"All right, yes, but you're avoiding the real question I was asking," he said.

"Which is?"

"Are you and I going to be okay?"

She nodded slowly. "I know you did everything in your power not to let me down. If we have problems, it won't be because of Kendra." She recalled his huddled chat with the girl right as they were leaving. "By the way, what were you two conspiring about?"

"She had a couple of last-minute questions," he said evasively.

"About?"

"Confidential," he said.

Molly wasn't buying it. "Judging from the fact that your cheeks are turning red, it must have been about the two of us. Was she matchmaking?"

He shrugged. "Like I said, our conversation was confidential."

She heard the finality in his voice and gave up. If he wanted to keep Kendra's secret, it was his prerogative. "Will you at least tell me what's going on back at Jess's? Based on what you said earlier, I assume you're expecting your brothers."

He nodded, his expression brightening. "Ryan called last night. He said they wanted to take another stab at working things out with the folks. They're all coming today, including the wives and kids."

"Oh, Daniel, that's wonderful," she said. "You must be so excited."

He gave her a wry look. "Maybe I would be if the folks had agreed to show up. I haven't even spoken to them yet."

"Because of Kendra," she guessed, aware once more of the significance of his having put Kendra's needs above his own. "Well, she's safely home now. Are you going to stop by and see your folks?"

"I'll drop you off, speak to my brothers, then go over there and see what I can work out."

She could tell he was dreading the encounter, probably because he was afraid they'd let him down. He'd been so loyal to them. They owed him this, at least as much as they owed answers to his brothers. She was prepared to tell them that, if it would help.

"I could come with you," she offered. "Your mom always liked me. Maybe I could help to convince them."

He shook his head. "She'd only be embarrassed that you know what she did. As for my father, he'd be even more appalled that I was dragging an outsider into family business."

Molly stiffened at his words. "Is that how you see me, Daniel? As an outsider?"

"No, of course not, Molly," he said at once. "But my father will. Hell, he didn't even think Patrick and I had a right to know about any of this. He's always been a pillar of the church here. He takes pride in the fact that people respect him. He's obviously afraid of losing that, if people find out what happened all those years ago."

Her flash of temper died as quickly as it had risen. "You're right. I can see how he might want to keep this private, but it won't stay private long, Daniel. This is Widow's Cove."

"Tell me something I don't know. Even if none of us said a word, all those men who look exactly like Connor Devaney would be a dead giveaway that something was up."

"You're right about that and about me getting involved. The gossip will get stirred up soon enough. I certainly don't want to make the situation any more awkward for him or your mom," she said. "What can I do?"

"Stay at Jess's," he requested. "Do you think you

could close the place for a private party this evening? I know it's a Saturday, but—"

Molly cut him off. "Of course I can. I think that's a great idea. It will put your folks more at ease, knowing that their neighbors aren't right in the thick of this."

"Thank you. Then you can spend some time with my brothers and their families this afternoon, try to convince them that my parents aren't ogres." He gave her a sideways glance. "Of course, that could be risky. Once you've spent some time with all these Devaneys, you might have second thoughts about me."

She laughed at that. "Hey, I always wanted a big family. Besides, I've met your brothers, at least briefly. I'm pretty sure these guys are a lot like Patrick, and I love *him.*"

Even though he had to know she was teasing, he frowned. "Just my luck," he said.

"It *is,*" she insisted. "I love your brother *like* a brother. What I feel for you moves into a whole other realm."

He visibly relaxed. "That's okay, then. Maybe there's time for a little detour back to that inn."

If his timing had been different, she might have been elated, but she caught on to the delaying tactic at once. "I don't think so. I'm not letting you put off this meeting with your folks. It's too important."

Daniel sighed heavily. "What if they refuse to budge on this?"

"Then you'll tell your brothers that. At least you'll have them in your life. And you know as well as anyone that very few bridges can be built overnight. You'll get a few pilings into the ground and work on the spans later."

He laughed. "Nice analogy."

"I thought so."

When he pulled into the parking lot at Jess's, there were three SUVs lined up next to Patrick's truck. Molly saw Daniel's jaw clench and realized that this man who could handle everyone else's crises was terrified that he'd fail at handling his own.

"You're going to work this out," she said, squeezing his hand.

He gave her a weak smile. "Thanks. I wouldn't put money on that, if I were you."

"I would," she said. "Now let's go see your brothers."

Daniel didn't stay long at Jess's. He reassured Ryan and the others that he was going to give his all to the attempt to convince their parents to join them, then left hastily, confident that Molly would do her part to make his brothers see another side of his folks.

He was in the parking lot when Patrick caught up with him.

"I know you're counting on this working out today," Patrick said, regarding him with what appeared to be genuine worry. "Don't be surprised if they let you down, Daniel."

"They won't," Daniel insisted with more confidence than he was actually feeling.

"I wish I shared your conviction," Patrick said. "They don't deserve a son like you."

"Yeah, well, they've got me," Daniel said.

Patrick frowned at that. For what seemed like an eternity, he appeared to be debating with himself about something. "Look," he said finally, shoving his hands in his pockets in a nervous gesture. "If you think it would make a difference, I could..." He sighed, then said, "I could come with you. It would be like an olive branch or something."

Daniel regarded him with surprise. "You would do that?"

"I want this to end," Patrick said. "Believe it or not, I don't like living with all this tension. Every time the subject of families comes up, Alice gives me this look, you know? Like she's disappointed in me. I can't stand it. I hate letting her down. And we've got a baby coming that I need to consider. I don't want my child to have grandparents nearby who aren't a part of his life."

Daniel grinned. "Yeah, I get that look from Molly a lot, too. Okay, if you're sure, hop in. We'll see if we can't catch 'em off guard and get them over here before they realize what they're getting into."

"You, Mr. Straight Arrow, are going to drag them over here without telling them who's waiting for them?"

"I'll tell them as much as necessary to keep Dad from having a heart attack," Daniel said tightly.

Patrick nudged him in the ribs. "Way to go, bro."

"Save the compliments. You're going to need all that charm to help me get Mom and Dad out of the house."

* * *

They'd inadvertently picked the perfect time, Daniel realized when he saw that his parents were all dressed up for five-o'clock Mass.

When he climbed out of his car, his mother regarded him with a quizzical expression. "Daniel, you never come by at this hour on a Saturday. You know we go to church. Is something wrong?"

Just then Patrick exited the car.

"Oh, my," his mother said. She took a step toward Patrick, then hesitated.

Patrick held back for a minute, then relaxed. "Hi, Mom," he said as if they'd parted on good terms only days before. "Daniel and I thought we might go to church with you and Dad."

Her expression brightened. "Really?"

Daniel realized that his sneaky brother had formed his own plan for getting them to Jess's. First, church, a lot of praying, and then the suggestion of dinner out. He wondered when Patrick planned to lay the rest of his scheme on the table. Probably not until they were at the front door of Jess's. Daniel thought that might be cutting it a little close. He figured the best time to do it would be on the drive over, when they were going sixty miles an hour. Not even his father would try to duck out of a car moving at that speed. And then no one could say they hadn't been warned. He subtly gave his brother a thumbs-up sign. So far, so good.

Just then his father stepped outside. He greeted Daniel, then caught sight of Patrick. "What're you doing here?" he asked warily, darting a look toward his wife as if to make sure she wasn't upset.

"Making peace," Patrick said.

"Yeah, right," his father scoffed. "What happened really? Did you run out of money?"

"Connor!" his mother said sharply. "Our son has come home. He and Daniel are going to church with us. This is something we've hoped and prayed for. Be grateful."

Daniel watched as his father bit back what probably would have been another scathing remark. Instead he reached for his wife's hand and gave it a squeeze.

"Well, let's get going," he said gruffly. "No point in standing around out here. The priest isn't going to wait for us to get there."

"I'll drive," Daniel said. "Dad, sit up front with me."

When everyone was seated, he drove to the small church where they'd attended services as far back as he could remember. He stood back as Patrick helped his mother from the car and saw her beam at him, looking happier than she had since the day Patrick had walked out of the house—certainly happier than she had on his one tension-filled visit a few weeks earlier with Ryan, Sean and Michael.

"Don't know why that boy picked now to come back," Connor grumbled to Daniel. "But I'm glad for your mother's sake. She's missed him."

"And you haven't?" Daniel asked lightly.

His father shrugged. "He was a good fisherman. Of course I miss his help."

Daniel shook his head. "Give it up, Dad. You know you've been every bit as miserable as Mom. Why don't you fix this?"

"Fix it? Fix it how? Never did anything to create the mess in the first place. It's that hotheaded brother of yours. He's the one who stirred things up."

"Actually, I'm the one who stirred them up," Daniel reminded him. "I found those pictures, Dad. Once I did, there was no point in denying that they mattered."

"I'm not talking about those pictures or about what happened all those years ago," his father said. "That's in the past and best left buried. If that's what this visit is about, you're wasting your time."

Daniel met his gaze evenly. "Maybe that's something you should pray about when we get inside, Dad. Keeping the past bottled up inside does no one any good. It certainly doesn't make it go away."

He let the matter drop then. He didn't want to get his father so angry that he wouldn't listen to reason once the service was over.

All during the Mass, Daniel noted that his mother's gaze kept straying to Patrick as if she couldn't get enough of the sight of him. More surprising was the fact that Patrick actually did seem to be at peace at long last. Sometimes all it took was that difficult first step to find forgiveness.

Once the service had ended and they were back in the car, Patrick was the one who said, "How about dinner at Jess's with Daniel and me? Alice will be there. I know she'd like to get to know you."

Their mother beamed. "I remember her so well as a child—I'd love to see her. I can see that she's made you happy. It's all right if we go, isn't it, Connor?"

He gave her one of the indulgent smiles that were so familiar to Daniel. It had always seemed as if there was nothing on earth their father wouldn't do to make their mother happy. Maybe that was because he'd done the one thing guaranteed to rob her of any real happiness and was trying desperately in his own small way to make amends.

"If it's what you want, Kathleen, I wouldn't mind a bowl of Molly's chowder." He glanced at Daniel. "Do you object?"

"Of course not."

His father didn't seem convinced. "There was a time not so long ago when the two of you were on the outs."

"A thing of the past," Daniel assured him. "We're back together, this time for good, I think."

His mother's eyes promptly filled with tears. "Oh, my, something more to celebrate."

Daniel exchanged a look with Patrick, trying to gauge if he had any clue about the best time to spring the rest of the news on them. Patrick shrugged, clearly leaving the really tough decision to him.

They were only minutes away from Jess's when Daniel turned to his father. "Dad, I think there's something you should know before we get there, you and Mom both."

Connor frowned. "What's that?"

"This isn't just about spending an evening with

Alice and Molly and us," he said quietly. "Ryan, Sean and Michael will be there, too, with their families."

Dangerously bright patches of color flooded his father's cheeks. "What the hell are you talking about?"

"Everyone's there, Dad."

"This is a damned setup?" he asked furiously. "How could you do this, Daniel? You know how I feel about dredging up all this ancient history."

"It's not a setup," Daniel insisted. "It's a chance, Dad, a chance to clear the air and get your sons back in your life. They're willing to meet you halfway. Can't you at least do that much?" He glanced in the rearview mirror and saw his mother's wistful expression. "Please, Dad. Do it for Mom."

"Yes, Connor, please," she said softly. "I want to see my sons. If it's possible, I want them back in our lives."

Connor regarded her with bewilderment. "Why, Kathleen? They hate us. They must." He scowled at Patrick. "This was your idea, wasn't it? You just want to humiliate us in public."

"Molly's closed the bar for the night," Daniel reassured him. "It will just be family."

"I still say this is a bad idea. I don't want to spend an entire evening listening to them berate us," Connor said. "Kathleen, you know it will only upset you."

"I'll be fine," she insisted. "It's time they get to have their say, Connor."

"I won't deny that there are a lot of strong emotions at work here, Dad, but the fact that they're here at all tells me they want this," Daniel said. "At the very least, help them to understand why you and Mom left them behind. Can't you at least give them answers to the questions they've had to live with their whole lives?"

His mother reached over the seat and clasped her husband's shoulder. "We must do this, Connor," she said firmly. "It's our chance to make things right, a chance we probably don't deserve. We failed them back then. Surely now we can give them the one thing they've ever asked of us."

Daniel saw that his father looked tormented. "Dad, it will be okay. They're good men. They really are. You'll be proud of them."

"I have no right to take any pride in the men they've become," his father replied, looking defeated. "They've accomplished whatever they've made of their lives in spite of me."

To Daniel's surprise, Patrick spoke up. "Maybe so, Dad, but there's Devaney blood running through their veins. If they're strong enough to overcome the past, it's because of that."

Their father sank back against the seat then and closed his eyes. When he opened them again, he turned to his wife. "This is what you want, Kathleen? You're sure?"

She nodded, tears in her eyes. "It's all I've ever wanted, just one more chance to see my boys."

"Then we'll go," he said. He frowned at Daniel, then at Patrick. "Not that I like the way the two of you went about this, mind you. Be warned that I'll have a lot to say about that later."

Patrick grinned. "I wouldn't expect anything less. The Connor Devaney who raised Daniel and me had a powerful sense of right and wrong."

Their father sighed. "Only because I was trying to make up for a great injustice I did to my other sons. I never wanted you two to be as weak as I was."

"Connor Devaney, you were *not* weak," Daniel's mother said fiercely. "You made an impossible decision and you did it out of love. I won't ever let you say otherwise. Maybe it was wrong. Maybe there was another way. But you were strong enough to live with the choice you made every day for the rest of your life. You didn't turn to drink, as many men would have. You didn't turn bitter and hard. You were a good father to the two boys we had left, no one here would deny that," she said, regarding Patrick and Daniel as if daring them to challenge her claim.

"She's right, Dad," Daniel told him. "I can't begin to understand the choice you made or what drove you to it...."

"And I hope to heaven you never have to make such a choice yourself," his father told him. "But now I'm about to face the consequences."

Daniel saw the real fear in his eyes and tried to reassure him. "It's going to be okay, Dad. We've all come a long way. I'm not sure if reconciliation would have been possible one minute sooner than this, but it is possible now. I believe that with all my heart."

"So do I," Patrick said.

"From your mouths to God's ear," his father said quietly.

"Amen," the rest of them said in a heartfelt chorus.

15

Daniel's gaze sought out Molly the instant they walked into Jess's. They made quite a little parade, his mother looking pathetically eager, Patrick wary, and their father as if he expected to be pummeled by a trio of outraged Devaney men. Molly gave him a reassuring smile, then came to meet him. She kissed his cheek, then gave his mother a warm hug.

"I'm so glad you're here," Molly told her, including Connor Devaney in the comment. "There are a lot of people here who are anxious to see you."

"More likely to lynch us," his father said in an undertone.

"Dad!" Patrick protested.

"Okay, okay, I'm giving this a chance. I said I would, didn't I?"

Just then a little girl's voice piped up. "Is that my grandpa?"

"Hush, darlin'," Ryan said, trying to maintain his grip on her.

But as he'd told Daniel on the phone, Caitlyn wasn't going to be put off a minute longer. The three-year-old broke away from her father's grasp and raced across the room, hurling herself straight at Connor. Startled, he reacted instinctively, scooping her up in his arms, then staring at her as if he wasn't quite sure where she'd come from.

"Are you my grandpa?" she demanded, gazing at him intently.

Connor drew in a deep breath, and his eyes filled with tears. He blinked hard to fight them. "Yes, I suppose I am, little angel. Who might you be?"

"I'm Caitlyn," she said without hesitation. "And that's my daddy and that's my mommy."

Daniel saw his father's gaze shift to Ryan, whose mouth was set in a grim line. Maggie had her arm tucked supportively through his, but her eyes were damp, and there was no question that her heart was with her impulsive daughter.

His own heart still in his throat, Daniel watched as a boy broke away from Sean and crossed the room. He frowned up at Caitlyn. "He's not just your grandpa. He's mine, too." He gave his new grandfather an irrepressible grin. "I'm Kevin. Me and Mom married Sean."

"I see," Connor said, swiping impatiently at the tears on his weathered cheeks. His gaze sought that of his second son and the woman who was openly crying beside him.

Connor turned slowly to the one remaining son, who looked as if he'd tried to disappear into the shadows. "Then you're Michael," he said softly, no longer even attempting to hide his tears.

"I'm surprised you remember my name," Michael said, earning a disapproving scowl from his wife.

Connor's gaze remained steady. "I deserved that." He looked from one son to the next. "I deserve whatever you think of me, whatever you want to say to my face or behind my back, but I'll tell you here and now that I won't tolerate you taking any of this out on your mother."

Daniel saw his older brothers exchange glances and knew they'd taken the warning to heart, knew that it was a reminder that their behavior at the house on that earlier visit wasn't to be repeated. It was almost as if they recalled a distant time when Connor Devaney's word had been law, when he'd earned their respect.

"Am I making myself clear?" Connor asked, pushing the point home.

"Yes," Ryan said tightly.

"Maybe we should all sit down," Daniel said, relieved that Michael's undisguised bitterness had been the worst of it so far. "Molly, how about something to drink?"

"Right away," she said.

He put an arm around his mother's waist and guided her to a table, then regarded her worriedly. "You okay?"

She nodded. "After they left so abruptly last time, I was afraid this day would never come," she whispered. "Thank you for making it happen."

Daniel grinned. "I think you should thank Caitlyn and Kevin. I gather from Ryan that they were adamant about meeting their grandparents."

Her gaze went immediately to the girl who still hadn't relinquished her hold on Connor. "I always wanted a little girl," she said sadly.

"Well, it's another generation, Mom," Daniel said. "A granddaughter will have to do."

"Oh, it does," she said, her eyes bright. "She's so lovely. She's like her mother, isn't she?"

Daniel looked from Caitlyn to Maggie. The resemblance was impossible to miss, but from all he knew, it went beyond being skin deep. "She has her mother's open heart and strong will, too," he told his mother. "That may be what guides us through this."

As soon as everyone was seated and drinks had been served, the room was filled with an awkward silence. Not even Caitlyn was chattering with her usual exuberance. It was Ryan who finally broke the impasse.

He looked at his father. "Since I'm the oldest, I'll be the one to ask. Why?" he asked simply. "Why did you leave us behind? After all these years, after the way it messed with our heads, I think you owe us an explanation. Weren't we good enough? Did I stir up too much trouble? Did Sean and Michael?"

"Never," Kathleen said with a shocked gasp. "Don't ever think such a thing. You three were my angels. From the moment you were born, Ryan, I knew you were going to make something of yourself. You came into this world with an independent streak. Of course, that landed you in scrapes from time to time, but you were a good boy. I won't hear you suggest otherwise."

"Then why?" he asked again. "For years now, each of us has had to live with being abandoned by the people who were supposed to love us unconditionally. The fact that we're all married now is a miracle. Not a one of us believed we were worth loving, because of what you did to us. Our wives believed otherwise and stuck with us till we came around. It's because of them that our hearts are finally whole."

In the silence that followed Ryan's bitter words, it was again Kathleen who finally spoke. "Then I'm grateful to you," she said, her gaze seeking out Maggie, then Deanna, then Kelly.

Tears streaming down her face, she turned to her husband and reached for his hand. "I can tell them," she said.

Connor looked shaken, but he raised her hand to his lips and kissed it gently. "No. You've shared the blame long enough, Kathleen. It was my decision. It's time I take responsibility for it." He met Ryan's gaze, then looked down at the trusting child in his arms. "You're a father now, so maybe you'll understand."

"God knows I want to," Ryan said. "We all do."

Connor cleared his throat, then looked to Molly. "I wouldn't mind another beer."

She jumped up at once. "Of course."

Only after she'd returned with the drink and he'd taken a long swallow did he finally speak. "When your mother and I were married, we were young. Too young, probably, but I fell in love with her the day I set eyes on her, and she felt the same. I had a job, a decent one with decent wages. A year later, Ryan, you were born. It was a joyous occasion. I looked at you the first time I held you and thought to myself, 'I would give my life to protect this boy.'"

Caitlyn patted her grandfather's cheek. "You're talking about my daddy, huh?"

Connor gave her a tired smile. "That I am, little angel. Your daddy was something else. He had one speed—full throttle."

Across the room, Maggie grinned. "Like someone else in the family," she said, gazing at her daughter.

Connor settled back in the booth, looking more at ease now that the telling was finally under way. He'd always had the gift of being a natural storyteller, and he drew on that now. Daniel knew he would paint a picture for Ryan, Sean and Michael that would make that tragic turning point in all their lives as real as if it had happened yesterday. Maybe it would lead only to more anger and blame, but there was also the chance it could finally lead to understanding and forgiveness.

"And then Sean came along," Connor said, looking toward his second born, who was wearing a Boston Fire Department T-shirt. "You were born without fear. If Ryan did it, you wanted to do it, too. Nothing was too high for you to climb or too risky for you to try."

"He's not scared of anything now, either," Kevin

said proudly. "He fights fires. That's how me and Mommy met him."

Connor nodded. "It doesn't surprise me in the least that you'd take chances, if it meant saving lives, Sean." He turned to his wife. "You remember the day he climbed up onto the neighbor's roof? Almost scared the life out of both of us."

Kathleen nodded. "How could I forget?"

Sean regarded them with bewilderment. "Why was I up there?"

"The neighbor's cat," his father said. "Poor, pitiful thing was meowing her head off, and you couldn't stand it. Everyone else was wringing their hands, and you slipped around back, found a ladder and scampered right up there."

Kevin was clearly intrigued, but Sean frowned at him. "Don't go getting any ideas."

"Amen," Deanna said, giving her son a forbidding look as the others chuckled at the disappointment on Kevin's face.

"We had two fine sons," Connor said, turning to smile at his wife. "But my Kathleen was aching for a daughter." He focused on Michael. "That would be you, son."

The laughter grew louder and less tense as everyone gazed at Michael, who couldn't have looked less feminine. His years in the Navy and his struggle to overcome injuries caused by a sniper's bullet had given him a powerful build.

Connor shook his head, his expression nostalgic. "If we thought Ryan was strong and Sean was fearless, you put the two of them to shame. There was nowhere they went that you didn't sneak off to follow them. If they took a risk, you took a more dangerous one. They were your heroes, but there was little question that one day you'd do something heroic yourself."

Daniel heard the words and felt a sudden twinge of suspicion. "Michael was a Navy SEAL, but you knew that, didn't you, Dad?"

Connor kept his gaze on Michael and nodded slowly. "I did. I kept up with each of you. I worried over your unhappiness and made myself sick thinking about the danger some of you put yourselves in. I blamed myself for making you think that your lives were worth so little that you might as well risk them."

Kathleen stared at him in shock. "You knew where they were? You knew what they were doing? You knew all of that and didn't tell me?"

He regarded her apologetically. "It was selfish, I know that now, but I thought I was protecting you, making it easier for you to bear being separated from them, if we never talked about them. I guess in the back of my mind, I thought that I would know if they truly needed us, and that then I'd tell you and we'd decide what to do together."

"But we did need you," Ryan said angrily. "Time and again."

"And I almost reached out," Connor told him. "I heard about the trouble you were getting mixed up in, the petty shoplifting and such. I was about to come for you myself and shake some sense into you, but Father Francis stepped in. He gave you what you needed."

Ryan still looked angry, but he nodded. "He was my salvation, no question about it."

"So, if you cared enough to keep track of all of us, why the hell did you dump us in the first place?" Michael demanded.

To Daniel's surprise, his father didn't take offense at his son's tone.

"You recall that your mother wanted a little girl. She'd just gotten pregnant again when I lost my job. I picked up work here and there, but I couldn't find a steady paycheck. Feeding three boys required more money than was coming in. We struggled over that and over doctor's bills and rent."

"And then you had us?" Patrick said, looking shaken. "Twins, when even one more baby was going to be a strain?"

"The timing was unfortunate," their father admitted. "But we looked at the two of you and you stole our hearts, just as your brothers had. For a long time, we told ourselves that things were going to get better, that I'd find another job and we'd land on our feet, but it didn't happen."

He gazed around the room at his sons. "I don't believe any of you have been out of work or desperate, but that's the way I was feeling. And Patrick and Daniel, bless 'em both, weren't easy babies, the way you other boys were. They had powerful sets of lungs and difficult dispositions."

"That hasn't changed much," Alice said, giving Patrick's hand a squeeze.

"I remember the fighting," Ryan suddenly said softly. "You and Mom were fighting for the first time I could ever remember."

"We were," Connor confirmed. "I knew that something had to change or I would lose my wife, lose everything that mattered to me. I knew we had to leave Boston and start over fresh."

Sean stared at him. "So you divided the family in half and tossed us aside to save the rest?" he asked heatedly. "What kind of choice is that?"

"A desperate one," Connor said. "The twins were little more than babies. They needed us. You three were strong. Young as you were, you were already independent. We knew you could make it without us, at least for a time. I hoped we'd be able to come back for you, but as time passed, it seemed best to leave things as they were. We believed you would find good homes, have a better chance than we could give you. I'm not saying it was a good decision, but it was the only one I could make at the time. Not a day has gone by that I haven't prayed to God to keep you safe. Not a day has passed that I haven't regretted what I did, but God help me, I didn't know what else to do."

Kathleen reached for her husband's hand and clung to it. "We didn't know what else to do," she said softly. "I don't know if you'll ever be able to forgive us. I don't know if we'll ever forgive ourselves, but we did the only thing that seemed to make sense at the time. We gave you three—Ryan, Sean and Michael—a chance at a better life than the one we could give you."

"You abandoned us," Michael said fiercely. "Okay, I was lucky. I wound up with a family that gave me all the emotional support a scared kid could need, but Ryan didn't. Sean didn't. How was that for the best?"

"If we'd kept all of you, there was little question that your father and I would eventually divorce," Kathleen said. "It was that bad between us. You'd have been no better off."

"We'd have been *together*," Michael said. "We'd have known what it meant to be a family, even if it was a family that had to struggle. Or you could have agreed to an adoption."

"That would have been so final," Kathleen said, her voice breaking.

Daniel looked into his mother's eyes and saw heartbreak, but he could barely sympathize. He was too caught up in his own sense of guilt, even though he knew it was ridiculous. He and Patrick hadn't been given a choice back then. They hadn't asked to be the ones chosen to stay behind. He glanced at his twin and saw that he was struggling with some of the same emotions. Because they'd been barely more than babies, because they'd been helpless and needy, they'd gotten to stay with their parents.

"If Patrick and I hadn't been born," he began.

"Don't you dare go there," his mother said, cutting him off. "You and Patrick brought such joy into our lives."

"More than Ryan, Sean and Michael had?" he asked.

"You can't trade the joy of one child for another," his mother responded.

"But you did," he reminded her. "That's exactly what you did."

He felt Molly's hand squeeze his, but it was scant comfort. He looked at his older brothers. "I'm so sorry."

Ryan scowled at him. "You have nothing to be sorry for. Don't be crazy. You and Patrick were barely two when all of this happened. I can see why Mom and Dad felt they had no choice but to look out for you."

"You can?" his mother said eagerly.

Ryan nodded slowly. "I look at Caitlyn now and know that I could never abandon her when she's so young. I think about the way I was at nine and I was tough. The truth is, I did make it—not without a lot of mistakes, but I made it."

"That's what we counted on," their father said.

Ryan held up a hand. "Wait, now. I'm not saying I agree with your decision or even that I can forgive it, but at least now I can understand it a little better." He looked around the room. "I think we're all pretty well wiped out now. Why don't we call it a night and sleep on all of this, maybe talk again in the morning?"

"What's left to say?" Connor Devaney asked. "I've told you what happened and why. I won't spend the rest of my days trying to defend it."

"And we're not asking you to," Ryan said.

"But we need to keep talking, Dad," Daniel said. "I don't want to lose this chance to know my brothers, and I don't think you want to lose this chance to know them and their wives and their children…your grandchildren. Please agree to come back tomorrow."

"We'll be here," his mother said, giving his father a look that dared him to challenge her.

Connor sighed. "If it's what your mother wants, we'll be here." He glanced at Molly. "I don't suppose you still have your grandfather's recipe for waffles, the old-fashioned kind?"

Molly grinned. "I do indeed. I'll make up a batch."

Caitlyn, who'd been half-asleep in her grandfather's arms for some time now, woke up in time to hear. She clapped her hands together. "I love waffles."

"Me, too," Kevin chimed in. "I can eat three of them."

"I can eat more," Caitlyn said.

Daniel saw his mother's eyes turn misty. "Mom, what is it?"

"They sound just like Ryan, Sean and Michael and the way they tried to outdo each other. It takes me back," she said. She smiled at Molly. "Something tells me you'd best be prepared to make a lot of waffles in the morning, but I wouldn't be surprised if quite a few of them wind up needing to be thrown out."

Molly squeezed her hand. "Not a problem."

"Just be sure I get mine first," Daniel said.

Molly rolled her eyes. "You really do need to learn to share," she scolded.

"Yeah, Daniel. I've been telling you the same thing for years," Patrick chimed in.

Suddenly the room was alive with teasing banter and laughter. To hear their wives tell it, sharing seemed to be a problem for all of the Devaney men.

Daniel leaned back and listened, suddenly content. It was noisy and chaotic, but he had Molly beside him and his family all in the same place. It wasn't perfect, but it was real. This was it. This was the way a family was supposed to be.

And God willing, it was the way his family would be from now on.

16

Molly had spent the entire morning making waffles. Even though she'd been running Jess's for years now, she'd never dealt with so many men with such huge appetites and the streak of competitiveness that seemed to drive them all to try to outdo each other.

Tired as she was, though, she couldn't help feeling satisfied that she'd had a small part in this reunion that meant so much to Daniel. She stood behind the bar and watched him with his brothers. There was still a certain reserve there on his part. She knew that came from his self-imposed and unwarranted sense of guilt over what had happened to them, but Ryan, Sean and Michael were slowly chipping away at it.

They were good men, she thought. And in time they would forgive, if not forget, what Connor and Kathleen Devaney had done to them. As their families grew and everyday stresses came along to challenge them, their understanding of that impossible choice would deepen, too.

She was putting away the last of the glassware when Daniel slipped up behind her and put his arms around her.

"You're awfully quiet this morning," he said. "Everything okay?"

She smiled. "I like watching you with your family. I always liked being with your folks, but it still seemed as if something was missing."

"It was," he said quietly.

"I think they've made progress this weekend, though, don't you?"

"I do," he said. "Michael's even lost that edge to his voice. And Caitlyn and Kevin are so enthralled with their new grandparents, who seem intent on spoiling them rotten, that they won't let Ryan or Sean be strangers."

She turned to face him. "You must be happy."

"I am," he said.

But Molly heard the hint of hesitation in his voice. "Daniel, stop blaming yourself. It's crazy."

"I know," he said. "In my head, I can hear how ridiculous I sound when I say it. I was two, for goodness sakes." He patted his chest. "But in here, I feel so responsible for costing them so much."

"Stop it," she said. "They gained a lot, too. And now you all have a chance to have what you should have had from the beginning, a whole family."

He grinned at her. "You're so smart."

"I know."

"And sexy."

"I know that, too."

"Think anybody would notice if I kissed you?" he asked.

"Do you care?"

He touched her cheek, his gaze darkening. "No. Come to think of it, I don't."

He settled his mouth over hers, kissing her in a way guaranteed to have her blood heating and her heart pounding. Her head was spinning when she heard the first hoots and shouts.

Daniel started to withdraw, then grinned. "Ah, what the hell?" he said, and picked up where he'd left off.

When they finally separated, Connor was standing next to them. "Son, you kiss a woman like that in public, you'd better be making a declaration," he said. He was scowling, but there was a definite twinkle in his eyes.

"I suppose I am," Daniel said, returning his father's gaze evenly.

A grin spread across Connor's face. "About damn time," he said, then lifted his glass. "To Molly and Daniel."

"Dad!" Daniel protested. "Hold on."

"What?" Connor asked.

"She hasn't said yes yet."

Molly blushed when Connor Devaney turned to her with blue eyes exactly like his son's.

"Well?" he demanded.

She wasn't about to let the two of them bully her into a quick reply. "I haven't heard a proper question yet," she said mildly.

Daniel's father grinned. "Guess that kiss didn't pass the test, after all, son."

Daniel frowned. "It was a perfectly fine kiss."

"It was," Molly agreed. "But I think the occasion calls for words, don't you? You're a glib Irishman. Surely you know how to woo me."

"Come on, Daniel," Patrick hollered. "Let's hear the pretty words. I'd kinda like to hear you do a bit of groveling."

"Yeah, Daniel," his brothers chorused.

Molly took pity on him. "You don't have to let them push you into anything you don't want to do," she pointed out.

"I want to do this," he said grimly. "I just hadn't expected to have an audience, but I suppose it's fitting that I do this right here and now, in front of the family I've wanted reunited for so long. They're proof that dreams can come true and that odds can be overcome."

Caitlyn chose that moment to join them. She gazed at her uncle with wide eyes. "Momma says you're gonna propose," she announced, drawing laughter. "Are you?"

Daniel grinned weakly. "That seems to be the plan."

Caitlyn nodded. "Okay. You got a ring?"

"As a matter of fact, I do," he said, catching Molly completely off guard.

"Can I see?" Caitlyn asked.

Daniel sighed heavily and drew a box out of his

pocket, but held it just out of the child's reach. "I think Molly should see it first, don't you?"

"How come?" Caitlyn asked.

"Because she's the one I'm asking to marry me," Daniel explained, his gaze seeking out Molly's.

Caitlyn seemed to accept that. She, too, gazed at Molly expectantly.

"Well?" Daniel prodded.

Molly wasn't quite ready to take pity on him yet. She turned to the crowd. "Did you hear a question? I didn't hear one."

"Neither did I," Maggie said.

"None I recognized," Deanna agreed.

"Come on, son," Connor urged. "My drink's getting warm while you fiddle around."

Daniel rolled his eyes. "Like there isn't enough pressure," he muttered, then sucked in a breath and regarded her with a serious expression. "Molly Creighton, it looks as if the time and place have been chosen for me to say this, but it's been in my heart for a long time now. I love you."

Molly felt her heart fill with joy.

"You complete me," he continued. "We've had our share of struggles, but we've grown stronger because of them. I doubt there's anything we can't weather as long as we're together and have faith in what we feel at this moment. Please don't be put off by this roomful of Devaneys. Something tells me they'll bring a lot of happiness into our lives." He glanced over his shoulder. "One of these days, anyway."

"If it would help you out, we could offer testimonials," Maggie called out.

Daniel waved her off, fighting a grin. "Thanks, Maggie. I'll handle this. Like Patrick said, I have some groveling left to do."

Molly fought a smile. "When, exactly?"

"Now, dammit. Stop rushing me."

She held up her hands. "Sorry."

He drew in a deep breath and lifted his gaze to meet hers. "What I've been trying to say so that you won't doubt it is that I love you. I always have, even if I acted like a fool a while back and lost my way. I'm praying with all my heart that you'll look past that and that you'll love me enough to marry me, to share this family with me, to have a family of our own. I know it's been a long time coming, but will you marry me, Molly?"

Molly swallowed hard and blinked back the sudden sting of salty tears. "Yes," she whispered, barely able to get the word past the lump in her throat.

"Can I see the ring now?" Caitlyn demanded impatiently.

Molly laughed. Being part of this huge family that was still struggling to find its way was going to present challenges, but as long as Daniel was by her side, every moment would be worth it.

She winked at Caitlyn, then said, "By all means, Daniel, show us the ring."

It was a simple emerald-cut diamond in a platinum band with baguettes on either side. It was gorgeous, far too beautiful to put on her work-roughened hands. She hesitated before holding out her left hand. Daniel slipped the ring on, then kissed her knuckles as if to put her self-consciousness to rest.

"I have another present," he said. "But it's for Retta and you."

"Oh?"

"I bought a dishwasher, so neither of you will spend half your lives up to your elbows in hot, sudsy water again."

Molly laughed. "Who said the man wasn't a romantic?"

Connor slapped him on the back. "Now, where was I?" he asked, lifting his glass again. "To Molly and Daniel, may there be years of happiness ahead of them."

Molly found her own half-filled glass on the bar and lifted it. "To the Devaneys," she said, fighting tears. "I hope that you'll continue the long journey back to each other. No matter the tears you've shed or the aches in your hearts, in the end you're family. I hope you come to find pride and joy in that."

Daniel's mother smiled at her. "Amen," she said softly, then looked at each of her sons in turn.

"Amen," Ryan said.

One by one the others chimed in, then looked to Connor.

"To the Devaneys," he said, his voice choked. "Together again."

Epilogue

The baby in Molly's arms squalled loudly enough to shake the rafters of the old church. Next to her Daniel grinned.

"If that's the way Patrick and I were, it's a wonder Mom and Dad didn't leave us behind in Boston," he said, gazing down at baby Connor, then letting his gaze drift to Molly's rounded stomach. "Do you suppose our firstborn is going to be as noisy?"

"Oh, I imagine we can count on that," Molly told him, just as Alice came rushing into the church to claim her son.

"Sorry," she apologized. "Kathleen was fussing up a storm, too."

"Where is our goddaughter?" Molly asked, even as she handed over her godson.

"With Patrick. He has a soothing effect on her," Alice said.

Daniel eyed the now peaceful baby warily. "I hope this twin thing is done for our generation."

"I don't," Molly said, her hand on her belly. "I think twins would be wonderful."

Her mother-in-law arrived just in time to hear her. "Twins are the greatest gift God can give you," she said, smiling down on baby Connor. "As long as you can survive the first, oh, eighteen years."

Alice groaned. "I was hoping things would improve a whole lot sooner than that."

"Depends on whether they got more of your genes or their daddy's," Kathleen Devaney told her.

Patrick arrived just then with a sleeping baby girl in his arms. "They're Devaneys through and through," he said. "Black hair, blue eyes, an appetite and a temper."

Molly gazed at Daniel. "At least they turn out okay once they're fully grown," she said. "Where is everyone, by the way? I thought this christening was supposed to start fifteen minutes ago?"

"We're waiting for Ryan and Maggie," he told her. "He called from the road. He said it's taken them longer because they've had to stop half a dozen times for Maggie to run to the restroom."

All three women exchanged a look. "She's pregnant, isn't she?" Molly asked, grinning.

"Has to be," Alice said.

Kathleen's expression turned nostalgic. "Never had a day of morning sickness, not with any of my boys."

Molly frowned at her mother-in-law. "You've just forgotten."

"No, I swear it. Not a day."

Alice scowled. "I could hate you."

"Me, too," Molly said. "And we definitely don't want to share that with Maggie."

"Share what with me?" Maggie asked, rushing into the church to take her place in front as baby Kathleen's second godmother. She looked pale but extraordinarily happy.

"Nothing," Molly, Alice and Kathleen chorused.

Ryan and the rest of the family came inside then, settling into pews as the priest joined them.

"It is always a joyous occasion to welcome a new life into the church," he said. "It is even more so when the family has been twice blessed."

Molly felt Daniel's hands on her waist as he stood behind her and listened to the timeless ceremony. She held baby Connor cradled in her arms once more. He was sleeping now and smelled of talcum powder. She gazed at him and thought of another baby who hadn't had a chance at life. Maybe God had known best, after all. Maybe she and Daniel had needed time to reach this moment, when their hearts were full and they were surrounded by family, so that a baby would be welcomed as it deserved.

In a few months they would be back here again with their own baby, asking God's blessing. Her heart filled to bursting as she envisioned it. She'd lost so much a few years ago, and she would never forget that. It made this moment—it made every moment she and Daniel shared—all the more precious.

She twisted to gaze up at him and saw the love shining in his eyes, the sense of anticipation and the faint shadow of sadness, and knew he was feeling all of the same emotions she was feeling. It had taken time, but they were in the same place now.

At the priest's words, she held baby Connor out for his blessing, then grinned when the baby awoke and squalled loudly as the cross was made on his forehead. Maybe that's what life was, in the end, a mix of blessings and protests, of struggles and joys.

As Connor settled down again, Molly gazed around the church, saw the private smiles between Ryan and Maggie, Sean and Deanna, Michael and Kelly. Saw the wink Patrick gave to Alice and the misty smile Kathleen shared with Connor. And then she met Daniel's gaze and saw the love brimming over in his eyes. There was her happily-ever-after ending, she thought, in his eyes.

"I love you," she whispered.

He leaned down and whispered in her ear, "I love you, too…but would you please, please try not to wake the babies?"

Patrick grinned at both of them. "Amen to that."

As if on cue, baby Connor and baby Kathleen both began to bellow. Patrick groaned.

"Never you mind," his mother said. "Your father and I will take the babies."

Connor was already reaching for his grandson. Molly handed the screaming baby over to him and watched in awe as the baby immediately fell silent.

"I'm booking you for baby-sitting for the next six years, minimum," she told her father-in-law.

"Oh, no, you don't," Alice said. "I have first dibs."

"I want him in Boston," Maggie chimed in, to Connor's obvious delight.

He glanced at his wife. "I think we have our family back," he told her.

She nodded, tears in her eyes. "It's been a long time coming," she agreed. "But I think we do at last."

* * * * *

Read on for a delicious excerpt from
THE SWEET MAGNOLIAS COOKBOOK
and a sneak peek at the next new
Sweet Magnolias novel,
SWAN POINT

The Sweet Magnolias Cookbook

Introduction

Throughout the Sweet Magnolias books—ten of them to date—food plays an important role. Southern food. Grits and gravy. Fried chicken. Red velvet cake. Peach cobbler. Bread pudding. Oh, my! I can gain ten pounds just writing about these things. As for eating them, it's best I not go there, at least on a regular basis. Moderation, that's the key. I try to remember that in real life, if not in my fictional world of Serenity, South Carolina.

The talk of food is particularly prominent in *A Slice of Heaven,* Dana Sue's story centered around Sullivan's—her regional success story, a restaurant known for putting a new spin on traditional Southern dishes. But food—and drink—also come into play at the infamous margarita nights held by the group of old friends who call themselves the Sweet Magnolias, at the café in The Corner Spa where less caloric offerings are available and in the many backyard get-togethers of the Sweet Magnolias and their families. These Southern gals are, you see—like the friends you have in your community or neighborhood—always ready to share a meal and have some fun.

As for myself, I have an interesting relationship with food: I love to eat! A little too much, perhaps. I also love to write about food. I guess I must be good at inventing things because the funny thing is, I've never really considered myself much of a cook.

While growing up, I didn't show much interest in learning to cook (I was too busy reading!), but by the time I was in my early teens, I was the default cook in my family. My working mother hated to cook. My dad enjoyed it, but he also worked. If I expected dinner at a reasonable hour, I figured out that I had to make it, so I set out to learn a few basics. I managed to get food on the table most of the time. At least until the night my parents arrived home to find me standing in the yard in tears and cradling my hand, which I'd managed to sear with hot grease, probably while attempting to fry chicken. That gave my mother pause. In the end, though, I kept cooking. Nothing fancy, mind you. No baking pies or cakes. No exotic, complicated dishes. Just get-it-over-with meals that were edible.

Once I was out and on my own, my repertoire expanded. I was, after all, trying to impress a date from time to time. I recall the first Thanksgiving dinner I made for friends. I had to call my dad, the grand master of the Thanksgiving meal in our household, to figure out what on earth I was supposed to do with the turkey. He also coached me through our family's traditional dressing and how to perfect our favorite sweet potatoes with marshmallows.

These days I do more writing about cooking than actual cooking, but I still like to get into the kitchen and try to impress some of my friends. It seems that a lot of them have taken cooking classes or belong to some gourmet club that hosts fancy monthly dinner parties. I'm traumatized every time I invite them to dinner, wondering how they're going to react to my dishes. My proudest moment came a few days after I'd grilled grouper and served it with a mango-papaya chutney I'd made from scratch. A friend reported having a similar dish at a fancy restaurant we all love and said, "Yours was better!" So, apparently I do have my moments of culinary triumph.

Then one day I was busy writing away—no doubt creating dishes on the page but not in the kitchen—when my publisher suggested that it might be nice to have a cookbook reflecting all the many occasions in which food plays a comforting or celebratory role for the Sweet Magnolias. While I was still trying to wrap my mind around the thought (how would I ever write a cookbook?), along came an out-of-the-blue email from a reader named Teddi Wohlford.

Teddi said she loved the Sweet Magnolias books, then added that she identified particularly with Dana Sue because she, too, is a Southern chef. She was also, as it turned out, the answer to my prayers. Teddi cooks! She caters! She's published a couple of Southern cookbooks of her own! Well, you can see how this might be a match made in publishing heaven.

Since the Sweet Magnolias series began, many of you have asked about recipes for some of the dishes mentioned. Here they are, along with many, many more created by Teddi, who (like Dana Sue) has put a new spin on many traditional Southern dishes and kicked 'em up a notch. I have worked my way through these incredible recipes and developed a whole new relationship with my treadmill along the way. But trust me, it's been worth it. I hope you enjoy them as much as I do!

Sherryl Woods

Mama Cruz's
Recipe File

When Helen, Maddie and I decided to open The Corner Spa, not a one of us knew a thing about proper exercise or working out. Oh, we'd take a jab at jogging from time to time or lifting an occasional weight over at Dexter's gym, but we were far from being experts. Truth be told, we weren't all that enthusiastic about exercise. That's when we decided we'd better hire personal trainer Elliott Cruz as an independent contractor to run the fitness side of our business.

I'd like to tell you we made that decision based solely on his résumé, which was rock-solid, but it was his equally rock-solid abs that really won us over. That man could be the poster boy for fitness! I swear, half the women who joined the spa did so just so they could watch him giving lessons. Even our seniors take a weekly jazzercise class just to ogle him and make the sort of smart remarks that make him blush. I'm not kidding! They'll tell you that themselves. Helen's mother, Flo Decatur, is the leader of this outrageous pack.

Still, it was mostly a business relationship (honest!) until Elliott started romancing Karen Ames, a struggling single mom who worked for me at Sullivan's. Then we all discovered the man could cook, and everything he'd learned in the kitchen, he'd learned from his mamacita, Maria Cruz.

As I understand it, Mama Cruz has always kept a tightfisted grip on her recipe secrets, using them as leverage to guarantee that all her children and their families show up every week for Sunday dinner. Karen says her mother-in-law has always sworn she'd take her blend of peppers and spices for her incredible mole sauce to the grave with her just to be sure they come visit the cemetery in the hope she'll communicate it from the great beyond. Somehow, though, Karen managed to wrestle it away from her to include here. Just wait till you taste Mama Cruz's enchilada casserole with classic mole sauce.

Elliott's the one who forked over the seafood paella recipe, a meal that makes good use of all the fresh Low-country seafood we have available around here. Add a salad and a nice white wine, and you have the makings for a fabulous party!

Since she's been married to a man who definitely likes a little spice in his life and in his food, Karen's taken to doing her own experimenting here in the Sullivan's kitchen, stealing a page right out of Mama Cruz's book. Her jalapeño mac and cheese has become a local favorite…and it's been quite a boon for our beverage sales, too! First Elliott and now his wife can't seem to go anywhere without generating plenty of heat.

Though I'm all about Southern cooking with a twist at Sullivan's, personally there's nothing I'd like better than having more ethnic specialties available right here in Serenity. When I was growing up, pizza and spaghetti were about as exotic as we got. A Chinese take-out place opened a few years ago. Now that I've sampled a few of Mama Cruz's specialties, I'm thinking there ought to be an authentic Mexican restaurant here in town. Maybe Karen and I need to talk. I wouldn't mind an exciting new business opportunity. Try these recipes, and see what you think.

Dulce De Leche Cheesecake Bars

Crust

*1¼ cups finely crushed Mexican "Maria" cookies,
vanilla wafers or graham crackers
½ cup butter, melted*

Filling

*1 (8-ounce) package cream cheese, softened
1 cup sugar
3 eggs, room temperature
1 tablespoon vanilla extract
½ teaspoon salt
1 (14-ounce) can dulce de leche*

Crust

1. Preheat oven to 350°F.

2. Grease a 13" x 9" x 2" baking pan.

3. Combine ingredients and press into bottom of prepared pan. Bake 15 minutes. While crust is baking, prepare filling.

Filling

1. Cream together cream cheese and sugar. Beat in
   eggs.

2. Stir in vanilla and salt, then spread the mixture
   on the hot baked crust.

3. Heat dulce de leche until very hot and melted,
   then drizzle it over cheesecake layer. Using a

skewer or the tip of a knife, swirl dulce de leche into cheesecake layer.

4. Cover pan tightly with foil and place in a large roasting pan. Add boiling water to roasting pan until water comes halfway up the sides of the baking pan. Bake 1 hour.

5. Remove from oven. Carefully lift pan out of water bath and place on a cooling rack, then remove the foil. Let cool to room temperature.

6. Cover and store in the refrigerator until ready to serve. Cut into 24 squares.

Makes 24

Chicken Enchilada Casserole
with Speedy Mole Sauce

Casserole

*6 boneless, skinless chicken breast halves
(about 2¼ pounds total)
1 envelope dry taco seasoning
2 tablespoons vegetable or canola oil
12 ounces shredded Mexican cheese blend
1 (15-ounce) can black beans, rinsed, drained well
1 (15-ounce) can whole-kernel corn, drained well
10 (6-inch) corn tortillas
1½ cups sour cream*

Sauce

*1 large medium-diced sweet onion
2 tablespoons vegetable or canola oil
3 tablespoons cocoa powder
1 envelope dry taco seasoning
2 (10¾-ounce) cans tomato soup concentrate
2 (10-ounce) cans mild RO·TEL tomatoes
1 milk chocolate Hershey's bar (no nuts)*

Garnishes (optional)

*Finely diced fresh jalapeño peppers
Minced fresh cilantro
Sour cream
Guacamole*

Casserole

1. Place chicken breast halves on a plate. Sprinkle both sides of each breast with taco seasoning.

2. In a skillet over medium heat, heat oil until hot but not smoking. Add chicken breast halves to skillet. Brown chicken on both sides, turning halfway through cooking, for a total cooking time of about 10 minutes.

3. Remove chicken from pan, and let stand 5 minutes before cutting into thin slices.

Sauce

1. Sauté onion in oil until crisp tender. Add cocoa powder and taco seasoning.

2. Stir together tomato soup and tomatoes. Add to the sauce, and blend well.

3. Cook over medium heat 5 minutes, stirring often.

4. Remove from heat, and crumble chocolate bar over top. Let stand for several minutes, then stir melted chocolate into the sauce.

Assembly

1. Preheat oven to 350°F.

2. Grease a 13" × 9" × 2" baking pan.

3. Combine half of the sauce with the thinly sliced chicken breasts. Add half of the cheese blend along with the black beans and corn. Stir to combine.

4. Spoon half of the remaining sauce in the bottom of the prepared pan. Set aside remaining sauce.

5. Divide chicken mixture among the 10 tortillas. Roll tightly.

6. Crowd the filled enchiladas in the pan on top of the sauce. Spoon all remaining sauce over top. Drop sour cream in dollops over the sauce.

7. Cover tightly with foil, and place in center of oven. Bake 40 minutes.

8. Remove casserole from oven, and remove foil. Raise oven temperature to 400°F. Scatter remaining cheese over top of casserole. Return casserole to oven, and cook an additional 10 minutes, until cheese melts and begins to brown.

To Serve
Remove casserole from oven, and let stand at least 5 minutes before serving with desired garnishes.

Serves 6–8

Jacked-Up Tex-Mex Macaroni & Cheese

1 pound breakfast sausage
1 cup chopped onion
1 envelope taco seasoning
1 (14-ounce) can spicy RO·TEL tomatoes
1 cup sour cream
1 pound elbow macaroni, cooked in salted water
until al dente, drained well
8 ounces grated cheddar cheese
8 ounces grated Monterey Jack cheese
4 cups milk
6 large eggs, beaten
Salsa of your choice

1. Preheat oven to 350°F.

2. Generously grease a 13" × 9" × 2" baking dish or other suitable casserole dish.

3. In a large skillet over medium-high heat, cook sausage, stirring to crumble.

4. Add onion and taco seasoning. Cook until onion is softened. Remove from heat, and stir in tomatoes and sour cream. Set aside.

5. In bottom of prepared dish, distribute half of the macaroni. Evenly spoon on half of the meat and then half of each cheese. Repeat layering once more.

6. Whisk together milk and eggs. Slowly pour over entire casserole contents.

7. Cover tightly with foil, and bake 45 minutes. Remove foil, and bake an additional 15–20 minutes, until cheese is melted and top is golden brown.

8. Remove from oven, and let stand 7–10 minutes before serving. Serve with salsa.

Serves 6–8

Pico de Gallo

7 finely chopped jalapeño peppers,
ribs and seeds removed
3 Roma tomatoes, seeded, diced
1 small white onion, finely chopped
¼ cup minced fresh cilantro
Juice of 1 lime
Salt to taste

Combine all ingredients, and stir to blend. Cover, and refrigerate up to 1 week.

Makes 2 Cups

Note: Brace yourself because this is one brazen pico! Fresh jalapeño peppers have so much flavor. By removing the seeds and ribs from these peppers, about 70% of their heat is removed. If you like this pico hotter still, leave in some of the seeds and ribs.

Smoky Pork-Filled Tamales

1 (8-ounce) package dried corn husks

Filling

1 (1¼ pounds) pork tenderloin
2 cups large-diced onion
3 garlic cloves, roughly chopped
1 (12-ounce) can beer

Sauce

1 dried ancho chili pepper
1 tablespoon vegetable oil
1 tablespoon flour
½ cup cooking liquid from pork
1 tablespoon smoked paprika
1 garlic clove, minced
1 teaspoon red wine vinegar
1 teaspoon ground cumin
1 teaspoon fresh oregano or ½ teaspoon dried
½ teaspoon crushed red pepper flakes
Seasoned salt to taste

Tamale Dough

1 cup lard
1 teaspoon salt
3 cups masa harina
1½ cups cooking liquid from pork

Husks

Place corn husks in a large bowl. Cover with hot water, and let soak about 3 hours (while the pork filling cooks). Use a dinner plate to help keep the corn husks submerged in the water.

Filling

1. Place pork tenderloin, onion and garlic in a large pot. Add beer and enough water to cover tenderloin. Bring to a boil.

2. As soon as water boils, reduce heat to simmer, and cover pot with a lid. Simmer at least 3 hours, until pork is tender.

3. When pork is done, remove from pot, reserving 2 cups of the cooking liquid. Once the pork is cool enough to handle, shred the pork using two forks, then coarsely chop.

Sauce

1. Toast the ancho in a skillet over medium-high heat. Keep a close eye on the pepper so it doesn't burn. Remove from heat, and let cool until you can handle it.

2. Remove the stem and seeds from the ancho. Crumble and grind in a clean coffee grinder or with a mortar and pestle.

3. Heat oil in a medium saucepan over medium heat. Add flour, and cook until the mixture has browned somewhat and begins to smell nutty.

4. Add ½ cup cooking liquid from pork, stirring until smooth. Add ground ancho and remaining sauce ingredients.

5. Reduce heat to simmer, and add shredded pork. Cover with lid, and let simmer 30 minutes.

Tamales

1. Using an electric mixer on high speed, blend together lard and salt until light and fluffy.

2. Add masa harina in several additions, and blend at low speed until fully incorporated.

3. Add remaining pork cooking liquid, a little at a time, enough to form a spreadable dough, similar to a soft cookie dough.

4. Remove the corn husks from their soaking water. Working with 1 tamale at a time, flatten out a corn husk. Have the narrow end facing you. Place a dollop (about 2 tablespoons) of dough in center of corn husk. Leaving an outer margin of about ⅓ the husk, spread dough to cover the remaining husk.

5. Spread a heaping tablespoon of pork filling down the center of the tamale. Roll up the corn husk, starting at one of the long sides. Fold the narrow end of the husk onto the rolled tamale, and secure with kitchen twine.

6. Layer tamales in a steamer basket. Steam over boiling water 1 hour. Add water to the steamer as needed during the cooking time.

Serves 6–8

Note: It's true love and indeed a labor of love when Mama Cruz makes tamales. She normally triples the recipe to feed the crowd. Any leftovers (yeah, right!) can be stored covered in the refrigerator up to 3 days, then steamed again to reheat.

Southern Seafood Paella

4½ cups chicken broth
1 (10-ounce) bottle clam juice
¾ cup white port or dry sherry
2 star anise (do not omit this seasoning)
2 teaspoons sea salt
1 teaspoon smoked paprika
¾ teaspoon crushed red pepper flakes
½ teaspoon saffron threads
1 pound arborio rice
4 tablespoons extra-virgin olive oil
2 large onions, cut into medium dice
*4 ounces Spanish chorizo sausage, casing removed,
thinly sliced*
3 ounces country ham, trimmed, cut into small dice
3 ounces smoked bacon, cut into thin strips
4 garlic cloves, minced
*4 ounces fresh green beans, trimmed,
cut into 1" pieces*
¾ cup frozen peas
10 large sea scallops, cut in half
12 ounces grouper, cut into 1" chunks
18 raw jumbo shrimp, shelled, deveined
1 pound live mussels, scrubbed, beards removed
*1 (10-ounce) jar roasted red peppers, drained, cut
into strips*
1 lemon, thinly sliced
½ cup minced fresh parsley

*For sanity's sake, have all ingredients prepped and
ready before starting this dish.*

1. In a medium saucepan, combine first 8 ingredients to make stock. Bring to a boil, then lower heat to a simmer, and cook at least 15 minutes. Remove star anise from broth. Meanwhile, proceed with recipe.

2. Rinse rice under running water until water runs clear. In a standard (12") paella pan or heavy-bottomed skillet of similar size, heat olive oil until hot but not smoking over medium-high heat. Sauté onions until crisp tender.

3. Add chorizo, country ham and bacon. Cook 2–3 minutes.

4. Stir in garlic, and sauté briefly.

5. Add drained rice, green beans and peas; stir to coat with oil.

6. Add seasoned stock to the rice mixture. Bring to a boil, stirring constantly. Reduce heat to low, and simmer for 15 minutes, cooking uncovered and without stirring.

7. Cover pan with lid or foil, and cook 5 minutes more. Most of the liquid should now be absorbed. If not, cover, and cook an additional 5 minutes.

8. Arrange all of the seafood on top, ending with the shrimp and mussels. Re-cover, and let simmer for an additional 5 minutes, or until the shrimp turns pink, the mussels open, and all liquid has been absorbed. Discard any mussels that do not open.

9. Arrange the red pepper strips and lemon slices over the top. Sprinkle with parsley, and serve immediately.

Serves 6–8
Note: Don't let the long list of ingredients scare you away from this recipe—it is heavenly! This classic Spanish dish gets all gussied up Southern-style. The intense flavors, vibrant colors and festive presentation are a feast for the eyes as well as the palate. This is truly special-occasion fare at its finest!

Black Bean Chili

1 pound ground pork breakfast sausage
1½ cups diced onion
1 tablespoon minced garlic
1 envelope taco seasoning
1 tablespoon dried oregano
1 teaspoon ground cumin
3 cups water
3 (15-ounce) cans black beans, rinsed well, drained
1 (15-ounce) can diced tomatoes
1 (15-ounce) can crushed tomatoes
1 tablespoon red wine vinegar

1. In a large soup pot, brown the sausage over medium-high heat, stirring to crumble.

2. Add onion, and cook until crisp tender.

3. Add garlic, and cook 1 minute before adding the taco seasoning, oregano and cumin.

4. Add the remaining ingredients. Bring to a boil, then lower heat, cover pot, and let simmer at least 15 minutes.

Serves 6

Note: *Can you keep a secret? Mama Cruz sure can! This is her quick-and-easy—but oh, so tasty—recipe for a super yummy and hearty black bean chili. The flavors are so well balanced and complex that you would swear she had been slaving over a hot* *stove all day. In truth, it can be made and served in about half an hour—start to finish! Another great thing about this chili is that the ingredients can be easily doubled (or tripled!) to suit your size gathering. Any leftovers freeze well.*

Roasted Corn & Mixed Bean Salsa

3 ears corn, shucked, silks removed
1 (15-ounce) can black beans, rinsed, drained
1 (15-ounce) can small red beans, rinsed, drained
3 green onions, minced
1 bell pepper, seeded, diced
2 jalapeño peppers, minced
(remove seeds and ribs for milder salsa)
1 cup diced tomato
½ cup balsamic vinaigrette
¼ cup minced cilantro
2 garlic cloves, minced
Salt and pepper to taste

Grill corn on all sides until done. Remove from grill to cool. Cut kernels from cob. Combine with remaining ingredients. Chill thoroughly. Serve with tortilla chips.

Serves 8–10

Caution: *Wear plastic gloves when working with hot peppers, and avoid contact with face.*

Tex-Mex Appetizer Cheesecake

Crust

1½ cups crushed Ritz crackers
¼ cup melted butter

Filling

2 (8-ounce) packages cream cheese, softened
3 large eggs, beaten
1 envelope taco seasoning
1 (4-ounce) can diced green chili or
chipotle peppers, drained well
1 (4-ounce) jar diced pimentos, drained well
8 ounces (2 cups) shredded Mexican cheese blend
1 cup sour cream

Garnishes (Optional)

Salsa
Guacamole
Corn chips

Crust

Preheat oven to 325°F. Spray a 9" springform pan with cooking spray. Stir together cracker crumbs and butter. Press firmly into the bottom of the pan. Bake 15 minutes.

Filling

1. In a medium mixing bowl, blend together the cream cheese and eggs until smooth.

2. Stir in taco seasoning, peppers and pimentos. Add the shredded cheese, and stir just until incorporated. Pour mixture over baked crust.

3. Bake 30 minutes.

4. Remove from oven. Immediately spread sour cream over cheesecake. Cool to room temperature. Cover, and refrigerate at least 4 hours or up to several days before serving.

5. Release cheesecake from pan. Slice into wedges, and top with your favorite salsa and/or guacamole. Serve with sturdy corn chips.

Serves 16

Tres Leches Cake

Cake

6 large eggs, separated
2 cups granulated sugar
2 cups all-purpose flour
2 teaspoons baking powder
¾ teaspoon salt
½ cup whole milk
1 teaspoon vanilla extract

Soaking liquid

1 (14-ounce) can sweetened condensed milk
1 (14-ounce) can evaporated milk
1 cup heavy whipping cream

Topping

2 cups heavy whipping cream
¼ cup sugar
1 teaspoon pure vanilla extract

Garnish

1 pound fresh strawberries, sliced or cut in half

Cake

1. Preheat oven to 350°F.

2. Lightly grease and flour a 13" × 9" × 2" baking pan.

3. Using an electric mixer, beat egg whites until frothy. Add sugar gradually, beating all the while, until stiff peaks form. Add egg yolks, 1 at a time, beating well after each addition.

4. Whisk together flour, baking powder and salt.

5. Add the flour mixture to the batter alternately with the milk, beginning and ending with the flour mixture. Stir in vanilla extract.

6. Transfer the batter to the prepared pan, and spread the batter level. Bake about 25 minutes, until golden and tester inserted in center comes out clean.

7. Remove from oven, and place on a cooling rack. Pierce cake all over with a wooden skewer.

Soaking liquid

Whisk together the soaking liquid ingredients, but do not incorporate any air into the liquid. Pour mixture over the hot cake in several additions, letting each soak in before adding more. When all the liquid has been absorbed, cover with plastic food wrap, and refrigerate at least 6 hours or up to 3 days before serving.

Topping

Combine all topping ingredients in a large mixing bowl. Using an electric mixer, beat on high speed until stiff peaks form. Spread over top surface of cake.

Garnish

Arrange strawberries on cake or on each individual serving.

Serves 12

Swan Point

1

Adelia watched with her heart in her throat as the moving van pulled away from the crumbling curb in Swan Point, one of Serenity, South Carolina's, oldest and, at one time, finest neighborhoods with moss-draped oaks in perfectly maintained yards. With backyards sloping to a small, man-made lake, which was home to several swans, the houses had been large and stately by early standards.

Now, though, most of the homes, like this one, were showing signs of age. She found something alluring and fitting about the prospect of filling this historic old house with laughter and giving it a new lease on life. It would be as if the house and her family were moving into the future together.

Letting go of the old life, however, was proving more difficult than she'd anticipated. Drawing in a deep breath, she turned to deal with the accusing looks of her four children, who weren't nearly as convinced as she was that they were about to have an exciting fresh start.

Her youngest, Tomas, named for his grandfather Hernandez on her ex-husband's side of the family, turned to her with tears streaming down his cheeks. "Mommy, I don't like it here. I want to go home. This house is old. It smells funny. And there's no pool."

She knelt down in front of the eight-year-old and gathered him close, gathered all of them close, even her oldest, Selena.

It was Selena who understood better than any of them why this move had been necessary. While they all knew that Adelia and their father had divorced, Selena had seen Ernesto more than once with one of his mistresses. In a move that defied logic or compassion, he'd even had the audacity to introduce the most recent woman to Selena while he and Adelia were still making a pretense at least of trying to keep their marriage intact. His action had devastated Selena and it had been the final straw for Adelia. She'd seen at last that tolerating such disrespect was the wrong example to set for her three girls and even for her son.

"I know you'd rather be in our old house," she said, comforting them with a hitch in her voice. "But it's just not possible. This is home now. I really think you're going to love it once we get settled in."

She ruffled Tomas's hair. "And don't worry about the funny smell. It's just been shut up for a few months. It'll smell fine once we air it out and put fresh paint on the walls." She injected a deliberately cheerful note into her voice. "We can all sit down and decide how we want to fix it up, then you can go with me to the hardware store to pick out the paint colors for your rooms."

The girls expressed enthusiasm for the idea, but Tomas remained visibly skeptical.

"What about the pool?" he asked sullenly.

"We can use the town pool," Selena said staunchly, even though there were tears in her eyes, too. "It's even bigger than the one at home and our friends will be there. And since we're living so close to downtown now, we can walk to the bakery after school for cupcakes, then stop in and see Mom at work. Or go across the green to Wharton's for ice cream."

Natalia sniffed, but Adelia saw a spark of interest in her eyes.

"I like ice cream," eleven-year-old Natalia whispered, then nudged Tomas. "You do, too."

"Me, too," Juanita chimed in. Until the divorce Adelia's nine-year-old had been boundlessly enthusiastic about everything, but this was the first sign in weeks that her high spirits were returning.

Tomas continued to look unconvinced. "Will *Abuela* be able to find us here?" he asked doubtfully.

"Of course," Adelia assured him. Tomas adored her mother, who'd been babysitting him practically from infancy because of all the school committees on which Adelia had found herself and, more recently, because she was working at a boutique on Main Street. "She helped me to find this house."

Amazingly, for once, her mother had kept her lectures on divorce to herself and professed to see all the positives in the new life Adelia was fashioning for her children. She'd told stories about the days when the elite in town had lived in Swan Point. There had been lavish parties in this very house, she'd reported to Adelia. She'd stuck to focusing on the possibilities in the house and the quiet, tree-shaded neighborhood, not the negatives.

Her mother's support had actually given Adelia the courage to move forward. To her surprise, Adelia had recognized that even in her early forties, she still craved her mother's approval. It was one of the many reasons she'd waited so long to act to end her travesty of a marriage.

"Can we still go to *Abuela's* house for cookies?" her son pressed.

"Absolutely," Adelia said. "You can go every day after school, if you like, the same as always."

Though he was starting to look relieved, a sudden frown crossed his face. "What about Papa? Is he going to live here, too? He won't like it, I'll bet. He likes our real house, same as me."

Selena whirled on him. "You know perfectly well he doesn't live with us anymore. He's not coming here. Not ever! He's going to live in our old house with somebody else."

Adelia winced at the disdain and hurt in her oldest's voice. Ever since she'd realized that her father had been openly cheating on Adelia, Selena had claimed she wanted no part of him. Her attitude had hardened even more when she'd overheard Ernesto describing her as her mother's child in a tone that made clear he wasn't complimenting either one of them.

Adelia had even spoken to a psychologist about this rift between father and daughter, but the woman had assured her that it wasn't unusual for an impressionable teenager—Selena had just turned thirteen—to react so strongly to a divorce, especially when Ernesto's cheating had been so public and when he'd shown no remorse at all once he'd been caught. In fact, he'd remained defiant to the bitter end, so much so that even the judge had lost patience with him.

At Selena's angry words, Tomas's eyes once again filled with tears.

"Enough," Adelia warned her daughter. To Tomas and the younger girls, she said, "You'll still be able to see your father whenever you want to." Like Tomas, Natalia and Juanita looked relieved, though they carefully avoided looking at their big sister, clearly fearing her disapproval. That was yet another rift she'd have to work on healing, Adelia concluded with a sigh. Ernesto certainly wouldn't make any effort to do it.

As hurt as she'd been and as much as she'd wanted to banish Ernesto from her life forever, she'd accepted that her kids deserved to have a relationship with their dad. It would be selfish of her to deny them that.

Besides, she'd had enough explaining to do to her rigidly Catholic family when she'd opted for divorce. Then, to top it off, she'd insisted on moving out of the huge house on the outskirts of town that Ernesto had apparently thought was reasonable compensation for his infidelity. Her sisters had been appalled by all of it—the scandal of Ernesto's cheating, the divorce and the move. Keeping her children away from their father—however distasteful his behavior—would have caused even more of an uproar.

Not that Adelia cared what any of them thought at this point. She'd made the only decision she could make. Her only goal now was to make this transition as easy for the children as possible. She'd do it with as much cheerfulness as she could possibly muster. She might not even have to fake it, since on some level she was actually eager for this fresh start.

For now, though, she forced a smile and looked each of them in the eye. "I have an idea," she announced, hoping to turn this difficult day around.

"What?" Tomas asked suspiciously.

"I think we all deserve a treat after such a long day."

"Pizza?" Natalia asked hopefully.

Adelia laughed. Natalia would eat pizza three times a day if she were allowed to.

"Yes, pizza," she confirmed.

"Not here, though," Tomas pleaded, wrinkling his nose in distaste.

"No, not here. The dishes aren't unpacked, anyway," she said. "We'll go to Rosalina's. I'll call your Uncle Elliott and see if he and Aunt Karen would like to join us with Daisy, Mack and the baby."

This last was offered especially for Selena, who

adored her uncle and who'd become especially close to his adopted daughter, Daisy. Adelia might not intend to keep Ernesto away from his children, but Elliott was the male role model she really wanted in their lives. Her younger brother was loving, rock-solid and dependable. She'd be proud to see Tomas grow up to be just like him. And she desperately hoped her girls would eventually find men like him, too.

Elliott had overcome all of his own strong objections to divorce to offer her the support she'd desperately needed once the decision had been made. She owed Karen for bringing him—and even her mother—around. Her own sisters continued to treat her as if she'd committed a mortal sin.

The prospect of pizza at Rosalina's with Uncle Elliott and his family wiped away the last of the tears and Adelia took a truly relieved breath for what seemed like the first time all day. Her family was going to be all right. There might be a few bumps along the way thanks to her determination to shed any of her own ties to Ernesto, but they would settle into this new house.

And, she concluded with new resolve, they would turn it into a real home, one filled with love and respect, something that had been in short supply with her ex-husband.

Gabe Franklin had claimed a booth in the back corner of Rosalina's for the fourth night in a row. Back in Serenity for less than a week and living at the Serenity Inn, he'd figured this was better than the bar across town for a man who'd determined to sober up and live life on the straight and narrow. That was the whole point of coming home, after all, to prove he'd changed and deserved a second chance. Once he'd accomplished that and made peace with his past, well, he'd decide whether to move on yet again. He wasn't sure he was the kind of man who'd ever put down roots.

Thank heaven for his cousin, Mitch Franklin, who'd offered him a job starting on Monday without a moment's hesitation. Recently remarried, Mitch claimed he needed a partner who knew construction so he could focus on his new family. He'd taken on a second family just as he'd started developing a series of dilapidated properties on Main Street in an attempt to revitalize downtown Serenity.

Gabe had listened in astonishment to Mitch's ambitious plans as he'd laid them out. Despite his cousin's enthusiasm, Gabe wasn't convinced revitalization was possible in an economy still struggling to rebound, but he was more than willing to jump in and give it a shot. Maybe there would be something cathartic about giving those old storefronts the same kind of second chance he was hoping to grab for himself.

"You're turning into a real regular in here," his waitress, a middle-aged woman who'd introduced herself a few nights ago as Debbie, said. "Are you new in town?"

"Not exactly," he said, returning her smile, but adding no details. "I'll have—"

"A large diet soda and a large pepperoni pizza," she filled in before he could complete his order.

Gabe winced. "I'm obviously in a rut."

"That's okay. Most of our regulars order the same thing every time," she said. "And I pay attention. Friendly service and a good memory get me bigger tips."

"I'll remember that," he said, then sat back and looked around the restaurant while waiting for his food.

Suddenly he sat up a little straighter as a dark-haired woman came in with four children. Even though she looked a little harried and a whole lot weary, she was stunning with her olive complexion and high cheekbones. She was also vaguely familiar, though he couldn't put a name to the face.

There hadn't been a lot of Mexican-American families in Serenity back when he'd lived here as a kid, though there had been plenty of transient farm workers during the summer months. For a minute he cursed the way he'd blown off school way more often than he should have. Surely if he'd gone regularly, this woman would have been on his radar. If there had been declared majors in high school, his would have been girls. He'd studied them the way the academic overachievers had absorbed the information in textbooks.

Instead, he'd been kicked out midway through his junior year for one too many fights, every one of them justified to his juvenile way of thinking. He'd eventually wised up and gotten his GED. He'd even attended college for a couple of years, but that had been later, when he'd stopped hating the world for the way it treated his troubled single mom and started putting the pieces of his life back together.

He watched now as the intriguing woman asked for several tables to be pushed together. He noted with disappointment when a man with two children came in to join them. So, he thought, she was married with six kids. An unfamiliar twinge of envy left him feeling vaguely unsettled. Since when had he been interested in having a family of any size? Still, he couldn't seem to tear his gaze away from the picture of domestic bliss they presented. The teasing and laughter seemed to settle in his heart and make it just a little lighter.

When his waitress returned with his drink, he nodded in the woman's direction. "Quite a family," he commented. "I can't imagine having six kids. They look like quite a handful."

Debbie laughed. "Oh, they're a handful, all right, but they're not all Adelia's. That's her brother, Elliott Cruz, who just came in with two of his. He has a baby, too, but I guess she was getting a cold, so his wife stayed home with her."

Gabe hid a grin. Thank heaven for chatty waitresses and a town known for gossiping. It hadn't been so great when he was a boy and his promiscuous mother had been the talk of the town, but now he could appreciate it.

"Where's her husband?"

The waitress leaned down and confided, "Sadly, not in hell where he belongs. The man cheated on her repeatedly and the whole town knew about it. She finally kicked his sorry butt to the curb. Too bad the whole town couldn't follow suit and divorce him." She flushed, her expression immediately filled with guilt. "Sorry. I shouldn't have said that, but Adelia's a great woman and she didn't deserve the way Ernesto Hernandez treated her."

Gabe nodded. "Sounds like a real gem," he said.

In fact, he sounded like a lot of the men who'd passed through his mom's life over the years. Gabe felt a sudden surge of empathy for Adelia. And he liked the fact that his waitress was firmly in her corner. He suspected the rest of the town was, too, just the way they'd always stood up for the wronged wives when his mom had been the other woman in way too many relationships.

Funny what a few years could do to give a man a new perspective. Back then all he'd cared about was the gossip, the taunts he'd suffered at school and his mom's tears each time the relationships inevitably ended. He'd witnessed her hope whenever a new man came into her life and, then, the slow realization that this time would be no different. His heart had broken almost as many times as hers.

Still, he couldn't help thinking about all of the complications that came with a woman in Adelia's situation. He had enough on his own plate without getting mixed up in her drama. Much as he might enjoy sitting right here and staring, it would be far better to slip away right now and avoid the powerful temptation to reach out to her. Heaven knew, he had nothing to offer a woman, not these days, anyway.

"Darlin', could you make that pizza of mine to go?" he asked his waitress.

"Sure thing," Debbie said readily.

She brought it out within minutes. As Gabe paid the check, she grinned. "I imagine I'll see you again tomorrow. Maybe you'll try something different."

"Maybe so," he agreed, then winked. "But don't count on it. I'm comfortable in this rut I'm in."

She shook her head, then glanced pointedly in Adelia's direction. "Seems to me that's just when you need to shake things up."

Gabe followed the direction of her gaze and found the very woman in question glancing his way. His heart, which hadn't been engaged in much more than keeping him alive these past few years, did a fascinating, anxiety-producing little stutter step.

No way, he told himself determinedly as he headed for the door and the safety of his comfortable, if uninviting room at the Serenity Inn. He'd never been much good at multitasking. Right now his only goal was to prove himself to Mitch and to himself. Complications were out of the question. And the beautiful Adelia Hernandez and her four kids had complication written all over them.

"Looks as if somebody has an admirer," Elliott commented to Adelia. Though his tone was light, there was a frown on his face as he watched the stranger leaving Rosalina's.

"Hush!" Adelia said, though she was blushing. She leaned closer to her brother. "That is not the sort of thing you should be saying in front of the kids. The ink's barely dry on my divorce papers."

Elliott laughed. "The kids are all clear across the restaurant playing video games. You're only flustered because you know I'm right. That guy was attracted to you, Adelia. I recognize that thunderstruck expression on a man's face. I wore it a lot when I first met Karen. I saw it in the mirror when I shaved. It happened every time she crossed my mind."

Adelia smiled at the memory of her little brother falling hard for a woman no one in the family had approved of at first simply because she'd divorced a deadbeat husband. Elliott had fought hard to ensure that they all came to accept Karen and her kids and love them as much as he did. After her own marital troubles, Adelia had even come to admire her sister-in-law's strength.

"You were a goner from the moment you laid eyes on her, weren't you?" she said.

"No question about it," he said. "I still am, and I don't see that ever changing. I want that happily-ever-after kind of love for you."

"Maybe someday," she said, not really able to imagine a time when she'd be willing to risk her heart again.

Elliott nodded in the direction of the door. "So, any idea who your admirer is?"

"Stop calling him that," she ordered, blushing again.

"Just calling it like I see it," he teased. "And it's nice to see some color in your cheeks."

She gave him a mock frown. "Don't make me sorry I called you tonight," she scolded. "There are some aggravations I can't avoid, but you're not one of them."

He grinned. "You needed me here to help you corral those kids. And don't even try to pretend that you didn't enjoy the way that man was looking at you. You're not just a mom. You're a woman. You've seen far too little of that sort of appreciation in recent years."

"That may be so, but I'm not even remotely interested in dating anytime soon," she repeated emphatically, though she knew she was wasting her breath. Her brother loved getting under her skin and he'd just found a new way to do exactly that.

"You didn't recognize him?" he persisted, proving her point that he didn't intend to let this drop. "You work right downtown. You're involved in every activity in the school system. You see people all day long."

She shook her head. "I've never seen him before. He must be new in town."

"And Grace Wharton hasn't sent out a news bulletin?" he asked, only partially in jest. Grace, who ran the soda fountain at the local drugstore, prided herself on knowing all the comings and goings in town and being the first to spread the word. "Or are you just pretending that you missed the latest edition?"

Adelia tried a stern look that on rare occasions worked with her kids. "Drop this, please. There's been enough turmoil in my life these past months to last a lifetime. These days I'm a mom first and foremost. I need to get the kids settled in our new house and on an emotional even keel. That's my only focus for now."

"You're still a vibrant, attractive woman," Elliott reminded her, clearly undeterred by her expression or her words. "You deserve to find a man who'll appreciate and respect you in a way that Ernesto never did." His expression darkened. "I still wish you'd let me teach him a lesson about mistreating my big sister."

She almost smiled at his zealous desire to stand up for her, but didn't because she didn't want to encourage him. "I dealt with Ernesto. Thanks to Helen Decatur-Whitney, he'll be paying for his misdeeds with those generous support payments for the kids for years to come. Every penny is going in the bank. They'll have enough money tucked away to attend any college they choose when the time comes."

"I still don't get why you refused any alimony," Elliott told her, his frustration plain. "The man owed you, Adelia. You have a business degree, but you never used it so you could concentrate on being the perfect wife and mother. Who knows what you might have achieved by now if you'd started a career after college."

"Being a wife and mother was the career I chose," she told him. "I don't regret that for a second. Now that I'm a single mom, I'll put just as much energy into working and being a good parent. Being independent is important to me, Elliott. I need to know I'm in control of my life."

"I'm just saying that Ernesto's money might have made it easier," he argued.

"Don't forget that Helen got enough money in a lump sum to pay for the new house and to keep our heads above water for a year, longer if I'm careful. I'm making decent money at the boutique, especially since Raylene made me the manager. I want to show my girls they can grow up to take care of themselves."

"I guess that's an admirable goal," he said, though his tone was doubtful.

She smiled at him. "Isn't that what your wife did after her husband left her with a mountain of debt? Karen made a life for herself and her kids. It was a struggle, but she persevered. That's one of the reasons you fell for her, because she was strong in the face of adversity."

"I suppose." He grinned. "But then she found me and now it's my mission to take care of her and our family."

"Funny," she said. "Karen seems to think you have a partnership."

Her brother winced at the reminder. "Sorry. Apparently the Cruz macho tendencies die hard."

"As long as they die," she told him. "But I'll leave it to Karen to teach you that lesson."

Elliott frowned. "How did we get off track and start talking about my marriage? We were talking about you and that man who just walked out of here after giving you a thorough once-over."

"While the idea of any man staring at me appreciatively is a welcome change," she conceded, "I'm not looking for a relationship now. Maybe never. How many times do I need to say that before you believe me?"

Elliott looked dismayed, rather than convinced, by her response. "Don't let what Ernesto did shape the rest of your life, Adelia," he said fiercely. "Not all men are like that."

"You're certainly not," she agreed. "And for that I am eternally grateful." She touched his cheek. "I imagine Karen feels the same way. She must count her blessings every night."

"*Most* nights," her brother corrected with a grin. "At least when she's not exasperated with me for one thing or another, like forgetting about that whole partnership thing, for instance."

"Yes, I can see how you might test a woman's patience," she told him. "As a boy you were certainly a pest."

"Gee, thanks."

She patted his cheek again. "Don't fret, *mi hermano*. We all wind up loving you just the same. Even though this conversation is making me a little crazy, I know you mean well and I love you for caring."

Elliott's expression suddenly sobered. "Adelia, promise me something, okay?"

"Anything."

"If a man comes along, you'll leave yourself open to the possibilities. I'm not talking about the man who just left here, but any man."

"Any man?" she echoed, amused.

"After I've checked him out thoroughly," he amended.

"Now *that* sounds much more like the overly protective brother I know and love," Adelia said.

"Promise," he repeated.

Though she couldn't imagine it to be a promise she'd have to keep, at least not anytime soon, Adelia nodded. "Promise."

Just then the pizza and the kids arrived at the table simultaneously and, thankfully, further conversation was impossible.

Time and time again, though, she found herself glancing toward the door and thinking about the man who'd cast a lingering look in her direction. Whether it was the openly appreciative way he'd studied her or her brother's teasing, she felt the oddest sensation stirring deep inside. It was a sensation she hadn't anticipated and didn't especially want, but it felt a whole lot as if she might be coming alive again.

REQUEST YOUR FREE BOOKS!

2 FREE NOVELS
FROM THE ROMANCE COLLECTION
PLUS 2 FREE GIFTS!

YES! Please send me 2 FREE novels from the Romance Collection and my 2 FREE gifts (gifts are worth about $10). After receiving them, if I don't wish to receive any more books, I can return the shipping statement marked "cancel." If I don't cancel, I will receive 4 brand-new novels every month and be billed just $6.24 per book in the U.S. or $6.74 per book in Canada. That's a savings of at least 22% off the cover price. It's quite a bargain! Shipping and handling is just 50¢ per book in the U.S. and 75¢ per book in Canada.* I understand that accepting the 2 free books and gifts places me under no obligation to buy anything. I can always return a shipment and cancel at any time. Even if I never buy another book, the two free books and gifts are mine to keep forever.

194/394 MDN F4XY

Name	(PLEASE PRINT)	
Address		Apt. #
City	State/Prov.	Zip/Postal Code

Signature (if under 18, a parent or guardian must sign)

Mail to the **Harlequin®** Reader Service:
IN U.S.A.: P.O. Box 1867, Buffalo, NY 14240-1867
IN CANADA: P.O. Box 609, Fort Erie, Ontario L2A 5X3

Want to try two free books from another line?
Call 1-800-873-8635 or visit www.ReaderService.com.

* Terms and prices subject to change without notice. Prices do not include applicable taxes. Sales tax applicable in N.Y. Canadian residents will be charged applicable taxes. Offer not valid in Quebec. This offer is limited to one order per household. Not valid for current subscribers to the Romance Collection or the Romance/Suspense Collection. All orders subject to credit approval. Credit or debit balances in a customer's account(s) may be offset by any other outstanding balance owed by or to the customer. Please allow 4 to 6 weeks for delivery. Offer available while quantities last.

Your Privacy—The Harlequin® Reader Service is committed to protecting your privacy. Our Privacy Policy is available online at www.ReaderService.com or upon request from the Harlequin Reader Service.

We make a portion of our mailing list available to reputable third parties that offer products we believe may interest you. If you prefer that we not exchange your name with third parties, or if you wish to clarify or modify your communication preferences, please visit us at www.ReaderService.com/consumerschoice or write to us at Harlequin Reader Service Preference Service, P.O. Box 9062, Buffalo, NY 14269. Include your complete name and address.

ROM13R